LAWSUIT
and
Leather

MINE TO KEEP SERIES
BOOK 1

VIVIAN MAE
MIDTOWN PUBLISHING LLC

Dedication

This goes out to all my Gemma's of the world. Believe in yourself, because you must be your own sturdy rock before you can become someone else's. And know in your heart that you will find the person you're meant to be with.

Disclaimer

* * *

This book contains content that some may find sensitive, including mental health disorders, signs of domestic abuse, and childhood trauma. It is filled with explicit mature sexual content which is recommended for readers who are at least eighteen years old.

CONTENTS

Playlist

Leisure - "Lonely Nights"
Sabrina Claudio - "Problem With You"
Adele - "Oh My God"
The Weekend - "Alone Again"
BENEE - "Supalonely"
Hailee Steinfield and Bloodpop - "Capital Letters"
Vicktor Taino - "Feathers and Wax"
GEMS - "W/O U"
Sabrina Claudio - "Wanna Know"
Kali Uchies - "Telepatia"
Fleurie - "Hurricane"
Ariana Grande & The Weeknd - "Love Me Harder"
Cigarettes After Sex - "Flash"
Gallant - "Talking To Myself"
Kali Uchies - "Que Te Pedi//"
Gallant - "Open Up"
Patrick Watson - "Je Te Laisserai Des Mots"
Lana Del Rey - "American"
Ariana Grande - "Safety Net"
The Weeknd - "True Colors"
Kali Uchies - "te pongo mal (préndelo)"
Leisure - "Beautiful"
The Weeknd - "Die For You"

Prologue

On the upper westside of Manhattan, wedged between a spiraling wood banister and two kissing lovers, I began to sweat. I was both excited and sick from the prospect of tonight and what I was about to do.

"Typical Columbia frat party," Dana, my college roommate and second closest friend, rolled her eyes as she snatched the freshly filled solo cup from a man's hand. "No beer, only bourbon. But it works even better though, so long as you don't mind the burn." She parted the lovers by my side like Moses, shooing them away.

"I just need to take the edge off, he's going to be here any second, and…" I trailed off as Dana passed me the cup, lifting it to my lips to shush me. I took a long sip, wincing as the spiced heat coursed its way down my throat.

"That's why we came early." Dana reassured me, combing a gold strand of her bobbed hair behind her ear, "It's my job to get you loosened up before he arrives. Plus, you have me, and do you think I'd let you break such big news without my support?" Dana tugged on her black fur coat, guiding my eyes towards hers. "Now, repeat the plan," she commanded.

I took a deep breath, inhaling the expensive scent of Ralph Lauren cologne, rich like juniper, cheapened only by the rhythmic pop of unfitting house music. "Once Parker arrives, I'll take him to the roof top where we always go." I recited the almost mantra Dana instilled in me since last week.

"Go on…" Dana encouraged with a wave of her hand, switching my empty cup with a full one.

"Then we'll have a few drinks and talk like normal. We'll laugh and be silly, just like best friends do, just as we have since we were kids." I shivered now, taking a long chug of my drink, welcoming the distraction of its unbearable taste. My stomach turned, it had always been weak, ever since I tried seafood in the Hamptons as a kid.

"I'm waiting…" Dana cocked her head, half smiling, half impatient. I blushed, my face reddened, no longer from the strong drinks alone.

"Then…" I squeezed the plastic cup in my hand, wetting my lips that suddenly went dry, "I tell him I *love* him." My voice fell out like a whimper. Even confessing out loud to Dana felt foreign.

Yes, I loved Parker Ellis Jones; the boy turned man who had been by my side since the age of six, inseparable even now as we attended different colleges. My quiet confession brought a new sense of self-awareness to my body, as if I were engulfed in one of Parker's protective hugs.

"How do I look?" I asked. "Do you think he'll like it?" I turned toward Dana, my hands delicately wrapped around my waist as I asked her for the twelfth time today.

"Are you serious?" She took the cup out of my hand

for a sip, "He's going to be a lawyer, isn't he? That means he has to be smart. So, yes. Unless he's a total idiot, he'll be drooling at your feet." Of course Parker wasn't an idiot, he was anything but. Not only had he finished his political science degree in three years, but he had already begun the first year of the juris doctorate program. He was tall, gorgeous, and beyond ambitious, leading as the captain of Columbia's track team. "Wait… that's the outfit you made?" Dana snapped my attention back to her as I nodded. She sighed, "I wish I could design like you; it's crazy how much better you are than the others in class." I blushed again, avoiding the praise she often gave, which I felt was far too kind.

Despite attending every one of Parker's Columbia frat parties, Dana and I did not actually study here. We were seniors at F.I.T., the best fashion school in New York City. This made the distance between Parker and me rather notable, but a small sacrifice we worked around. And even though Columbia had its own subway stop on 116th street, Parker never once wanted me to ride it, and insisted Dana and I take a cab.

"It's not safe." He'd sternly announced, *"And I can't accept it. Not today, not ever."* Of course he'd never let me pay for my fare; it was just like Parker to think he needed to take care of me. He gave Dana and me enough money to get to the parties and back and extra for food, in case we ever got hungry. This was Parker, relentless and protective, observant, and caring in the most precise ways. *"As long as I get to see you, I'll pay whatever it takes."* The memory of his words was sweet, and the fact that he made time to see me despite the

demand of his schedule. I grinned to myself, settling in the thought, allowing the bourbon to ease the tension along my shoulders.

"You girls enjoying the party?" The familiar coastal tone of a California man sauntered by. He arched a dark brow, his hair combed back, uniformed like the other polo wearing men in the mahogany trimmed living room. "Gemma..." He nodded with a toothy grin. Dana blinked as if annoyed.

Tommy Romero was a clean-shaven man with dark eyes and a bent nose. Despite the scar above his eyebrow, and his rather clumsy approach to women, Tommy was a sweet guy. He tried pursuing me before, but seemed reluctant around Parker, whose presence always carried an unspoken dominance with the pierce of his emerald green eyes.

"Not now, Tommy," Dana widened her expression, shooting an interpreted message only close girlfriends could decipher as— *Oh my god.*

"The party's great." I took another sip of my drink, which no longer burned, but rather sat sweetly on my tongue.

As Tommy flirted with an unimpressed Dana, I glanced down at the small silver band around my finger, the one with a tiny butterfly at its center. Parker surprised me with it the night I turned thirteen. In fact, it was the first piece of jewelry I ever owned, and best of all, it came from him. Not many people knew the reason behind it, but the ring was far more specific than most even realized.

In Mrs. Tempton's third grade class, Parker and I

were assigned to pick an animal which best suited our personalities. I wanted to be a pigeon, who's mundane nature I appreciated, along with the almost metallic shine of their wings. Parker disagreed, though, and maintained I was too pretty to be a pigeon, so he called me a butterfly instead.

Parker picked a rattlesnake, prefacing he'd only bite if he felt threatened; a stern distinction he made as a child, and the leading reason he picked that over a shark. This stayed with us, especially any time we'd say goodbye. "Better shake, Rattlesnake," I'd always tell him, to which he'd return, "Bye, bye, Butterfly."

Yes, I was his Butterfly, and he was my Rattlesnake; and this ring meant the world to me. I always wore it, specifically because it always felt like a piece of him was with me, especially in moments like now as I waited in the discomfort of large crowds.

When Tommy asked earlier if I was enjoying the party, I actually lied, and seeing my ring was a reminder of that. In fact, I was never one for parties, even for my birthday. When Parker gave me the ring, I told him the only thing I wanted to do was see a movie; one above the standard PG rating that stopped us before. Not only did he surprise me with the gift, but he came with me to the midnight premiere of *Twilight*.

It was one of the first real things we did alone as young adults, and I wouldn't have done it with anyone but him. He wasn't just a companion, he was an active participant, passing the time with thumb wars, middle school gossip, and eating gummy peach rings while waiting in line.

That was perfect, much better than any party.

"Why don't we sit down?" Tommy nodded, pointing to the newly purchased leather sofa where everyone stood. Dana scrunched her face, absorbing the hollering cheers of an arm-wrestling competition close by.

"And risk getting their sweat on us?" Dana shook her head.

"You know me. It's a little crowded." I added.

"You and Parker both," Tommy groaned, "What's the point of a party if you two just leave every time?" He teased as if daring me to stay.

Parker and I were the same—a little more reserved —which is why we spent our time upstairs away from others. Although the frat house was a meeting point, we'd always end up on the roof, sitting on an old yellow couch that never got donated.

"You know I caught them falling asleep up there one night?" Tommy scoffed to Dana, "Like seniors after their early bird special."

"I think it's cute," Dana defended, "and I bet Parker was quite comfortable." She winked in my direction, a not so subtle clue even for Tommy. I'd do just about anything to spend moments like that with Parker, especially on cold nights like this. Often I'd get close enough to fall asleep, using the support of his large shoulder as my personal pillow.

"Wouldn't be the first time." I confessed, reminded again of when Parker gave me my ring. That night on my birthday, I was completely enamored, barely watching the movie, spending the entire time looking down at my silver butterfly. I rubbed my thumb on the foreign feeling of a band, slowly yawning, resting my head on Parker's shoulder as I fell asleep. I wasn't sure if he intended for me to know, but he kissed me that night. Right there in the theatre, as I slowly shut my eyes, he pressed his lips on the top of my head.

"See, she's blushing." Tommy winked in my direction, misinterpreting my thought as some excitement for his presence.

"Go away, Tommy, we have important things to do tonight." Dana shooed him once more, her attention focused on being my wing girl for the evening. *Important* was an understatement as I was hours or even minutes away from finally confessing my love to Parker. My stomach dipped into a loose knot, an uncomfortable combination of adrenaline and fear.

Yes, I was afraid, and I had every right to be, considering the life I lived, the mother I had, and the father that left.

A man in the corner rolled his thumb along the flint wheel of a Bic lighter, causing a familiar flicking noise that triggered so many bad memories. I studied him as he lit a cigarette, puffing a stale grey cloud of smoke into the air. The odor was similar to that of dirt and burnt tires, each being more pleasant than what it truly reminded me of: home.

Your heart is a piggy bank, Gemma, but a man is always a hammer. Claire, my mother, would always say this, amongst other things, smoking cigarette after cigarette. *They'll take it all, and they'll leave you, too. Don't say I didn't warn you. Someday you'll end up like me.*

The sudden smoke that filled the room twisted in my

gut. The fear of rejection, the fear of who my mother was and her disorder, fueled me with a paranoia I'd seen and heard my entire life. I still remembered the night my father left, the thing she had done to me, what I witnessed. Parker was always there no matter what, and though he knew me the best out of anyone, not even he knew the details of what happened that night.

I stroked my neck, soothing it from the stench of smoke as I stared off. I couldn't acknowledge the hold she had on me for so long and how it prevented me from ever confessing to Parker how I felt.

"Are you sure? You think he loves me?" I whispered into Dana's ear, clinging onto a bit of hope. Dana encouraged me to do this. The confidence she exuded was far more profound than what I had in myself, and I envied her for it. I needed that reminder, I needed to remember why I chose to do this now, to risk it all for the man of my dreams.

"I'm positive! There isn't a doubt in my mind." Dana practically shouted, confirming her certainty as if it were her final answer on a game show.

"Positive about what?" A voice so deep and warm questioned Dana from behind my back, pricking along my neck like hot velvet arrows. I turned around, still amazed each time I saw him, the towering and built frame of Parker, peering down with an unmatched white smile. "How's my Butterfly?" My toes curled from his greeting, caused by the sight of his dirty blonde waves. His hair sat unkempt, loose and sexy, perfect for the bronzed look of his dimpled smirk.

"Parker!" I shouted, my voice hitched as he pulled

me in for a hug. Whereas others wore polos and slacks, Parker sported a grey Columbia sweater and dark denim jeans. His casual style put him so in contrast to the others in the room, if not obvious already from his staggering height and striking green eyes.

"Is this the outfit you talked about, the one that landed you the internship?" Parker pulled away and stared down along my body; his large hands softly gripped my shoulders into position.

"It's all from scratch." I admitted, unlike the intention I wished to confess. Though I couldn't be as vocal with my feelings as I wanted, fashion had always been a way to express myself, which was probably why I worked so hard at it. This look in particular was no different, and my outfit carried secret meanings. Would Parker notice my wool skirt as an homage to his eyes? Plaid but green, short of brilliant like the white pleated blouse I wore in honor of his smile? Or perhaps my cami, whose texture and hue was similar to the golden brown waves of his soft hair? The look was designed to say it all, *I'm thinking of you, and I'm yours, reach out and take me.* "Do you like it?" I asked, his eyes still observed every inch of my body.

"It was the first thing I saw when I entered. I haven't stopped staring since." He assured, his voice low but defiant to the music. He'd been watching me? The realization elicited goosebumps across my arms, his admission perhaps more profound for me than the people listening by our side. I tucked my shoulders close to my ears.

"Internship?" Dana interrupted, her eyes puzzled.

"Gemma got a position styling for Gerard Halt. She'll start in spring after graduation." Parker answered before I could, his voice assertive with an almost unmistakable pride. "As if there were any doubts, I knew she'd get it, and her look convinced him." *If only it could convince you too*, I thought, and the way his eyes stayed fixed along my neck made me feel as though it were coming true.

"I got the news today actually, I know it's just styling for now, but I hope it leads to designing." I reached up and adjusted the collar around Parker's neck, a habit I formed for correcting looks. I was excited to be interning for Gerard, a small-time designer with a big ego, one which impressed some, but not yet many. "And if I work as hard as this guy, I'm sure I'll be designing in no time." I bumped into Parker, who wasn't shy about hiding his smirk. I was ecstatic about the position, but couldn't enjoy it, not till I could confess to Parker and ease this anxious tension in my stomach.

"Congrats Gemma!" Tommy announced, raising his glass, meeting Dana's extended hand as he reached to pat my back. Instead, the cup smacked loose from his grip, spilling directly onto my chest and down my cami. I gasped as the ice cubes fell down my top, instantly perking my nipples with their chill. I shivered quickly, allowing them to fall through the bottom of my skirt. "Fuck!" Tommy winced, "Gemma, I'm so sorry." With a napkin in hand, Tommy reached toward me, but Parker grabbed his wrist.

"It's ok." Parker warned, his tightened grip squeezed for just a moment before letting go. Tommy looked absolutely frightened, startled more by Parker than from my gasp. "I can take care of this. Why don't you get Dana a fresh drink?" He looked over at an amused Dana, who was equally enamored by the charm Parker had. "These ladies are always honored guests within this chapter, and I want to make sure they are treated as such." If Parker wasn't already intimidating, the fact that his father, Albert Jones, was both a notable alumnus and a legal powerhouse, provided an extra heir of authority to Parker's family name.

"Of course." Tommy nodded, "Can I get anyone anything else?"

"You're good, Tommy." Parker assured him, his eyes not once leaving mine. I wanted to stare forever, my heart raced at the possibility of saying the sweet words I held in for so long.

"You two going to the roof?" Dana slipped the question, a subtle reminder of our foolproof plan.

"Yes! These boots are killing me." I half grinned, "You know I wear them for the look not the comfort."

"I'm not taking you to the roof like this?" Parker laughed. "You're soaking wet, and it's far too cold to be wearing wet clothes. I'm cleaning you up first." *Cleaning* me up? Dana wafted her face, her hand acting like a fan to his words.

"You feel dirty, Gemma?" Dana asked, her unconcealed meaning enough for me to melt from embarrassment.

"Sticky." I replied, but how the words fell out felt less innocuous than I hoped.

"I'm taking you upstairs, let's go." Parker reached

for my hand, engulfing its tiny size with the care of his grip. I held onto my cup as he divided the crowd, reaching the dark spiraling stairs which led to the private rooms above. I sipped my drink, feeling the faintest of buzzes kicking in as we ascended along the wall of regal grey decor and polished dark paneling. There was something about the dimmed lighting, how its subtle and warm tones made me feel more prepared, as though secrets could easily be told in the shadows. He couldn't see my face, which made me feel more secure than in the light. Without realizing, I squeezed his hand harder, and my action reciprocated as his grip tightened.

"Right here, Butterfly." Parker held the door open to a rather clean bathroom. Its honeycomb tile was marked in a mosaic, showing the year of the chapter's establishment: *1942*.

"I smell like the bar on 94th street, remember how we snuck in for New Year's Eve?"

Parker sighed at my words, recalling the colossal hangover he suffered.

"Teeeeequila." I slowly dragged out my words, teasing the memories from that night.

"Just hearing the word." He crinkled his face, the line of his brow visible. Even when his face scrunched with disgust, he was handsome. "I'll never drink it again, and if I do, it better be for a damn good reason."

"I happen to like it a lot." I chirped, but my smile quickly shifted into shock as Parker placed his hands around my hips, lifting me into the air and onto the porcelain counter. It happened so quick and with such ease, he didn't even bat an eye. It was as if I were weightless, his attention turned to the cabinet where he pulled out a towel.

"Well, if you like it, it can't be that bad." He conceded, wetting the towel at the faucet.

"Ugh, I think my outfit is ruined." I muttered, catching a glimpse in the mirror. My curled auburn hair was pulled back with golden pins, my hazel eyes crowned with a smokey look just for Parker. I checked the stain. My black bra was visible through the cami, transparent from bourbon and ice.

"I'll fix it." Parker rolled up the sleeves of his grey sweater, just before wringing out the excess water from the towel. His thick brawny arms flexed from the force, defined by fine hair and a thick vein.

"You promise?" I asked innocently.

"Promise." He assured, leaning closer to dab the towel along the top of my chest. His words were scented like soft mint, complimented by the warmth of his proximity. Right where the heat of his hands had been, my hips screamed to be touched again, to be pulled by his strength. A loose golden strand of hair fell before his eyes, cradling the glisten of his brow. "And when I promise something, I keep it."

"I know you do, Rattlesnake." I replied, my eyes focused on him, watching as one of his hands slowly slipped up my thigh. I curled my fingers into a ball, as his hand firmly squeezed, as his stare diverted down to my thin porcelain leg.

"You're not eating enough." He scolded, as his hand measured the width of my thigh. "After this I'm taking you out for food, and I won't accept no for an answer."

"I'm eating, but sometimes I just forget! You know I get so busy with designs. I lose track of time." I shrugged off his words as if it were innocent, but the truth was I had little to no money. This was another attempt to shield Parker from the ugliness of my private life, and though he knew I grew up poor, he assumed I was doing ok at the moment. The truth was, I was used to skipping meals, especially with a mother who was almost never present when I needed her. But Parker was very observant and fooling him was no easy task. He was onto me as he flashed me a warning stare, something I imagined would be useful when questioning others in court. If he even suspected I was low on money, he'd insist on giving me some. I couldn't let him do that though. I couldn't share the shame it made me feel about who I was and where I came from.

"We'll get you fed soon enough, especially when you come over for Thanksgiving. Mom keeps reminding me to tell you, and I keep assuring her you wouldn't miss it for the world." He dabbed my shirt a little further, "She needs her special girl to make the potato salad." He laughed, a nod to a childhood story recited at every dinner.

"I can't wait to hear the Spuddington story again. It's literally my favorite part of any gathering."

"Why do you torture me?" He asked, dreading the family tradition, pulling away to admire his work.

"I love to see you squirm." I grinned, indulgent in his stern yet cheerful face. He glanced up from my chest and into my eyes. *Love.* The word was said, but only in relation to how I loved to make him *squirm*. That wasn't the only thing I loved though, and there was no list big enough to detail the intricacies of my feelings. We grew up together; he held me when I cried; he stayed with me when I felt alone; and despite shielding him from the details of my ugly past, he bared with me through it all. It wasn't just him, it was his family, the very people who had welcomed me too. It all felt so perfect, and after a lifetime of messy, I was ready for *perfect.*

Suddenly, as fast as I could realize, I knew everything I hoped to believe was true. Parker loved me, there was no mistaking it. Dana was right, I was right. Everything would be great, and nothing could go wrong. It crept up in my chest; the blood rushed in my face with the beat of my pounding heart.

"Parker…" I said softly, staring into his green eyes, the ones I had modeled my skirt after, my most intimate form of expression, until now.

"What is it, Butterfly?" He asked, his face leaned closer toward mine. I swallowed, unsure of this new sensation, a heightened sense which made my ears ring and hands tremble. It was as if the whole world lit up, defined in clarity so sharp yet intimidating that all I could do was say the words.

"I'm in love with you…" I whimpered, the sound of the electronic music outside far too faint in comparison to the pound of my heart. Parker's skin burned red, mirroring my own, his eyes perplexed, blinking as if sending morse code. What did it mean? I cringed as his face appeared shocked as he absorbed the weight of my words.

"Gemma… I…" he muttered, the towel dropped

from his hand, as his lips hovered near mine. He was so close I could taste them with the slightest sense of imagination. "I love you too..." He admitted, his head leaned against mine as his hand gripped even tighter around my thigh. He pinched his fingers to the point it burned. I winced at what I thought was a confession, but instead was a clarifying stab to the gut. "Like a sister..."

Sister?

I hadn't realized my mouth dropped open, leaving me perched on the counter like some surprised doll.

"Sister?" I stated, half a question to Parker, and half a question to the universe, to everyone and everything. A sister? Why didn't he just call me his grandma, or even his dog? It was all just as awful, the complete other end to a spectrum of my feelings.

They'll take it all, and they'll leave you too. Don't say I didn't warn you, someday you'll end up like me. Claire's voice popped into my head, a mocking and jubilant taunt that turned my stomach. She was right, I was the fool.

"Gemma." Parker sighed, visibly frustrated at my lack of response. "These things are complicated, you're my best friend."

"I got to go..." I stuttered, and the room visibly spun as I stood up. I should have listened to the fear, the one Claire instilled so long ago.

"You don't understand, it's for the best." Parker panicked, reaching for my arm.

"Let me go, I have to go..." I shoved him away quickly, completely stunned. This was not supposed to happen, this wasn't what Dana promised. I was wrong, but worse, I was a fool.

"Gemma, goddamn it, please!" He begged, gripping my shoulders to face him.

"Parker…" I wavered, my vision blurred while the walls and lights spun like broken clocks. I could feel it, my years of contemplation and anxiety rising, filling my neck. "I'm going to be sick." I gargled, my lip trembled not from sadness, but from embarrassment and horror. Right then and there, the perfect ending, my words interrupted as I puked all over Parker's clean white shoes.

SIX YEARS LATER...

Chapter 1

Businesses don't fail, people do; that was what I'd been told anyway. The screeching sound of the packing tape reverberated through my clenched teeth, as I tore it away from my boxes. I hated that feeling, the one that gave me shivers in the presence of unpleasant noises.

"Where do you want this box, Gem?" Parker shouted from his living room.

"What does it say?" I yelled back, slightly annoyed. Not at Parker, but at this damn box.

"Uhhh… you wrote, 'kitchen, living room, bedroom, and misc.' So, I guess it goes everywhere?" His laugh made its way to the semi-empty guest room, the one where I'd be living out of for the next few months.

It was a harsh truth, one that was becoming more real with each unpacked box. My business failed, and I had no choice but to move in with Parker. This felt like more than a step back; no, this was a leap and jump in the wrong direction. Crouched near a large box by my new bed, I pulled out an old, wrinkled purse. It was a knock off Coach bag, whose logo of horses were clearly missing a set of legs. It sat completely empty, and I couldn't help but feel the same. Both of us penniless, both of us cheap attempts to be something greater than what we really were.

But despite this loss, I still had the one thing that was greater than any dream, Parker. Sure, I was broke, borderline homeless, and impossibly single, but here he was, saving me once again. He never stopped being there for me, not even after my drunken confession on that awful college night. I cringed silently, remembering the past like an embarrassing ghost.

Next to my purse lay a fresh pack of business cards, taped shut in a little bag. These were unused, and I wasn't certain if they ever would be. After graduating at F.I.T., I spent two years interning as a stylist for Gerard Halt, who's name made me twist the fake bag in my hands. I just wanted more, to actually design and be seen, but when his clients started preferring my sketches over his, that was when it all changed. He hated me, no question about it, and when I decided to leave, he didn't let me forget it.

I grabbed my old scheduler, scanning through the names of recent cancellations, each one slashed with a thick red line. Another client snatched, a string pulled by Gerard, to spite me in the most viscous of ways. Was he that petty? How could an ego so big be so fragile? I found it hard to believe I was at all threatening, seeing how small my business was.

"Gem?" Parker called out once more, his tone peeked for my attention.

"Fine! On my way, Park!" I shoved my box aside, running down the hall in my socks. Parker still carried the mystery box in his hands, the sleeves of his dress shirt rolled along his thick arms. He winked as I got closer, acknowledging my presence as I rushed to his side, "Set it over here and we'll take a peek." I instructed, unsure of what was actually inside. The move from my small place in Soho to Parker's Midtown apartment was a rushed and sudden chain of events, leaving my packed boxes as uncertain as my future.

I tore off the tape from the top, allowing the contents inside to billow out like a sigh of relief. I was beyond confused as to what I'd placed inside, knowing I was either exhausted or drunk when I packed it. Inside was a random assortment of things: tubes of mascara, a pizza cutter, a sock with no matching pair.

"Oh, these are perfect." Parker's deep voice hung with an impressed tone, removing a stack of playbills tucked inside. "I love how you keep these, not a single one missed." He thumbed through each one, fanning them open to be read out loud, "*Wicked*, *Rent*, *Chicago*…" He paused, "But what about?"

"In the very back." I assured him, "I'd never get rid of it."

"Is this *the* original?"

"Of course." I scoffed at his question, "Like I would ever not keep a piece of our past."

"*Phantom of the Opera*…" He looked up with a smoldering tease of his voice, "A child's worst fear." I laughed, recalling the moment I first met Parker.

"What were they thinking? Taking a bunch of first graders to see that?" I questioned, remembering the distinct moment when two classes of Brooklyn's Archer Elementary school were invited to watch the play on Broadway. In an attempt to foster meeting new friends, each class was paired with a partner, mine just so happened to be Parker.

"As soon as the lights went out, half the class started screaming." Parker smirked, "Given most of us slept with the lights on still, I guess it wasn't surprising."

"But not us." I reminded him, "In fact, we were both giddy. What was wrong with us? Two little kids, excited by the idea of seeing a monster, or so we thought."

"I learned two things that day," Parker motioned with two of his fingers. "One, I was always going to be by your side, and two, we were both a little creepy." I slapped his arm, his deep chuckle warmed my cheeks with the crease of his smirk.

"You're right, we were," I agreed. "Guess that's why we love horror movies so much." This of course was true, but for me, it involved reasons much more important than monsters and gore. It was a chance to sit in the dark, to cuddle close to Parker. In these moments, he'd confuse my pounding heart as an affect from the movie, when, in reality, it was from him. His eyes returned to the box as he bit his lip.

"What do we have here?" His unassuming tone left me in shock, as he pulled out a familiar hot pink toy. I felt sick immediately. How dare I put my vibrator in a random box? It had serviced me so well, and here it was with the pizza cutter. It buzzed in Parker's hand as he switched it on. "Still charged." He announced.

"Don't you dare!" I screeched, snatching it from his hands and throwing it into the box, "Parker!" His name was all I could get out, my face popped like a red balloon. Ten minutes into living with each other, and I already wanted to die from embarrassment.

"No judgement here." He flashed me a grin, the one that caused me to melt time and time again. Even after the rejection all those years back, we still managed to find our way to normalcy. My confession didn't ruin our friendship, but something changed within me. I felt myself building up a wall again, the one my mother encouraged. I couldn't lie, it killed me to hear his rejection, and moving in was a small reminder of that feeling, like he was taking in his little sister. But despite how I felt and what I confessed, Parker never once shut me out or made me feel weird. We were still just us, Parker and Gemma, best friends and overall trouble.

Parker held my gaze, his bold green eyes attempting to pierce the armor of my walls. He was as handsome as ever, his face more refined, older with slight creases. His once smooth jaw was now replaced with fresh stubble, his look more rugged, appearing like a man of strong labor before slipping into a suit. He always cleaned up before a big case, shaving his beard, returning to the polished lawyer of great prestige. What a man. It felt as though we stared so long, that both of us forgot what we were doing.

"Ummmm..." He laughed, massaging his strong chin, still bent on his knees. "I got a surprise for you," he chirped, almost as if he'd forgotten.

"For me? Parker, you shouldn't have." I waved him off.

"I didn't, but someone couldn't resist." He shot to his feet, quickly making his way to the kitchen and back with a bouquet of flowers. "Mama Meg sends her housewarming regards." He rolled his eyes, still holding a mischievous grin.

"No, she didn't!" I exclaimed, reaching up to smell the arranged cream roses and assorted baby's breath. Mama Meg was no ordinary mother; she was Parker's mom, but in many ways mine too. She always had me by her side at family gatherings, seating me as if I were her daughter, showing me the love I never knew I deserved. "I'm her favorite." I announced, yanking the basket from his hands filled with assorted goodies.

"I won't argue with that." Parker exchanged, knowing full well his mother and I were close. I plucked out a handwritten card from the crystalline blue vase.

Gemma dear,

Thrilled to see the adventures to come, and know in your heart greatness will follow wherever you go. Have Parker mind his manners, or else send him to me.

Love, Mama Meg

My cheeks were in pain, caught in an unbreakable smile. I owed her more than she could ever know, and in reality, if it weren't for her real estate endeavors, I would have never met Parker. Back in the early 2000s, when rates were low and the market was hot, Meg Jones invested in blocks of real estate in the heart of Brooklyn. It was no secret the Joneses had enormous wealth, but Mama Meg's humble beginnings were never fallen short on Parker. She made her family relocate from Manhattan for the entire length of the project, investing millions into the renovation of older brick apartments and impoverished communities. For over a decade, Mama Meg forced Parker to live a normal life, to be a child in the public school system, just as she had growing up. This of course was in exception to the lavish Hampton vacations they took each summer. I peered down at a postscript below her signature:

P.s.

Sent a vintage Fendi skirt with Parker, found it at the thrift store for $14.00. What a thief I am.

Her eye for fashion was equally matched with her need to stay frugal, maintaining that wealth was no excuse to spend unnecessary money. She was a thrifter, and a style icon in many ways, stealing designer looks for fractions of the price. When I first met her, I loved everything about her, and it began with the welcoming hues of her styled looks. Sophisticated browns, grey tweeds, and white tops tucked into skirts. Her eyes were always framed in dark chic glasses, highlighting the glow of their welcoming green tone. Before she could ever say a word, her fashion said it all. I knew it the moment I saw her, she was a kind, sophisticated, and elegant woman. I wanted that power too, to communicate like her, to express how I felt through design. I loved her, and then from that love, came fashion.

"Dibs on the candy." Parker fished out a bag of

peach gummy rings from the care package, splitting it open.

"Of course she remembers these." I sat the flowers down by the side table, reaching in for a ring, "Anytime I eat these it reminds me of vacation, of lying out by the pool with your family." I took a bite, remembering how we would eat these until we were sick as children.

"We always pretended they were some type of treasure." Parker continued, reenacting a tradition we began as children. He reached out for my hand, gripping my wrist, propping it on display as he slipped one onto my finger. The sugary crystals tickled along my skin, a momentary sensation until Parker reached down and removed it with a bite. I laughed, chewing the original gummy I still had in my mouth.

"I'm calling Mama Meg today, catching her up on the move." I said nonchalantly, avoiding the wave of heat I felt from Parker's lips near my fingers. He stifled his expression, combing his golden hair back, almost sighing.

"Speaking of moms…" He motioned back to a box, avoiding the question I knew he didn't want to ask, but felt compelled to do so, "Have you told Claire about moving in?"

Claire. My mother. If it weren't apparent enough in the awkwardness of the question alone, I didn't enjoy talking about her or the memories she brought.

"I checked on her." I stated quickly, "She's doing ok, still taking her medicine as instructed. But honestly, the less she knows, the better." Not once did I glance up at Parker but assumed my position back on the floor with a box. I wanted to brush this away, and though he was always there to support me, I didn't want him exposed to too much of my reality.

If my past were one of these boxes, I'd choose to keep it sealed, to tuck it away in the closet, as to not spoil the charming decor of Parker's home. Within that box would be shame, exhaustion, but most of all, fear of being vulnerable. That side was ugly, and out here with Parker, it was pretty. "I have so many boxes, and they're totally in your way." I laughed, dispelling the tension I felt over my mother.

"They're not a problem, Gem. If anything, they're exciting. I'm happy to have someone around. Especially you." Parker lifted two large boxes on his own, placing them in a corner with little effort. I couldn't help but appreciate what I saw, his ass sculpted from years of athletics, placed perfectly in fitted grey slacks. He was incredibly sexy, and though he was both generous and helpful, I needed to remind myself, the longer I stayed the harder it'd be to leave.

"Well, I don't want to be in your hair too long, you're already going out of your way with helping me unpack. Just don't go snooping around my other boxes, got it." I teased.

"You can stay in my hair and my house. Honestly, it's yours too. You've had a key since I got it, haven't you?"

"Yes, but that was for emergencies," I corrected. "This is different, I'm in your space. My interview is tomorrow, and I'm hoping it'll go well." I mumbled, realizing the dreaded words that just slipped from my mouth.

"With Gerard?" Parker asked, his voice dropping an octave. This was the shift in his mindset, from perfect friend to vicious lawyer. "I don't like what he did, and I especially don't like that he's stringing you along for this interview."

"I know…" I sighed. Parker wasn't wrong. My business was so small, shopping for clients and styling them for events. It wasn't even worth Gerard's attention, yet he seemed so relentless with his pursuit, propositioning my clients with lower prices. After all, his name was bigger than mine, how could they refuse?

"You really want to go back to him and beg for your job? Gemma, you have time now… you want to be a designer, I know you can do it. You're not a stylist, you're a creator, so stay here and chase your dream."

"It's not that simple." I replied, reminding myself staying longer meant growing more attached to the idea of being closer to Parker. Couldn't he see that? It made me wish I was still in contact with Dana, who left before graduating to study fashion in Paris. We lost touch, and it had only been Parker and me for years. But despite my urge to leave, his offer was tempting. And he was right, styling was not what I wanted to do, and though my business consisted of that, it was only a means for income, nothing more.

Starting a business was supposed to give me more time to design, to live on my own and make my own hours. But I couldn't even do that, not with Gerard looming in the shadows. More than three years out on my own, and he stifled every opportunity that came my way. I felt like I was on some blacklist, and getting in his good graces felt both pathetic and necessary, especially if I wanted to leave Parker's sooner.

"Why isn't it simple?" His tone pressed.

"Because... I'm a guest. I need to be able to have my own space and be an adult. Besides, what if you have someone over, a girl perhaps?" I asked.

"So?"

"So? Doesn't that look weird? I want you to have the freedom to do whatever, to have a love life uninterrupted. You don't need to be a single man with your loser friend living in your luxury apartment."

"Stop," he commanded softly. "One, you're not a loser. You're Gemma Rose Harrison, future fashion icon. Two, my love life is..." He contemplated almost shrugging, "It's nothing. I'm happy right now, and even more happy to have you here. Just promise me if you don't want the job, you won't take it." Parker arched his brows into a sweet frame around his eyes. He cared, and that made me happy, but still I was determined to do what was best for me, and my walls.

"I promise..." I conceded, but not before cutting in quickly, "as long as you promise not to let my presence stop you from living your life. If I sense that, I'll leave..." I tried to be stern, but the confident wink he shot made me melt.

"I promise." He shook his head, staring down at his watch, "Shit!" He groaned, reaching over the couch for his suit jacket. "I gotta get going, I'm meeting with a client for a big case." He slung his arms through the jacket, adjusting the cuffs by his wrists.

"A *big* case?" I asked, adjusting the pocket square of his jacket.

"Maybe the biggest one yet." Two years after graduating from Columbia with his Juris Doctorate, Parker was already one of the most well-known lawyers in Manhattan, having landed a position with the city's most prestigious firm. When people saw Parker, they saw his father, New York's retired Chief of Justice, Albert Jones, who was equally tremendous and unequivocally dominant in court. Parker stopped before turning away, his eyes scanned over the flowers his mom sent. "You know you can always talk to me, Gem." He nodded, "About anything. Claire included."

It was sweet, but the thought scared me. I wasn't ready, and I wasn't sure if I'd ever be. I knew he would never judge me for what happened, but that wasn't good enough. How could I share what I wished never came true? I rarely invited Parker to Claire's when I was a kid, and if he ever showed up, I'd always make him leave. I hated his surprise visits, especially if I caught him talking to Claire. Seeing them together always gave me such anxiety, leaving me uncertain of what was said and what was known. That was my world, not his. I wished it on no one.

"You better shake, Rattlesnake." I finally said, not truly acknowledging his words. He nodded, knowing once again I slipped from his persistent charm.

"Bye, bye, Butterfly." He winked and waited for a moment, allowing the silence to fill our space before turning away. I followed behind, locking the door as he left.

Parker's apartment—despite my mess—was very neat, leaving the guest room as no exception. I stretched my neck, observing the dark navy walls and white crown molding. Very masculine but softened by the thick white rug that covered over the cold wood floors. This was his home, but a part of me was still here, evident by the photos of us all around. Regardless, I returned to my mess, organizing fragments of my life into various piles. Poking out of one of the boxes was a sea foam green sewing machine. It'd been so long since I'd used it, since I even had the time. By its side was a Vogue magazine, featuring a yellow and pink pencil dress from my favorite designer, St. La Vie. I wish it was him I was interviewing with, but that was a dream, and in reality, I was meeting with Gerard Halt, designer turned hitman.

Still, I pulled out the sewing machine and carried its massive size to the desk in my room. Maybe Parker was right, perhaps I could take time to work on my true passion. But what would that cost, if not the possibility of painful hope? Time was not on my side, and I knew myself too well. I had to get over Parker, and part of that meant getting out as soon as I could.

Tomorrow would be the most important interview of my life, despite the overwhelming feeling of dread it most certainly caused.

Chapter 2

The cabbie slammed his hand on the horn mercilessly. I peeked out the window and watched as traffic was re-directed once again. A man with a headset waved us away, blocking our path with the authority of a steel fence. My phone buzzed with an alert, reminding me of the hell to come: *Interview with Gerard Halt (professional asshole).*

Having missed breakfast, I resorted to stuffing my face with a bag of cheap yellow cookies. Marcello's Galletas were my favorite, but I never ate them around Parker. No, they weren't just cookies, they were a guilty segue from my past. Admitting I liked twenty-five cent bodega cookies was not shameful, however, admitting these cookies were all I had because my mother rarely made dinner was.

"What's the hold up?" I shouted, catching bits of crumbs that fell from my lip. I was beyond nervous and chewed like an observant squirrel as I looked out the window.

The cab driver sighed loudly, "They're filming another movie again. Streets are closed for the next half mile, so you better get comfortable," his hoarse tone seemed annoyed, as if he shared the sentiment of my outrage. I watched as he placed the car in park and pulled out a half-finished crossword puzzle.

Get comfortable?

I gazed down at my oversized tote, filled with swatches and designs. My entire short-lived career was crammed into its confines, stitched with the letters VIP.

As if.

I knew I couldn't be late to meet Gerard, I refused to give him another reason to hate me. I thought of everything at stake, my future home, the job I barely wanted, and getting out of Parker's house. Where would me and my big box of miscellaneous items go if this didn't work out? I panicked, digging into my purse past the cookies for a wad of cash.

"I can't be the homeless, vibrator, pizza cutter lady!" I shouted, visualizing my future kicked to the curb. "Stop here!" I threw a slew of singles at the cabbie as he craned his neck, startled in the rearview mirror.

"Lady, I am stopped!" He cursed, but I was too distracted, attempting to leave with my seatbelt still on.

"Thank you, I love you!" I replied, confusing both him and myself, feeling completely rushed and out of my mind. I was at least twelve blocks away from Gerard's, a distance already sizable without the added chaos of a New York morning. Quickly, I checked my watch in horror. I had to do it, and as much as it pained me, I removed my Louboutins and placed my bare feet onto the rough, almost grimy concrete by the curb.

"I love you too, sweetie!" The cabbie rolled his window down just for me, but I was already gone.

Hastily, I sprinted. My bag and cookies jostled like stolen goods, while my feet morphed into the hue of black sticky tar. Even after leaving Parker's early, here I was, screaming down the street, excusing my shoves for a job I already knew I'd hate. And why? Because of another movie set? It felt like every day someone was filming something new, popping up like mold, ruining peoples' lives, just like mine, just like now. My bag slammed along one of the barricades tracing my path, emitting a loud ting that annoyed me further. I groaned as my foot landed on what felt like gum but was possibly something worse.

"Why god?" I asked, crossing a busy street, defying a red glowing hand urging me to stop. I didn't, but rather continued, staring up for an answer, met only with a condescending billboard for expensive cologne. In it, a man—who's name escaped me, but face seemed familiar —stared down from the clouds as if summoned. A finger from his golden hand traced the stubble on his face, its color refined like strokes of dark ink, but unmatched by the piercing chocolate eyes that followed me along. I scowled, reading the quote hovered above his slicked black hair.

"*It's me, baby, deal with it.*"

"Deal with it?" I groaned, repeating his words as if it were meant for me and the many detour signs that cursed my morning. I swiped at the sweat on my face, more agitated than before, as I reached the corner of Gerard's boutique. My watch confirmed everything I knew was already true, I was almost twenty minutes late and impossibly frustrated. I tried to collect myself, dropping my heels to my feet, slipping them on with what felt like a rock between my toes. I puffed a strand of hair from my face, scurrying along to the now propped entrance.

"After you." A tall and looming man with a Dodgers cap held the door open, his eyes concealed behind a pair of thick black shades.

"Yup!" I sighed, half paying attention to his smirk, noticing the hue of minty green gum he casually chewed. I passed him, his scent lingered like cherry and spice, centering me as a gust of cool air blew through the entrance. I straightened my posture, recognizing the familiar orange glow of Gerard's darkened skin.

"So she lives." He announced, exaggerating his expression of shock, up from an array of fabric swatches. The way his eyes magnified behind the thick lenses of his designer frames gave him the appearance of an animated doll.

"I ran here." My smile twitched as I approached the large counter where he worked. The letters of his last name hung above his desk, reading more like a command than a welcome. He glanced over my body, placing a half-chewed pencil behind his ear.

"That explains the sweat," he added with the scrunch of his nose, "and despite the nature of our business, being fashionably late is never a good look. But *happy* to see you nonetheless." His greeting extended far past a courteous hello. He was happy to see me, back in his presence, out of options, and in his palms. I combed a strand of wet hair behind my ear, attempting to look presentable.

"Happy to be back," I lied. "It's apparent I have lots to learn, and what better way than being with the best." I flattered him, and my soul buckled under the weight of my words. Gerard huffed with a laugh, pulling out a large pair of shears, clipping along a strip of tweed. He didn't even look at me anymore, he merely returned to his work as I continued. "I have plenty of new sketches and ideas, things I think you'll really enjoy." I pulled out a large book, covered in tags for quick access, "You know I'm serious, and I really want to impress…" I hesitated, choosing my words carefully, "you, that is…" I added, my eyebrows raised. Gerard glanced up, dragging the book into his tiny hands.

"Pretty bold assumption." He said flatly, licking his finger before flipping the pages. All I could do was stare, his face studying each new look and sketch. There was no denying it, the expansion of his lids, the unconscious nod of his head. He liked them, that was for sure. He cleared his throat regardless, as if to reboot his intentions for having me over. "No." He announced, the word itself almost caught in a cough.

"No?" I questioned, "Well I have more. I've been drawing up designs in my spare time and these are the fabrics I'd use." I pulled out a thick binder, flipping it open. "I could see this for Fall fashion week, or even The Met Gala!" I announced, showing a swopping satin dress, its bottom sprawled like a trumpet with sleeves composed of hand stitched feathers. Sleek, wild, a bit crazy, much like my morning.

"No." He winced, ruthlessly committed to dragging me down. "Your look is dated, I'm not sure what era this is even from." He closed it shut, not sliding it towards my direction, but rather all the way towards the other end of the table.

"Dated?" I asked. "I don't understand."

"And you wouldn't, that's why you're here and not with your clients. Like you said, Miss Harrison, you have lots to learn."

"Oh, ok…" I drew out my voice, buying the time I needed as to not whimper. "Well if you don't like my designs, then at least let me style for you again." I conceded. I didn't want to style, but if it took me starting from the bottom up again, I would.

"Oh," he laughed, "I'm not hiring you, Gemma. Not for anything." He answered, the quick clip of his words matched each sharp compression of the shears in his hand. "You're crazy if you think that."

My body boiled, not from the tone of Gerard's voice, but rather, the inescapable sensation of being watched. It pricked at my neck, teasing like a hot dagger, the sense of lingering eyes. Quickly I peeked up, recognizing the figure close by as the man in the Dodgers cap. He stood near a rack of clothes, his shoulders held in a tight leather jacket. His stare sat guarded, shielded with dark shades, but directed at me. I grimaced, feeling the cringe of embarrassment, knowing he witnessed the entire failed interview. I was sweaty, on the brink of tears, and completely disheveled from the run.

"But I thought you wanted to hire me?" I questioned, returning my attention to Gerard. "I guess… I'm just confused."

"You certainly are." He scoffed. "I wouldn't hire you

to fetch my coffee, Gemma. The fact you showed my clients your *own* designs while working for me was completely disrespectful. How could I forgive that? I couldn't. So instead, I taught you a lesson."

"Gerard, that was a complete accident." I reminded him, recalling the moment one of his A-list clients caught me sketching and begged for the look to be made. "It happened once, and I even gave you all the credit."

"I'm not listening," he plugged his ears. "I had to remind you that you were never truly anything special." His smile curled into an ugly smirk, "Besides, you were late today, just like before. Back when you were here, it was always something new, running off to help your poor mommy in some crummy Brooklyn apartment," he seemed disgusted. "I don't need that garbage around my shop, or your second hand looks."

My mouth dropped; his words stung in the most viscous of ways. To even bring up Claire, to drag her into this. Why would he, or more importantly, how could he? That was over four years ago, and it was hell. Claire was on the wrong medication, and I had to be there to put her back together. Gerard had no idea the extent of my leave, but he knew enough to allow me to go. And now, he asked me to an interview, and for what? To watch me struggle, after stealing my clients and ruining my business? A big, fat *fuck you* teetered on my tongue.

"Any questions?" He blinked rapidly. The urge to leap over the counter and wring his neck was overwhelming, to say the least. I hated him, but most of all, I hated how he made me feel, like I was a little girl again with no control.

"Just one." A thick, steady voice hummed in the air, diverting my attention to the end of the counter. It was the man from before, standing unfazed, flipping through the pages of my designs. "Does this come in black?" He asked, the hint of dark tattoos peeked from his cuff, his hand imprinted with a black rose. He pointed towards a Polaroid, a Calvin Klein suit I styled for an event: navy jacket, burgundy tie.

"Yes…" I muttered, still reeling from the effects of Gerard's attack.

"And you can curate this? If I need *it*?" His voice deepened, steeped in an accent like Latin silk.

"Well… of course." I fidgeted, looking back at Gerard who was not amused.

"I'm sorry, sir, we're in the middle of something right now." Gerard chimed in, almost apologetic. The man looked up at me, only me, staring in silence as if Gerard didn't exist. He closed the book, lifting it with one hand, who's weight required two of my own.

"I'm here for a stylist, and I'm short on time." He announced. His black boots clicked with a heavy thud, perfectly matched with knee slit denim jeans, as he approached.

"Well, I can style you sir, that's no…" Gerard's words stopped, blocked by the motion of the man, who said nothing at all, but instead, raised a single finger to his lips. The implied shush startled me, as Gerard's face turned from orange to red.

"I'm not sure if you're what I was looking for, but

you may be what I need." He said, curiously eyeing me as he set the book by my side. I reached for it, but he stopped me. He placed his hand on top of the cover. His skin glowed like bronzed honey. "Like I said, I'm short on time, and I'm ready to make a decision."

"She doesn't even work here," Gerard interrupted, "and you need to leave. In fact, both of you leave, or I'll call the cops." His absurd threat warranted a smirk from the man, who slowly reached up to remove his shades.

"The cops? Now this is a party." He chewed his gum ever so slightly, revealing who he was beneath. Gerard gasped, the noise of his breath more startling than my own realization.

Those eyes.

I knew them.

They were the same from the man in the billboard, dark and familiar, those that judged me as I ran across the street. He was here, more apparent than ever, his knitted brow impossibly calm.

"Alex Rivers..." The tremble in Gerard's voice shook between my ears, but all I heard was the rush of my own blood. I stared, hopelessly lost in the unbreakable gaze of the man who challenged me with an undefined intention.

"Alex Rivers?" I asked out loud. It was a name I knew, but almost forgot, whose face covered more than just a billboard. Yes, I knew his name, I knew his clout. He carried it like a heavy stick, an aura concealed clearly from the public, disguised in the simplest of ways.

"I need you to be quiet now." Alex instructed

Gerard, as he calmly gazed down at the silver ring on his thumb, toying with its rotation. "I have what I came for."

Have what I came for? Did he mean me? I stared at a panicked Gerard, whose own fear felt somehow contagious. What was I supposed to do? Alex lifted my binders from the counter, placing them into my tote.

"You don't need to do that," I laughed nervously, but Alex continued.

"I know." He wrapped the handle of the tote along his tight grip. "You can thank me outside." He walked off, carrying my life's work in his hands, leaving me to stare as he reached the door. Gerard shouted, but I ran, chasing to keep up with Alex's loud clicking boots.

"Where are you going?" I asked, reaching for my tote as he stopped by the curb. I pulled it from his hands, gently coaxing his release. The weight seemed heavier than I remembered, fooled by how easy he held it.

"What's your name?" He asked, as I set the bag down on the floor, kneeling to ensure its contents were secure. As I stared up, I was met with a firm expression, the creases along his eyes left me in doubt about the tone of his question. Was he angry or eager to know?

"Gemma." I mumbled, allowing the weight of his presence to settle in. This was a celebrity, one evoking fear from Gerard, but I felt nothing. I didn't know his work or anything he'd done, except appear in ads. This celebrity aspect didn't have an effect on me, but the command of his voice did.

"Gemma…" He repeated my name with such slick

conviction, almost as if he wanted to test the way it rolled off his tongue.

Even in heels, my nose barely reached his chest. I tilted my head, just as I had when I saw him in the billboard. I couldn't resist the urge to divert my eyes from his, his stare was as powerful as it was fiercely dark. His broad shoulders and fitted jacket, opened to a pristine white V-neck. Its contrast fit snuggly against his olive skin, teasing a coarse tuft of pebbled chest hair. I felt small in his shadow and how his eyes stared from above.

"What?" I asked, brushing my hair behind my ear. "Why are you staring at me like that?" He cocked his head, narrowing his eyes as his tongue clicked the gum in his mouth.

"Does it make you uncomfortable?"

Uncomfortable? I wasn't sure how it made me feel. Nervous, warm, almost as if I had slipped into a hot bath. Though his face was stern, his presence was anything but. Assertive, yes, but how did it make me feel? I wanted to say *safe*, though admitting it felt absurd.

"It doesn't." I answered.

"And where you from, Gemma?"

"Midtown."

"No." He hushed.

"No?" I asked, puzzled by his refute. "I live in Midtown… currently."

"You're not from Midtown though, are you?" His eyes finally looked away, slowly scanning the entirety of my body, shamelessly lingering at my lips. The brief pauses between his questions made me feel as though I was being studied. I returned the courtesy, taking a longer glance at the black rose tattoo on his hand. "Tell me, where are you really from?" His eyes motioned towards my purse, as he removed the gum from his mouth. I froze as his hand dropped near my waist, digging into the yellow bag of Marcello's Galletas. He pulled out a cookie, slipping it between his soft cupid lips. The way he stared between the bag and me, it almost felt like he knew something more. He sensed it, subtly hinting at my quiet truth with the crunch of a sweet vanilla crisp.

"Brooklyn." I corrected, mortified at his discovery of my poor bodega cookies. He licked his thumb.

"Where in Brooklyn?"

"Bushwick."

"Is that where you take care of your mother?"

I scrunched my face, a part of me immediately annoyed by his prying questions and how Gerard made that comment so loudly. I shook my head, reluctant to answer any further.

"I don't take care of her," I said swiftly. "And that's none of your business." I cleared my throat, reminded of Gerard's words and all the trouble living with Claire caused. Reaching up, I stroked my neck, already suffocated from the scent of imaginary cigarettes. Alex's eyes shifted, fixated on my hand.

"Hmmm…" he hummed.

"Hmm, what?"

"Now you're uncomfortable."

"No, I'm not." I pulled my hands back to my side. He grinned, and for the first time, it seemed like a genuine reaction to my stubborn dispute. The way his eyes creased, kissed by the sun, smooth, yet rugged, had the appearance of age but none of its timely wear. If I had to guess, he was much older than me, perhaps ten years the difference of Parker and me.

"If you say so…" he said unconvinced, "you're here for an interview, and that's what I'm giving you." He stared passed me, observing for any oncoming traffic, or possibly the sign of people. "Why were you late?"

"Half the Upper East Side is blocked," I sighed, "another movie, another headache."

He laughed, and the sound of his deep rasp tightened my chest. "Apologies are in order," he replied, "and be glad. I don't do that often."

His laugh irked me, realizing the gravity of his confession, "Wait, you mean… it's *your* movie?"

"Most of them are…"

"Well, you're the reason I was late, the reason I took my heels off and ran through the dirty streets of New York." My lip twitched in disgust, feeling the grime between my toes. "And why aren't you there? Entire streets are blocked, and yet you're here at a small boutique?"

"They shoot when I'm ready." He replied calmly. "And I'll be ready, once this is taken care of first."

"Well, you being late caused me to be late." I shrugged, "It's unprofessional."

"Maybe… but it's my choice, and I have so few already, except for one, of course," he paused, "the one I'm making right now."

I stepped backward, reaching my hand behind me to

steady myself against a parking meter. I felt as though I could fall at any moment, clutching my oversized tote between my knees. He moved in closer, studying me once more. "And what would that be?" I asked.

"You." He stated, so matter of fact.

I laughed. "What about me?"

"I have some upcoming events that require a stylist. I came here by word of mouth, and here you were. So now you're my stylist." I laughed again. He couldn't be serious, not like this, but I could tell in the way his eyes narrowed, he wasn't joking at all.

"Do you do this often?" I asked, completely suspicious of his words. He was too smooth, too confident, completely unhesitant.

"Do what exactly?"

"Ask girls to be your stylist?" I shrugged, "Don't you already have a team of people? This just seems odd. Like some pick up line." I cleared my throat, asserting my position. But why would he be hitting on me? I looked like I just escaped a fire and ran a marathon.

"Don't be ridiculous." He scoffed, leaning closer, the faint rise of cherry scent lifted from his skin and into my nose. "If I wanted to *pick* you up, I'd merely lift you in my arms and take you." The way his voice rolled, appeared both foreign and alluring. I felt as if I could buckle, my body both stiff and loose. "This is a serious job," he added, "with serious expectations. I don't do charity. I see what I want, and I take it." His eyes peered down at the bag of unused business cards I held the day before. He plucked them from my purse, "This is you?" He asked, nodding at the bag.

"That's me," was all I could say, as Alex bit into the plastic, the white fang of his tooth pulled a seam to access a card. He held it up, reading my name aloud with a smirk.

"Gemma. Rose. Harrison." He growled, his eyes met mine once more, "*Piedra preciosa.*" The unfamiliar words buzzed like a drug in my veins, his voice far too intoxicating for me to make sense of.

"What did you just say?" I stammered as his eyes looked up at an oncoming crowd. He flashed a quick but stressful grin, slipping his glasses back onto his face.

"Don't be shy. Soon everyone will know your name." He tucked the card into his pocket, leaving me no chance to inquire further as hordes of people took notice of the apparent star, Mr. Alex Rivers.

Chapter 3

"**S**he'll need Tabasco." Parker warned the waitress as she placed our food on the table.

"And he'll need more half and half." I added, ripping two pink packets of sugar for his freshly filled coffee.

Breakfast at Bennes' was the culmination of every simple pleasure that a diner could have. If it wasn't the sizzle of a fried egg, or the chatter of revolving guests, then it was the charm of anointed Christmas lights that hung above our tiny booth. These were the things that caused Parker and me to return like a habit, and I loved it, especially since it was something we shared together.

"Every time," Parker laughed with a shake of his head, "why is it that you always forget Tabasco and I forget the creamer?" He stirred the sugar in as his spoon clinked against the ceramic lip of his mug.

"I don't know, I think that's why we make a good team." I replied, knowing full well the reason. For me, it was a ritual. I'd always forget Tabasco on purpose, anticipating whether Parker would remember or not. He always did, and I in turn ordered the creamer. As silly as it felt, I enjoyed how he cared to remember both me and my taste. I wondered if the same was true for him, though I had the feeling it was purely by accident.

"Speaking of tradition…" I said out loud, as the thoughts in my head spilled over into real spoken words.

"Tradition?" Parker questioned, placing his suit jacket over the top of our booth.

"Oh, nothing." I corrected, removing the cap of hot sauce placed on the table, "I'm just wondering what you did wrong." I teased, dabbing dots of red liquid over my bed of hash browns.

"Wrong?" Parker asked, pouring the creamer. "Are you the lawyer or me?" He took a sip.

I glanced over at his plate, my brows knitted in suspicion, "Clearly you did something wrong, why else would you be punishing yourself? Exhibit A." My potato filled fork pointed to a square cut of salmon on his plate, its pink hue sat atop a heap of steamed zucchini. "What's with the change? Or better yet, where is Parker, and what have you done with him? You hate seafood!"

Parker took a bite, his face turning sour as he tried to answer. "Broadening my horizons." He sneered. He chewed like he was avoiding his tongue, keeping the salmon on a path from teeth to stomach. I slid a piece of hot bacon onto his plate, giving him a wink.

"For when you come to your senses." I watched, making sure he took a bite, relishing in the joy the flavor gave him. "You'll need your strength for work," I noticed, of course, his formal attire, and how he filled the lines of his fitted white shirt. "I still can't believe you're going in on a Saturday. My god, you've been so busy, I haven't even seen you all week! What time did you get in last night?" I sacrificed another piece of bacon, just to see him smile once more.

"Late." He chewed, "You won't even believe what's happening. I've been busting my ass on this new case, and I'm hellbent on making a statement." He pushed his zucchini around, unimpressed. "Winning this case means maintaining my reputation. It's a big fish. I'll leave it at that."

My eyebrow arched, and Parker sighed, knowing my affinity for his job and the gossip it included. "What did they do?" I leaned in, curling a loose whip of hair that fell from my bun.

"No…" Parker raised his hand, "I'm not a true crime podcast; I have a code of conduct."

"Lawyers have a code of conduct?" I joked.

"Ouch." He grasped his chest as if struck.

"Kidding!" I smacked his hand as he reached for another piece of bacon. The dimple on his cheek creased as I pursed my lips.

"Honestly, I want to just fast forward, to win against this asshole and ruin his day. Consider it my championship fight." His jaw clicked at the word *fight*. He reached up, assessing the smoothness of his cheek, his wrist wrapped in a sleek leather watch. He wasn't stressed, but rather focused, his clean-cut appearance a hallmark to a new mental state. This was the lawyer, the man who already made a name for himself within such little time.

I feared if I stared any longer, my admiration would be too apparent. I adjusted in my seat as the skin that peeked from my short, floral skirt stuck to the booth. He made me sweat with his words as I crossed my legs.

"Well, before you take over the world, remember I got us tickets to see the *Phantom of the Opera…*" I wobbled my head, enjoying the taste of cheesy eggs.

"I wouldn't miss it, but I wish you had let me pay. You can save money since you're with me."

With me, the way he said it felt so close, its interpretation different than intended. Enjoying breakfast was a routine pleasure, allowing me to keep the fantasy of us alive in my head. Living with him was different though, I knew it'd be tough, especially with comments like that. Honestly, it made my belly ache.

"It's no problem. It was my turn to pay. You got last year's tickets, remember?" I brushed my thoughts away, "I had them on reserve, anyway, and I got the same seats from when we first saw it."

"Just like every year."

"Exactly." I confirmed, his eyes were so tender, disrupted only by the taste of salmon entering his mouth. I'm sure the flavor was awful, but I would've kissed him regardless if he asked. I'd take any excuse to feel his lips on mine.

Stop it, Gemma.

"Tell me." He announced, as if catching my thoughts.

"About?"

"About your interview? Please tell me you said no to that parasite." He placed his empty coffee mug at the edge of the table, eagerly looking back. "I know I've been out all week, but I was tempted to wake you up and ask." He stated, but quickly clarified the reason he didn't, "but your rest is most important, Butterfly, so I waited."

I fought the urge to suck on my lip, "Well… I certainly didn't get the job, and actually I'm happy about that."

"That's good." He sighed, his shoulders lowered in ease.

"Yes and no. Well, something else happened, but I don't think it's anything real." I added, unsure if it was even worth the explanation.

"Now I'm interested. Tell me."

"I was propositioned." I teased.

"Stop."

"What? I was. Well, rescued is more like it. This guy needed a stylist; apparently, he has some events coming up. No idea on the pay, no idea on if it will even happen. Honestly, he may have just been flirting…" I added but debated. Was he flirting? He was incredibly persistent and wildly confident. It was as if I had no choice in the matter, he was there to take me, with or without my approval. He mentioned being short on time, so perhaps it was out of convenience rather than something more?

"Flirt?" Parker asked, his excitement more tamed.

"Maybe? It could have just been his personality. You know celebrities better than I do."

"Celebrities?" He concealed a laugh, leaving me unsure if he was confused or excited. "Local New Yorker?"

"Definitely not."

"Anyone I know?"

"Probably, I think he does actions movies. You like those, not me."

"Well yeah, but how do you know him?"

"I don't really. I mean, his face looked familiar, I'm sure you've seen it around New York."

"Name?" Parker was interrogating, fishing his way as if filing a report. I wanted to string him along for a bit of fun; his face intrigued as if it were a game.

"Guess…"

"Gemma…"

I hummed for a moment, acting as if I didn't know, but in reality, I truly forgot. I wanted to say Alec at first, but reminded myself it was Alex, having initially noticed that his height was similar to—if not slightly taller than —Alexander Skarsgård, who himself was already six-foot-four.

"Alex," I said, mustering as much nonchalance as I could. "Alex Rivers." The waitress from before approached with a pot of coffee. Parker held up his hand, his green eyes haunting like cursed jewels.

"Not now." He instructed her, causing her eyes to widen before turning away.

"Ok? That was rude." I chirped, adjusting a strand of hair back into my bun.

"What are you doing with Alex Rivers?" He asked, the mood no longer felt like a game, but instead a concern.

"Nothing yet. He has my business card, so now I'm waiting."

"You gave that to him?"

"Well, no... he took it."

"What do you mean he *took* it?" He pressed further, his elbow leaned on the table. This movement alone caused a reaction in his bicep, and its structured size popped into sight.

"I mean, he reached into my bag and pulled them out... practically tore them apart with his teeth." It sounded weird the way I admitted it, as if he were more of a dog than a man.

"No." Parker folded his napkin onto the table, making a decision I was not yet privy to.

"No?" I asked. "No to what?"

"You can't work with Alex Rivers."

I pulled my head back, craning my neck to see if anyone was listening. Parker ensuring my Tabasco was ordered was cute. I loved when he looked after me that way. However, telling me who I couldn't work with felt different. I didn't care for it.

"I can." I replied, angrily retrieving my half-eaten bacon back from his plate. "There is no reason to say otherwise."

"He's the guy, Gemma." Parker announced, his finger delivering a quick jab to the table. "My big fish; the case I'm working on at this very moment." I stopped chewing, swallowing a large piece of toast that slowly scraped my throat. It felt uncomfortable, much like Parker's confession.

"He's harmless." I assured, knowing the ability of my own strength, along with the things I'd seen and experienced in my lifetime. How bad could he be?

"He's violent." Parker furrowed his brow, thumbing

the sterling fork in his hand, "He's already spent plenty of time in court, I've read the files. Did you know he can't even return to The Pierre Hotel? Not after what happened, the damages that occurred. Some fucking party he threw got way out of hand, and it's not just the hotel that's coming after him anymore. It's bad, Gemma, you have no idea what a world of shit this guy's in, especially after I'm done with him." Parker stole the bacon back, taking a definitive bite from its length. "He has no regard for being professional, always late when his lawyers request him and leaves when the tough questions get asked. As soon as it gets heated, he's gone. He has no control, for himself or his women. You understand?" He arched a brow, "Don't get involved."

"He's unprofessional? I thought you weren't a true crime podcast? Yet, here you are now, judging him." I reminded, "Code of conduct?" I could tell this bothered him; his lip twitched as if to say more.

"This is different, I know too much." He retorted, "Outside of this case, he's been charged with assault. The man acts like he fights for a living. I don't want you around that."

"And what about me? Can't I be professional?" I challenged, assessing his perception.

"Of course, but he's different. He's cunning."

"And… what? I'm naive?"

"Fuck, Gemma no…" He sighed, slightly frustrated.

"He can't be that dangerous, has anyone died?" I asked, tilting my head as if that was some convincing argument. It wasn't.

"People have been hurt, that's all I can say at the moment."

The truth was, this scared me, but the assertive tone Parker used rubbed me the wrong way. I wasn't even sure if Alex would call, but the idea of Parker already shooting it down felt disappointing. I wanted that choice, not Parker, who lived his life without being told what to do.

"I need to decide what's best for me," I said plainly. "That includes the opportunities I'm given."

He sighed with frustration. "Why can't you just trust me on this one?"

"And why can't you? There's a lot I've been through and I'm stronger than you realize. I can handle myself around some celebrity."

"It's not about being strong or not, it's about…" It pained him to even say, the words failing to come out, replaced with a breath. "I just… want you to be safe."

"And I just don't want to be a burden. Parker, I don't really have many choices. I'm not having any luck, and even if he called, what would I say? Oh, sorry, my roommate doesn't approve? I'm trying to get out of your hair."

"I've told you before, you're not in my hair." His voice mellowed softly.

"But those are my feelings, and that is what I'm entitled to. I just don't feel comfortable staying rent free. I know it'll somehow prevent you from living a normal life, even if you won't admit it."

"Like what?"

"Like I've said before, what if you brought a girl

home? How would you even act, knowing your third wheel best friend is close by? I won't do that, not to you." I stated, wanting him to live his life while avoiding my feelings from getting hurt.

"Fuck that," he snipped. "No opportunity is worth your safety, I won't hear that. Anyway, why are you obsessed with me finding a girl and being normal?" He shook his head.

"Why are you obsessed with my safety? You can't tell me who I can and cannot work with, Park. We're not dating…"

Parker's soft lips parted, my words caught on his tongue. He fell silent as I turned my attention to the runny yolk of my split egg. I didn't want him to feel as if I were holding a grudge from that awful college night, and I was afraid that felt apparent with my last remark. Wasn't he just being honest when he said I was only like a sister to him? He didn't owe me anything, in fact, he gave me so much, and all I could do was keep him in a box in my head, guarded like a secret fantasy.

"I didn't mean it like that." I apologized.

"I know…" he sighed, "we're not dating, but…" He adjusted the knot of his tie, scrambling with a thought before coming to some conclusion. "There's something I want to talk to you about. Let me take you out somewhere special tomorrow night." He caught my attention, the annunciation of his words deliberate and cautious. It appeared he was still pondering what to say but leaned forward with confident poise.

"Special?" I asked, the idea almost forbidden.

"Yes, somewhere we can discuss more, and maybe I

can put you at ease." He checked his watch, annoyed at the time. "I have to go, but promise me you won't be mad at me?" He asked, refusing to leave until I responded.

"I promise." I replied, unable to resist the adorable way his cheek creased and how a loose strand of hair swooped over his face. He was cute, and when he wasn't, he was handsome, but more so than that, sexy. The most powerful lawyer by my side, eager to defend, even against Alex Rivers, a man who'd probably never call. He slipped on his jacket, folding a hundred dollar bill by the coffee mug.

"Be sure to eat lunch, Butterfly." He winked, turning away, slipping passed the seated crowd.

Something *special?* The way his face dropped when I said, *we're not dating*, made me feel as though I had struck a chord. Was this my imagination, or was the vague request of *wanting* to talk about something else somehow related? I wasn't nervous about Alex, or even upset at Parker's persistence, instead, in this moment, all I felt was a strange glimpse of hope. What else would he want to talk about, if not the possibility of us?

"*Put me at ease.*" I mussed, taking a bite of the same bacon that touched both our lips.

Chapter 4

I t was impossible to focus, all day I'd been in a haze, thinking about tonight, about Parker. Something felt magical about yesterday, the calm in his voice, the almost suppressed excitement in his eyes.

What could he possibly want to talk to me about?

I sat in front of the round mirror of my bathroom, applying a thin strip of black eyeliner. I turned my cheeks side to side, loving how the contour matched with a sexy blend of blush and gold. For a moment I observed, staring back into the mirror, unable to quit my beaming smile.

A loud knock sounded at my door, as my lips pursed for some color. "Come in!" I shouted, peeking past the doorframe.

"You almost ready?" Parker stepped in. I stalled, glancing in the mirror, placing a pair of gold hoops into my ears. Really I wasn't ready, and though I had all day to be, I spent it shopping instead. Tonight was special, Parker made that clear, so spending the entire day hunting for the perfect look was my main priority. The current predicament lied in what I wanted to say, not with words, but with style. I found two dresses, both of which asked the same question, *which Gemma should come out to dinner?* The answer was either the sweet innocent one, or the sexy sultry one? I bit the corner of my nail, contemplating this life changing decision.

"Almost, just have to get my dress!" I exclaimed, concealing the fact it wasn't as easy as it sounded. I popped out of the bathroom, tightening the belt of my floral silk robe. "How much time do we have?"

"Twenty minutes," Parker stood by my old oak desk, his thumb grazed the shadowed look along his jaw, "but take your time, I want to show you off tonight." I nearly tripped from his words, my blush far too profound for him not to notice. Show me off? I parted my lips, stuck in an apparent gawk, lost in his mesmerizing words and the sleek fit of his navy suit. He glanced down, his large hands adjusted a dark sapphire tie. It was a sign, a tie only worn on special occasions, the one I had gotten for his twenty-fourth birthday. It was actually going to happen, he was going to ask me to be his girlfriend. "Gemma?" He laughed, breaking the spell his eyes held on my body.

"Yes!" I held up a finger, "One second, I promise," I rushed into my closet and was greeted by the two dresses. Parker wanted to show me off, and knowing that alone pulled in my stomach. I wanted to deliver the perfect message, so the question was asked once again. Sexy or innocent? One, a sleeveless black Valentino, shaped with a plunging dash across the bust. Sexy? Very much so. The second, an indigo blue Oscar De La Renta with angel sleeves and bright gold poppies. Innocent, but also very sweet. Both vintage, both a thrift store find, but equally costing more money than I truly had.

"Are you excited?" Parker asked. The noisy springs creaked as his large body sat atop my bed. I quivered. What was going through his mind while he stared around my room? Did he notice the old cut out magazines pinned along the walls, showing the latest styles of my favorite designer, St. La Vie? I wondered if this made me look too young, like a teen with her posters hung around.

"Nervous." I admitted, skimming the two dresses before my eyes. Though the black Valentino was hot, I wasn't sure if I was ready for it. I felt as though it gave too much away, not my flesh, but more my feelings. I always imagined Parker as a lover, to be sweet and gentle, but also, I imagined more. He wasn't just a kind guy, he was a feared lawyer, a viscous and protective man who never settled in court. This side was more rough, a version of Parker I'd fantasized about with my hot pink vibrator, at least three times since being here.

"Don't be nervous, I'm right here." Parker said in a low sexy tone. Each word a deliberate slip, falling softly like velvet. I wanted my dress to say both, 'Fuck my brains out,' yet 'kiss me softly.' The sudden thought of him taking me, of the word *fuck*, felt so dirty, like it belonged to someone other than myself. But hell, I wanted it all. I tightened my lips.

"What's so special about a regular ol' Sunday night?" I fished, begging to hear his voice once again.

"You'll see soon enough, like I've said, I think this will put your mind at ease."

My mind at ease? It was anything but. When defending my decision to make the choices I wanted, I reminded Parker we weren't dating; at least not yet. All this over Alex, a man who hadn't even called. I didn't care about that right now, tonight was something better, the cumulation of everything I ever wanted. To put me at ease would be to make us official, making my move into his apartment a blessing in disguise.

The bedspring creaked again, as if Parker moved to get closer to the closet. Purposefully, I left the door open, leaving myself perfectly in sight of the large mirror on my wall. I could almost sense his eyes, his movement on the bed, giving him the advantage needed to silently watch me undress.

"I hope so. Actually, I'm not nervous anymore, I'm excited." I slipped my finger through the knot of my silk belt, pulling it loose. My body straightened at the realization, the allowance I gave Parker to watch. It could be a secret if he wished, something he could keep to himself. My robe slowly swept off my shoulders and onto the floor. I stood still in my heels, adjusting the band of my black lace thong high on my hips.

"You should be excited. I can't think of a better time than now." He replied. My imagination ran wild as I heard the bed squeak once more, his subtle movement surely for me. I couldn't help myself, the thought of being a tease, a sight to get him off. I stretched my body up, extending the reach of my length as my legs pressed together. A perfect glimpse, a sight of my ass popping into place, hitched in a thong.

"Will there be candles?" I asked, my tongue played with the side of my cheek.

"With five hundred dollar bottles of wine on the

menu, I'd assume the mood would be fitting." His voice appeared much closer than it was just moments ago. The creak from the bed wasn't from his adjustment, it was from him standing up. "You know, I love the way that looks." His breath grazed my neck, surprising the skin along my shoulders. I held my response, unprepared for his sudden voice.

"Parker?" I cooed but was hushed as his large hands brushed my hair off to the side of my shoulder.

"Don't turn around." He moaned, "You're perfect where you're at." The trace of his fingertips trailed along my skin, moving from my neck and up towards my chin. He adjusted my gaze with the tilt of his wrist, meeting the mirror that sat in the closet. "Actually, *we're* perfect where *we're* at." He stated.

"What about the reservation?"

"Fuck it," he said. "I'm hungry now." My fingers knitted through his hair, granting a silent permission with my back still turned to his chest. He let me know his intent as his hands surrounded my entire middle, leaving me speechless as he pressed himself against me. My eyes fluttered back. I shivered at his size, the unmistakable erection caught in his slacks, a frustrating barrier pressed against my nearly naked ass.

"Were you watching me?" I asked, my breath fell short of a whisper.

"I always am." He growled, clawing at my torso, twisting my navel as he reached below, "And I'm about sick of waiting…"

"Waiting for what?"

"Waiting to take you, to make you mine."

"How?" I begged for an answer, his hand reached lower than I could ever imagine, stinging with an unfamiliar intensity. After years of waiting, he was here, touching parts of my body I only dreamed of. I wanted to know how he'd make me his, how he'd claim me.

"In the only way possible," he quivered, the reflection of his lips parted and nipped near my ear, "with my cum leaking between your legs, of course." His finger slipped down as he groaned, passing my panties and into my wet slit.

"Park…" I gasped, his size plunged into me, causing me to buckle forward with a whimper.

"Stay with me," he instructed, correcting my posture with a firm grip of my jaw. "I want to see my Butterfly enjoy herself." I obeyed, staring into the mirror, almost shutting my eyes from ecstasy alone.

"I'm so…"

"Wet?" He moaned. His fingers slithered the lubed noise from my lips, unique like the smack of new bubble gum. His strength alone lifted me up, pulling me to my toes as a second finger slipped inside. "We don't eat dinner till I make you mine," he directed, "and that starts with you screaming my name."

"I will." I promised. My hips moved to the motion of his finger. Impatiently he reached up, his loose hand yanked on my bra, freeing the pink blush of my perked nipple with a pinch.

"I know you will," he motioned, kissing down my neck, "I've said your name too, under my breath anytime I touched myself."

"Just like me." I confessed, admitting how I've

thought of him while masturbating, which I'd done countless times already. If only he knew how many orgasms he'd already given me, simply from the thought of his dick stuffed between my lips. His erection pressed into me further, its head big just like I imagined, round and full.

"No, not like you." He challenged, "Do you bite your lip? Do you twist your sheets in resistance, fighting the urge to find me, to fuck me? Cause I do for you, and it takes everything I have to stop that."

"Then don't," I pleaded, his fingers slipped out, swiping the slick wetness along my swollen clit. My climax was unbearably close, his words alone building me higher than I was prepared for.

"I won't," he moaned. "Just give me permission."

"To fuck me?" I asked, my voice hoarse, dry from the lack of spit.

"To bend you over," he inhaled, "to make you hold my cum." I pinched my thighs around his fingers which were inside me again, pumping slowly, forcing me to drip from the pressure of his size.

"I'd keep it inside." I whined, his cum a newly given treat I desperately wanted. "I'll stop it from leaking, I'll even hold it in for as long as you want."

"Every ounce," he instructed. "I'll knock you up, Butterfly, I'll take that pretty pussy of yours and make you my wife." He bit my shoulder, his erection almost painfully pressed against my cheeks, as if at any moment the length of him could slip inside my ass. "But before I do, I'll make you feel my hot breath. I'll burn you alive, starting from your neck until I'm between your thighs.

It's the only place I'll ever kneel, where I'll fucking worship."

"Worship?" He spoke as if I were an alter, a position to pray, or possibly give thanks.

"A place to atone, Butterfly, for all the wicked shit I wanted to do but never could. Not anymore though. Now, I'll lick you like the fucking wet treat that you are, tasting you as deep as I can fucking get." His description was as arousing as it was vulgar, knowing that at any moment he'd spread me open for a taste.

"Just like that…" I gasped as his fingers rolled the nub of my clit like a gentle dial.

"Shit," he moaned testing the swelling that he caused, "I got you fucking puffy, so wet that I might just slip out. I bet you were leaking before I even fucked you with my fingers."

"You on the bed was all I needed." I admitted, almost in pain from the intense pleasure the tip of his finger provided.

"That's my Butterfly, getting wet for me, knowing it will be easier to stretch you out. Neither of us will last long, but I promise, you'll taste my cum from just how hard I'll shoot inside you."

"Stop, you're going to make me come." I cried at his threat. I could feel it throbbing, something far more intimate than ever before. I wanted it in the closet, bent over and rough, his grip in my hair, his lips on my neck. Yes, Parker Jones, the lawyer, the god, filling me up, breaking me in.

"You ready, Butterfly?" Parker's voice appeared at the door, his cheerful question startled me into focus. I was in a fantasy, lost in the thought of him taking me in the closet. Literally, I was caught, almost reaching down into my own panties, seduced by my imagination.

"Park!" I screeched, pressing my elbows closer to my body. I concealed any true peek, betraying the confidence I just had while fantasizing. "I'm picking out something special," I assured, suddenly far more shy than I realized. At most in our lifetime he had seen me in my bathing suit, possibly my bra in the heat of a quick change, but this was different, he was not coy like me, he was merely confident in everything that he did.

His broad shoulder leaned in the doorway, while his cool green eyes studied mine, lowering to my chest with an encompassing glance. I allowed the silence to fall between us, tempting my mouth to ask the question, *do you want to see me*? What did his eyes say, if not silent admiration? I looked at his tie and knew exactly what to wear. I was not yet the hot sexy Gemma, but rather, the shy sweet girl who loved her best friend.

"Help me zip it up?" I asked, turning away to remove the blue Oscar De La Renta off the hanger. He stepped forward, accepting the request, the tanned dimple of his cheek appeared.

"Looks special to me." He smirked, as I stepped into the dress and pulled it up to my waist. "Wait," Parker stopped. "Let me." He hummed, the softness of his hand gently lifted the dress up to my shoulders. The way his thumb brushed against my skin tingled, vibrating from my toes to my neck as the top clasp clicked. "There." He finished, his voice still low.

I turned to face him, and his eyes assessed the dark

blue shine of my silk dress. I adjusted the strap, the skintight fit hugged along my curves and small chest. Parker's eyes swept over my body then down at his own tie, "You look... really great," he attempted to cover a groan by clearing his throat. "We match like a couple."

"Don't we though?" I asked, hoping to skip dinner and go straight for the kiss. I adjusted his tie, the designer in me ensuring his look was correct, but also an excuse to touch him briefly.

"Now we're ready." He confirmed, "Tonight you'll know this is your home, and you'll never have to feel weird. I'll show you what you've been waiting to see. I promise." The conviction of his words were true. When Parker made a promise, he never broke it.

Chapter 5

April showers in New York were a problem for some, but not for me. I loved the rain, in exception to the thunder, whose booming noise felt too close to the shouts I heard while growing up. Like other unpleasant noises, such as the flick of a lighter, I'd find myself flinching, or even avoiding a space all together. I tried to ignore this fact, reminding myself that rain often signaled the season of spring, along with the fashion that followed.

While others wore heavy coats, I wore a tight dress with gold poppies, their meaning a little confusing depending on the interpretation. To some it resembled peace earned through death, but to others it was the symbol of love between a new couple. Tonight, it was the latter, it's former meaning something I ignored. Regardless, they were a nice touch, adorned with blooming petals I'd never cover up.

We pulled up to the curb of a massive building, its exterior made of glass and warm lights. It towered above, piercing the sky, halting the rain which fell just moments ago.

Parker offered his arm which I gladly accepted as we stepped out. "So, now that we're getting closer, can you finally tell me what tonight is all about?" I asked, my hand filled with the size of his bicep.

"Not yet, but you'll see once we get to the rooftop. You'll be so excited. I promise."

I snuggled close against his arm as we walked, "I cannot believe it! We're actually dressed up for a dinner. You know we've never gone anywhere fancy, right? It's always been pizza slices or breakfast." I laughed.

"That's not bad!" He tilted his head toward mine, combing the untamed wave of his hair. "I actually prefer that. It's so us, simple and comfortable."

"Simple? Like, predictable?" I twisted my lips, questioning his choice of words. "Should I take that as a compliment?" I wasn't sure if it was.

"Simple?" He asked. "Simple has a bad rep. Life is so complicated, so messy. There's nothing wrong with simple, in fact it's a luxury in my eyes." Parker nodded, "I suppose simple isn't the right word, but in my heart, it makes sense. But I get it, sometimes we need to try new things, even if it makes us uncomfortable."

"That's true, I suppose it's how we grow."

If Parker and I were supposed to be with each other, we would have to escape our comfort zone. Maybe I wasn't the sister anymore, I was the risk he was willing to take. My stomach twirled in anticipation.

For a moment, we faced each other, and I feared he could sense the nervousness in my eyes. The pumping in my neck was almost a dizzying dream. I felt both incredible and beautiful, just from the way he stared at me. I wasn't just happy, I was loved by the man I'd dreamed of calling mine since the day we met.

He placed his hand gently on my shoulder. "Gemma…" He finally let out.

"Yes?" I answered immediately, consumed by the silence between us. I couldn't take it, the tension in my body, the alignment of a grand reveal.

"I've been meaning to tell you something." He sighed, a little excited, but a little unsure as well, "You'll be happy to know something. Something you've been pestering me about."

"Something I pestered you about?" I asked. All I could do was nod my head, urging him to continue. I was lost, ready for his words. This was the moment I'd been waiting for…

"Parker!" Someone shouted from across the lobby. A complete stranger caught my attention. "Over here, babe." A beautiful petite woman dressed all in black approached. She appeared like a chiffon dream, her sashaying hips hugged in the skintight sequence of a black liquid dress. The hypnotizing toss of her hair was enough to make me twitch, it's black waves as dark as her eyes, encompassing the glow that graced her honey-kissed skin.

Babe? Parker? Wait…

I couldn't have imagined, I couldn't have dreamed, the absolute worse alternative to everything I expected.

My blinking slowed as she fastened her manicured fingers around Parker's arm, pulling herself closely as I let him go. Gently she reached up, her palm rested on his chest as she kissed his lips ever so softly.

What. The. Fuck.

She stared back with slow blinking eyes filled with joy and glamour. She kissed him as if they were lovers in the midst of a honeymoon, completely lost in their own world, with me, their lone spectator. Was this what Parker meant to tell me? Parker pulled away softly, his eyes a little more concerned.

"Gemma, this is Mila… my girlfriend." He stared right into my eyes, searching for a reaction. His face mirrored mine, mild shock, mild uncertainty.

She stuck her hand out to shake mine, "*You* can call me Camilla. I can't believe I finally get to meet the amazing Gemma." She emphasized my name. The chirp in her voice appeared tamer, addressing me with a distance in her tone. "My Parker has told me so much about you," she rolled her large chocolate eyes up at him, jabbing his side with her finger, warranting a nervous smirk. He looked at me, seeking some approval, some reaction to confirm my excitement, but all I could feel was the sudden chill that anchored into my core.

He laughed at one of Camilla's precise pokes, displaying an intimate understanding of both the part of his body and the reaction it created. My skin instantly sweat, feeling the simultaneous sensation of hot and cold along my bones. I was sick. Parker just studied me, ignoring the fact I somehow couldn't address her as Mila.

I shook her hand back, "It's nice to meet you, Camilla." My eyes squinted in pained pleasantries, "I wish Parker said something, I had no idea we were meeting you tonight." I fidgeted with the butterfly ring on my finger, rotating it around inconspicuously with sudden embarrassment.

"I'll make him remember next time." She said confidently as her eyes fixated on mine.

"Ok," Parker laughed, breaking the silence that lingered for a moment, "I'm sure we're all hungry. I called ahead and reserved a special bottle of Cabernet, they should be letting it breath as we speak." His hand reached for my back but quickly switched to help guide Camilla inside.

The elevator ride was silent and awkward with a strange, thick tension. Trying my best not to get caught, I glanced at Parker, whose observant gaze was set on me before darting away. What the hell was he thinking, what even possessed him to suspect this would be some pleasant surprise? Was my persistent nudging of living a normal life a total backfire? I frowned for a moment, hoping he'd catch my eyes again, but was met with Camilla's. Of course she was in a black dress, she could pull it off. I had the choice too, but instead my vintage Valentino sat in the closet, unworn because of how I saw myself; the shy timid girl with St. La Vie magazine clippings on the wall.

"It's a long ride." Parker cleared his throat, creating no traction in anyone's response. If I could, I'd pull him by the ear, I'd scold him for such a stupid approach. And to think I'd possibly confess my feelings once again, to be vulnerable like an idiot.

You trust a man and trust you'll be disappointed. The lingering words Claire once said came flooding back into my head. She was right again, her stupid words like unwelcome fortune cookies. Fuck, I wanted to scream. Was there something to it? One of these days I'd get too close, I'd get hurt just like her and maybe I'd snap. I touched my neck, the thickness forming at the fear she caused. I had to protect myself; I was all I had, all I could trust.

I relaxed my face to hide the expression of doubt as the elevator opened. When we stepped out, our bodies were illuminated by the glow of scattered string lights and tabletop candles. This was the mood I prepared for, my dress enhanced by the floral surroundings and quaint trees which sprouted from the concrete like magic.

"Do you like it?" Parker asked, looking back at me.

Yes, Parker, this surprise suckerpunch was fantastic. Another please.

A hostess in a uniformed black vest greeted us at the podium, thumbing through menus.

"It's what I imagined." I said, giving a partial truth. I imagined much more, including a kiss, but not the one I witnessed.

"What more could you want?" Camilla chimed in, gesturing her arms toward the beautiful rooftop and fantastic views, "I know you're used to pizza slices, but I think you'll like this much better." How much did Parker say about me? Camilla's tone was so flat, as if pointing out my taste was simple—simple like how I was made to feel before walking inside.

"Pizza is simple. Simple's a luxury. Right, Park?" I mirrored his sentiment from earlier, watching as he chewed his lip nervously. It seemed as if he regretted his surprise plan. We were both at opposite ends on romantic feelings, that much was clear.

"It is." He assured, his shoulders tightened, bracing as Camilla held him close. I knew I should've been happy for Parker, hell, I'd been telling him to find someone great, how he should live a normal life. And while he may have found his someone, I never truly thought he'd find that person unless it were me. A disappointed sob choked in the back of my throat, thick but not threatening enough to my restraint. I forced a smile.

"My apologies," the waiter presented a small table, "the reservation was only made for two." He looked over at Parker, "This is the only table left, I'm not sure if it will seat three…"

"Mila?" Parker asked, "What happened?"

"A mistake, but a small one," she beamed, watching me curiously, "I must have been on autopilot when I called in. You know how busy it can be working a full-time job?" She spoke to me, as if she knew I was unemployed. She didn't forget, this was on purpose. Parker stood by my side as a chair arrived, and we all took our seats. I immediately opened the drink menu, knowing the Cabernet would never cut it.

"Parker, babe," Camilla craned her neck, "You know what to order if they come by. Don't forget the Mignonette sauce and extra lemons." She pursed her lips, "I need to fix my face." She winked, almost laughing before leaving us alone. I wish she had stayed, I could have fixed it for her. I was about to scold Parker when I immediately got the strange whiff of pungent fish and ocean tide.

"Wait, this is an oyster bar?" I frantically flipped through the menu.

"It's Mila's favorite…" He was slow to respond.

I laughed, but the corners of my lip twitched as I nodded. Of course it was her favorite, a romantic New York view meant for Parker and her alone.

"Since when do you like this type of food? I thought you didn't like oysters or slimy things or… seafood for that matter?" I asked flustered, seriously questioning the man I'd known for twenty plus years.

"You're not wrong." He winced, but almost pleaded with his eyes. "I'm trying something new though and I figured it was something we could suffer through together. Besides, I want to make a good impression." He closed the menu, "You've been obsessed with this idea that living with me will somehow ruin my life. That somehow it'll prevent me from living some definition you have on how I should be."

"That's not what I meant, and not what I pictured."

"And how's that? You've reminded me any chance you got. You made it clear that this was important."

"Are you happy?" I looked around, knowing this was not the scene Parker and I were used to. Yes, we were simple; yes, we ate pizza and watched horror movies; but that wasn't wrong, and now I felt like I messed up.

"I told you I was happy, and things would be fine, but I felt like I had to prove it. I thought you'd be relieved about this. You talk about me being with a nice girl, and I feel like this could be that chance, right? Wouldn't that be nice?"

"Yes?" I said half unconvincingly.

"Tell me I'm wrong, and we'll go home. I'll make an excuse. But just tell me the truth."

He looked at me with an unfamiliar stare that both

questioned and challenged my beliefs. I wasn't sure if I wanted to say yes, or if *he* wanted me to say yes. But I couldn't, not without implications or Claire's foreboding words in my head. I failed to be brave, unable to muster the courage, just like I had in the closet before leaving.

"You're right, Park." I shook my head, "Of course, this is great. Thanks for bringing me out to *meet* your girlfriend." It pained me to hear just as much to say it. It all made sense now, the breakfast and salmon. Parker was prepping his pallet for another woman, one to show off. "There's only one problem," I shifted in my seat, "remember the Hamptons as kids? We ate that godforsaken fish we thought was a good idea to catch from your dock? I totally got sick that summer, you even had to hold my hair!"

"That's different than oysters, you ate cod that night. Plus, it didn't help that we ate an entire bag of licorice that day." He wasn't wrong. "Also, I called ahead, they do have a filet mignon for you, I made sure of it before agreeing to this place." He bargained, "Please just try this with me, and if you hate it, I swear we can both chow down on pizza after this. Simple. Luxury." I didn't need to have oysters to know I didn't like them. Little cold shells with slimy blobs. They were the cum of the ocean.

"Promise?" I asked, knowing he could never break his word.

"I promise, if you do, too."

"What?"

"Promise me you'll make a good impression and give this a try. For me?" He asked. I hated this, I hated everything about what he was asking me to do. It pained me to see the man I loved be taken, to be forced to watch him kiss and hold hands with another woman. I pinched the skin on my wrist, hoping this was all some terrible nightmare.

"Hmmm..." I hummed.

"Promise me?" He asked quickly as Camilla approached.

I stared into his eyes. Even with all this, the pain and hurt, I couldn't let him down, I wouldn't. I'd do anything for Parker, even suffer through my own personal hell. He'd do the same for me. We had a close-knit bond, a friendship filled with years of having one another's back.

"Ok... I'll try. I promise." I muttered in a quick hush.

"What'd I miss?" Camilla asked, her sultry voice addressed us with authority.

"Nothing," we said in unison. She eyeballed us suspiciously but opened her menu back up.

I shifted uncomfortably in my metal chair, watching as our waiter filled our glasses with dark red wine. I half expected a basket of bread, depending on it as my entree for tonight, but was greeted only with a plate of brown crisp crackers and grains.

Camilla pulled Parker by the tie, bringing him in for a kiss. My tie of all things, the one I got for his birthday. I instantly felt so dumb, the buildup I caused myself, seeing the hidden signs which weren't there. Parker pulled away, giving Camilla a stare as if to calm her down. I cleared my throat, feeling more like a third wheel than ever before.

"So sorry, Gemma. For a moment, I forgot you were here. You're so quiet, like a cute little mouse." Camilla stated with a pouty lip.

"It's easy to forget things when you're overworked. Your makeup must have taken all night to put on," I adjusted the tie on Parker's chest, placing it back in order. "It's so romantic here, I can't believe Parker insisted I come. I guess it's because we're just so close." I declared, speaking with my truest authenticity. "Are you sure you want me here?"

The moment the words slipped out of my mouth, Camilla's lips curled as if she claimed some small victory. Parker didn't hesitate, resting his hand on my wrist, gesturing for me not to move.

"This isn't just for Mila and I, this is about us, all together for a dinner. Please." He mouthed the word *try*, reminding me of my promise.

"It's a dinner you won't forget," Camilla hummed, "a chance to expand your horizons." She placed her hand down on Parker's thigh, giving it a squeeze. Camilla was flaunting him on purpose, sensing my clear jealousy from the very beginning. I was not here for this, or her sea witch energy.

"I'm sure you're right," I cut in quickly, "Parker has so few important women in his life, me and Meg included."

"Meg?" Camilla panicked, as if he were friends with another woman.

"My mother." Parker laughed, gauging her reaction.

Ah yes, what would Mama Meg say about Camilla? Mama Meg was one of the sweetest women around. I imagined her here, sipping on her signature sangrias, probing Camilla's genuine self.

I picked up the menu, trying my best to appease Parker. "So," I sighed towards Camilla, "What do you recommend? I'm not sure I can do the oysters, but I'm open to something different."

"You *can't do* oysters?" She scoffed. Without a care, she glanced at Parker for a moment then brought her eyes back towards me. "Be brave, Gemma! How can you call yourself a New Yorker when you haven't had oysters?"

Brave? I didn't realize eating oysters was equivalent to going to war. Brave was her shade of lipstick, which clearly clashed with her foundation. That was a lie, it didn't clash, but it felt good to say in my head regardless. She spoke to me like a bratty sister, as if I was too naive to enjoy the sophistication of her god-awful taste. I twisted the napkin in my lap, opening my mouth, but was interrupted.

"Gemma doesn't need to eat oysters. But she's welcome to if she wants." Parker sipped his wine, "They'll be for the table."

"They are nature's aphrodisiac," her dark eyes peeked out at Parker, her lashes full and gorgeous, "isn't that right, babe?"

I closed my eyes, allowing a silent breath to seep out. If Parker wanted me to make a good impression, then I would, but Ca-milla sure as hell wasn't making it easy. The waitress appeared, cheerfully asking around for our orders, while I stared at the menu, skimming it for the filet Parker mentioned.

"You'll love it, Gem, I promise." Camilla's soft words squeaked as I looked up.

"It's Gemma." I took offense. I'd be polite as long as she was, and I promised to only mirror what she felt was right to give. As I stared, I noticed the waitress had already left, "I didn't even get to order..." Parker looked up too, realizing the same.

"I placed the order for us, they'll bring oysters first, then entrees later. If you're still hungry that is."

"Awesome." I sucked in my lips. Pretending to be happy was a challenge, but I did owe Parker my best attempt. "So... Camilla, what do you do for a living?" I asked quickly.

"I'm a journalist for *New York Prestige*. I cover the pop-culture column. I guess Parker has held off on bragging about me?" She pursed her lips together, snapping a quick glare at Parker. "Actually, that's how we met. I was doing an article on a local case, and one of the appointed lawyers that took my interview was Parker. Obviously, he's so gorgeous," she laughed, looking to the heavens as if giving thanks, "I had to make a move like a total boss babe. I asked to use his phone and texted myself." Camilla giggled.

"More like she pried it out of my hands," Parker interrupted. "I wasn't sure I had a choice."

"Let's not get into hasty details. Anyway, since then, we've been inseparable. Right?"

"We've been texting," he corrected, his addition more for me than for Camilla. "The only thing I'm inseparable from is the case at the moment." Camilla pouted. Honestly, I just wanted to parachute off the building, land on a hot dog cart, and call it a night.

"What do you do, Gem-ma?" She over-emphasized my name.

"It's Gemma." Parker corrected, giving her an authoritative expression that lawyers tended to have. Camilla pulled her lips together, sensing his annoyed tone.

"I'm a fashion designer." I confessed, but the way I said it was as if I didn't believe it myself. It was flat, embarrassing even. I didn't want her to think any less of me, even if I hesitated. "I'll be working with Alex Rivers very soon." I blurted out, sounding almost excited with something that wasn't even true.

Camilla stopped what she was doing and leaned in across the small table. "Alex Rivers? You don't say. How do you know him?" Camilla clenched her jaw tightly. I wasn't sure she realized her initial expression because she softened it with the bat of her eyes.

"I don't know him well. He kind of came to my rescue recently and offered me a job. He's here in New York filming."

"Amongst other things…" Parker chimed in, his eyes set on me and the excitement I displayed. "Mila knows he has legal business here, not sure how long he'll stay."

"He's a hard man to get ahold of," Camilla confessed, "and after talking to Parker, I don't blame him. I wouldn't want to answer the tough questions either." She traced the lip of her wine glass with the tip of her finger. "Well, you better be careful with him… it's not a smart move to work with that guy."

I leaned back in my chair, eyeing her. "And why is that?"

"He's an actor and a bad boy. An arrogant rich man, who only wants one thing from women. Does that make it clear for you?" She scoffed, as if validated, "If you can't handle oysters, how do you expect to handle a temperament like Alex Rivers?"

"Enough." Parker snipped, but I retorted.

"I'm not surprised you can handle oysters, you look like you're used to swallowing on the first date." I snipped as Parker massaged his temple, most definitely regretting his decision for our meeting.

"Jesus Christ, Gemma." Parker sighed, as Camilla yanked her hand from his thigh. I felt bad, but I also felt defenseless, so my words came out like an angry child. I didn't want to be here; I didn't want to witness whatever the hell this was. "Can you both just relax?" Parker asked, but his eyes shot to my phone as it buzzed loudly along the table. I looked down at the apparent lifeline, a random number glowing across the screen and onto my face. Parker knitted his brows, as if knowing what it was.

"Stop…" I warned, holding my finger up before he could begin.

"It can wait." He persisted, not wanting me to pick it up.

"No, it can't actually. I've got a business to revive." I dismissed him with my hand, turning my body to the side as I answered the call. "Hello?" I greeted, doing my best to avoid Camilla's scoff.

"Is Miss Gemma Harrison available?" A woman on the other line asked, clicking away on a keyboard.

"This is she."

"Gemma, this is Ivanna. Alex Rivers' personal assistant. I'm sorry to call so late, but we'd like to request your services for upcoming events. I'm calling to check your availability."

The urgency to confirm the only job I could get was almost paralyzing. The timing couldn't be more perfect, right here, like a gift to escape.

"Perfect, any dates in particular?" I asked, not needing to check my calendar, which was as empty as Camilla's head.

"He's wanting you for a shoot coming up, and future events are contingent on that. Would you be available for this upcoming weekend?" I looked over at Parker, his leery expression was far more rattling than the call itself. He knew what this was about, he knew what I was doing, but this was my chance.

"I'm available," I said definitively, not once breaking my stare with Parker. "I'll have my schedule cleared for that day."

"Great. I'll email you the complete details of where you'll be and what you'll need." I recited my email address, confirming it twice before ending the call.

"What's happening?" Parker asked quickly, causing a look from Camilla. I turned back to the table, my face almost righteous.

"Alex Rivers wants me." I confessed, almost a little too proud, allowing the words to float across the table. *Wants* me, as in I was being chosen now. Yes, it was a job, but for Parker it was a display of my independence. "I'm sorry, lovebirds, but I have to go. It's a work emergency."

Parker shook his head, standing from the table as I scooted back. "You can't stay?"

I leaned up to give him a hug. "Raincheck?" I asked. "This is really important to me. Sometimes we need to do new things, even if they're uncomfortable. It's how we grow." I repeated the advice he gave me before my night was ruined. I turned to Camilla, flashing my sincerest smile as I stepped away.

Parker made the choice to put me at ease, to show me in the most profound way he could live a normal life. I couldn't help but blame myself, feeling partly guilty for pushing this idea upon him. But it was true, maybe change was needed in order to live a normal life. I was stuck on Parker, that much was apparent, and starting a new job could begin the journey for something special, or so I hoped.

So much had been said about Alex Rivers, and when I met him, his presence was unlike anything I'd seen. I wasn't impressed, I wasn't afraid, I knew I could do this, with or without his bad boy reputation. But would he make it easy, or would he be all the things I was made to believe? The big bad wolf, wrapped in leather, luring me into his next endeavor.

Chapter 6

"**W**e need at least a hundred more black roses. No… just do your job and get them here. Got it?" The photo shoot coordinator, Nevia, yelled at the florist over the phone. I just met her, and, so far, she may have been the most stressed out person I'd ever met. She was a machine, powered by caffeine and anxiety, her curly black hair slicked into a bun: no makeup, only rage. "Where the hell is Alex Rivers?"

It was no surprise Alex was late, seeing how Parker warned me about his unprofessional habits. But this wasn't an ordinary job for me. This was a brand defining photoshoot for a major corporation that could change my life. Alex was hired to endorse Drip, a lime-flavored soda, now bigger than Pepsi. But he was nowhere to be seen, and the stress had everyone on edge.

"Fuck! Where are the goddamn napkins!" Nevia screamed, wafting away the hot coffee she just spilled on her blouse. I took that as my queue to leave, pushing my large rack of clothes out of the way of her assistant, who rushed over with some paper towels. I thought of how chaotic the evening was, my clicking heels distant to the frustrated staff.

Parker was right about Alex, especially now, but was

he right about everything? He had no reason to lie, no reason to scare me about the violent threat Alex supposedly posed. Parker merely wanted to protect me, regardless of my self-sufficient ways. I took a moment for myself, shamelessly hiding behind the rack of clothes, slouching in a dark corner. If Alex was truly a bad boy, then the results would speak for themselves. I pulled out my phone, typing the letters of his name into Google, curious to see how the world saw my new boss.

The first result that appeared on the screen was a *New York Prestige* article, posted merely five hours ago. It was Alex, his face harshly illuminated with light, his raw smolder tucked into the back of a town car.

"Oh my god." I covered my mouth, reading the thick red letters of a screaming headline:

Brooklyn Brawler, Alex Rivers, Knocks Out DJ at Bushwick Nightclub - No Charges Pressed.

My jaw dropped as I scrolled down, focused on a photo of a man whose nose appeared to be warped, busted like a purple turnip. The image popped up so suddenly it turned my stomach. I couldn't believe how fresh it was. It all happened last night in Brooklyn, of all places. No, not just Brooklyn, but Bushwick, my neighborhood. There was nothing to do there, nothing particularly special that wasn't already in Manhattan, especially a club. Interestingly enough, the man wasn't pressing charges and considering how rich Alex probably was, it seemed odd how this would just slip by. I studied it once more, realizing how extensive the beating was, enough to sour my face with its sight alone.

Nevia moaned as another batch of flowers tumbled

off the wall and onto the floor. I thought she was going to explode, but the surprise in her eyes struck me as relieved as she faced the entrance. "Oh my god, he's here." Nevia swirled her finger into the air, as people rushed around the warehouse. "Everyone, places, now!"

Calmly, I stood from my corner, sliding the rack of clothing toward the tent where Alex would change. I kept my eyes down, not wanting to see the man who broke the nose of some DJ out in Bushwick. The thought alone made me shiver, though I was unsure how that knowledge truly made me feel. Suddenly, I was nervous, not out of fear, but by the simple fact I now knew something about the infamous Alex Rivers.

Before, he was just a man on a billboard, a stranger really. Now, he was fighter, a piece of gossip stuck in my head. I knew if I looked up too quickly, my face would reveal the secret of what I had read. I bit my lip and averted my eyes as the rhythmic pound of his heavy boots mirrored the beat of my heart.

Thump, thump, thump.

He was close, I could feel him, and perhaps it was the torment of his insistent eyes. I collected my reaction before acknowledging his imposing presence.

"Where the hell have you been?" Nevia snipped, but Alex persisted in my direction. I glanced up and stared, studying the movement of a man who was almost two hours late. He was unfazed by Nevia's frustrated voice, using the claw of his hand to correct the direction of his slicked back hair.

"Busy," he responded, the rasp of his voice lying heavy like a boulder. "But I'm here now." His broad shoulders were draped in a black leather jacket, his tight shirt and jeans matched the tone of his raven hair. Not once did he stare at Nevia, but instead towards me. My heart sank. How long had he been staring before I had the courage to look up? He approached my side, reaching to remove his shades as his body cast a formidable shadow onto my face.

"Hi." The smallest voice fell out of my mouth, my fingers wringing together, soothing the sweat within my palm. He smirked so softly I almost missed it. He smelt like cherries and mint, rugged like a sex-filled room.

"For you, Gemma, apologies are in order. Sorry for the wait." He said it with an almost stern expression, and had it not been such a sweet gesture, I would've confused his seriousness as an attempt to intimidate. But this was how he was, his face kissed with a furrow, a brooding scowl as handsome as it was chilling.

"She gets an apology? What about the rest of the staff?" Nevia barked, following both Alex and I into the changing tent. Alex leaned back in a large, tufted chair, crossing his legs as he stared up at Nevia. He sighed as if exhausted from what he was about to say.

"It's me, baby, deal with it." The words fell out of his mouth, with little conviction, though Nevia swooned. *It's me, baby, deal with it...* Those were the same words above his head in the billboard. An Alex Rivers catchphrase? This seemed to calm the rage in Nevia's eyes, as she stared over to me.

"Gorgeous, but frustrating, wouldn't you agree? I need him ready in five minutes, but that shouldn't be too hard by the looks of him," she raised a single eyebrow. "Easy enough, right Gemma?" She asked, as I glanced at Alex. His dark eyes peered into mine, shooting a look that hoped to approve what Nevia said.

"Yes, *I'm* easy." I mumbled, lost in a momentary stare. I shook my head from how ridiculous I sounded, "I mean, this should be easy." Alex smirked, and Nevia agreed, ignoring the obvious slip of my tongue as she rushed away. Now, it was just Alex, me, and the rack of clothes I brought for him.

"I really do apologize," Alex started, "for this afternoon, for your time."

"This *evening*," I corrected, pointing to my watch. "It's well past lunch, and more dinner time than anything."

"I suppose you're right. But this won't take long, I swear it."

"What does a swear from Alex Rivers look like?" I asked, sifting through the rack for his first look.

"Guess you'll see," he said flatly, the clarity of his voice masked with a rough grit. "I trust you have everything I need."

"I believe so," I answered, "but your assistant didn't send too many details. It felt more like she wanted me to assume what you'd like, rather than advise."

"Good." He reached into the pocket of his leather jacket, "That was by design." He pulled out a small auburn box, an unfamiliar brand of cigarettes that made my heart skip. He smoked? His movement was so meticulous, intentionally smooth, as he slipped one between his lips and reached for a gold lighter. "I wanted to see what you see." He cupped his hand around the flame, clicking it shut with a sudden snap.

I flinched. The sound of the lighter frightened me with a reminder of Claire, who began smoking like a fiend shortly after my father left. The smell of cigarettes had always turned my stomach, but his was different, something unlike I'd ever smelled before. Through the grate of his teeth, Alex exhaled a plume of smoke, only to inhale it back with the snap of his jaw. He stared at me, savoring the flavor, studying my moves. It was *cherry* scented, sweet but spiced, calming a disgust I often loathed to feel. This was nice. Still, I reached up to my neck, the sound of the lighter bringing an uncomfortable memory to mind.

"Does my smoking make you uncomfortable?" He asked as he studied the cigarette in his hands, held in place with the tip of his thumb and middle finger. I swallowed, pulling my hands away, knowing how observant he was.

"What was it you wanted to see?" I clarified, "You mentioned that this was by design?" I avoided his question, evoking a subtle smirk on his face. He was letting me off the hook, but maybe, just this *once*.

"I want to see the clothes you pick. To see what you think of me." His tongue played with the corner of his lip as he stood up from the chair. "I want to know, what is it that you have, what is it that you think? I don't usually come across people like you."

"Like me? Well…" I completely hesitated, unsure of how to approach what he wanted, or what the hell he even meant, "I have a lot of things to show you." I began to sweat. This felt less like a job and more like a quiz. How was I supposed to know what it was I saw in him? I saw nothing, I knew nothing, except the possible facade of a Hollywood star.

He placed the cigarette in his lips again, exhaling with the stretch of his neck, patiently waiting as I combed through the rack. Everything had a different message, picked from various merchants whose samples were loud in color. This job was to help define the image of a new soda, not Alex specially. I figured he was complaisant with whatever I had picked, which were actually really good looks. Even Nevia approved them, using corporate lingo to describe my choices as, "on brand" for their "targeted audience." *Did I miss the assignment?* I worried, realizing as I sifted through the looks that my selection was more for Drip the product, than Alex the person. He lowered his gaze, staring at the shirt I pulled out for him. "This could be a contender, I know you have a wild side…" I said half unconvincingly, lifting an animal print shirt up to his chest, "paired with some tawny slacks, gold accessories…" His Adam's apple bobbed, swallowing what I imagined was cherry flavored spit.

"Leopard?" He asked. "Wild?"

Yes, wild, like the man who fought strangers for no reason, though I couldn't say that. Unlike his assistant, Drip sent a packet of mood boards to be inspired by, though Alex seemed less interested in the keywords I was using. Was he expecting something else? Suddenly, I felt uncertain about my choices. Maybe he wanted to see what I thought of his onscreen persona, considering he had a catchphrase that made people swoon.

"Yes! Like the action star that you are."

"And what do you know about that, Gemma? Humor me."

His movies? Was he really asking me this? Maybe he thought I was a fan, which would be a serious misunderstanding. Not only did I not watch action movies, but I avoided them. I didn't like the explosions, or any loud noises for that matter. I could have lied, but he was too clever for that, so I told the truth.

"I've never seen any of your movies." I admitted, revealing how little I truly knew about him as a character that people saw.

"Good, neither have I." He coaxed me with his voice, not intentionally, but by the gravity of his growling accent. It slithered, slipping like a pill that melted my mind. "Look at me now, and ask me what you want to know." I clung the shirt to my chest, as if to shield myself from the burn of his eyes, which made me feel both scared and protected.

"I'm not sure what to ask… this job was specific for a brand. I figured the clothes were…"

"Never mind that," he interrupted. "I'm asking you to stop what you're doing, to look at me, and ask a question. What do you want to know?"

I wasn't sure what I would do if he stepped any closer. All I could do was stare at his hands, their massive size, wielding the sweet-scented cigarette that teased my senses. His knuckles were scraped, bruised with a red hue, as if pounded against a wall. They were clues to his night, to the nose he ruined in Bushwick.

"Does that hurt?" I nodded toward his hand, asking a question just like he wanted. "They look... sore." Alex followed my eyes, his head not once moving as he observed the stinging wounds.

"I've had worse." He replied.

"From?"

"Harvesting in an agave field." He massaged his knuckles with his large, calloused fingers, proven to be tools for more than I expected. "The plants have needles, they're thick spikes that cut if you get too close, but they're necessary. It's everything needed to protect the stem, but it's the stem you want, it's what you're harvesting for."

"So, you're a farmer too?"

"No." He laughed, twisting his jaw, "Not necessarily, but I've put in my fair share of hours from the past couple years. I'm a busy man."

I assumed so. According to Parker, Alex was consumed with lawsuits, though he didn't act as if this was even true. I would've been a mess, but he was out here unbothered and apparently harvesting, an unlikely hobby for a Hollywood superstar.

"I can't picture you doing that, especially in Los Angeles."

"*Jalisco.*" He corrected, extinguishing his cigarette on the marble table by his side, "In *México.*"

"Is that where you're from?"

"No." His quick words snipped, "Fresno, California.

It's not as strange as you think, I was raised by harvesters. Immigrants."

"So your family is still with you in California then?" I asked, but Alex was slow to respond, taking a subtle but noticeable deep breath. He concentrated his eyes into mine, his dark brow and full lashes squinted in thought. He didn't like the question and remained silent as my phone buzzed loudly. I glanced down to see a text from Parker but silenced it, returning my eyes back to Alex. "I'm sorry about that."

"Have you been to *México*?" He avoided my comment by asking a question instead.

"No, that would require money. Though the idea sounds nice."

"Then where do you vacation?" He pressed, as I pondered the question, shrugging.

"The Hamptons during the summer. That's about the only place I ever go."

"The Hamptons?" He laughed, almost puzzled at the contradiction. "Lots of money there, now isn't that true?"

"Yes, but not mine."

"Whose?"

"My best friend's… family." I didn't want to get into this and was determined to avoid his question as much as he avoided my comment. "This endorsement of yours is for Drip; it's a bold company, a little edgy and fun. I figured the leopard print would be a good idea."

"It's not," he corrected, "Drip isn't edgy, it's an idea of what others think I should be. They believe since they added a *hint* of lime to their drink, the only way to promote is by using a Hispanic actor. But it's not mine, it's their perception of me and who I am. They see my skin, they hear my voice, and they see a stereotype." He gently pulled the shirt away from my body, placing it back onto the rack. "It's not me though, just like the Hamptons aren't you, Gemma."

I tensed at the thought, his cool perspective and voice snapped me into place like a puzzle. The Hamptons aren't me? He wasn't wrong, but he wasn't right either. The Hamptons had Parker, it had Mama Meg and Mr. Jones, those were extensions of me, or so I'd thought.

"What makes you say that?"

"I saw it in your face, the moment Gerard mentioned your mother and home. He put you in a box, yes, but you weren't disagreeing with him. You come from somewhere else. The way you carry yourself, your clothes, it's all a presentation, but I still haven't decided yet, is it a front or is it a truth? I need to know."

I scowled at his presumption, this idea I could be fooling the world with my look. It wasn't true; it was an idea he had of me, just like Drip had of him. It's not like he knew me or who I was with Parker. Just because I avoided my past, didn't make my choices less true, did it?

"You're right. You're not a leopard." I turned away from Alex, searching the rack quickly for something new. "You're cooler than a leopard, but you're not as bold as one either. In fact, I find you more guarded than you think." I pulled out a black shirt, its cuffs and buttons detailed with a small gold design. "If you ask me, you're a shadow, but there are glimpses beneath the facade that you put on, Mr. Rivers." I handed him the shirt, "This suits you... for now."

Alex was no different than what he accused me of. He was, in fact, the agave he described. A man guarded with needles and spikes, protecting the stem where the good stuff lived.

"For now..." He repeated my words with a contemplative smirk that caught me off guard. Did he like this? Pushing me to snip?

Alex pulled off his jacket, tossing it to the chair before removing his shirt. His bruised knuckles tightened as he reached up over his head, his back and shoulders evoked into a flex.

My lips felt the sting of adrenaline, a rapid pump of blood that burned along my ears. "I'm sorry." I turned away, embarrassed by the apple red hue torturing my cheeks.

"Of?" He asked.

"I should leave, you need privacy." I turned to walk, but his words caught my steps.

"Are you a child?" His deep voice caused me to blink, halting my steps as if the question itself were a demand to stop.

"Pardon?"

"You don't need to be shy or courteous. You can stand there and advise. If you don't want to answer my question, I'll answer it for you. You're not a child, but if you act like one, then I'll ask you to stand there like the good girl you are."

The hairs on my neck pricked into fine pins, raised

at the audacity of his words. I turned to face him, his size almost startling as he approached. Everything about him grazed the surface of my skin, climbing from my toes to my scalp, not once ever truly being touched. My reaction was an instinct, charged with wide eyes that attempted to ward him off, but unintentionally may have invited him in. I worried I may have looked startled, a disadvantage that I always took as weakness.

"I don't need to be told what to do." I hissed as confidently as my parched tongue would allow.

"No? But I bet you'll listen, you'll like the things I tell you to do." The light above formed a contour along the cuts of his body. Each muscle a defined ripple, pronounced with the rough edges of a strong man, gripped in a sleeve tattoo of dark ink and gold skin. "Am I wrong?"

His tapered jeans dipped far below his waist. The suggested band of his Armani underwear appeared lost, almost replaced by the strong V-cut shape of his taut abs. I stared too long at the thick vein that traveled below, coiled like a road map into the darkness of denim. "Put your shirt on," I commanded. "You've kept enough people waiting, and now you're wasting my time."

"I bought your time. I'll use it as I please." He replied, his thumb tested the softness of his lips. What was he thinking as his eyes searched mine with an observant glare that dared me to protest? He placed the shirt over his thick arms, their strength formed not only by the gym, but by the labor of an apparent agave field.

"Payments still need to be discussed." I retorted,

observing the tattoos on his body. Near his chest was a black outline of angel wings, filled with the initials *AA*. Maybe a past lover? I figured his violent side was as true as his womanizing one.

"I'll take care of you." He assured, slowly buttoning up the shirt. "You'll see soon enough." His boots once again thumped like my heart, stepping closer than before.

I'll take care of you? The conviction of his voice felt both assertive and calm, as if I had no choice but to accept it. With the chance he offered to ask any question, I wondered if I chose correctly, not being more direct than I should have. I wanted to confront him about Bushwick, what business he had out there. I needed to know it wasn't because of me. Suddenly I felt conceited, as if he'd travel to the middle of nowhere just because of what I told him in front of Gerard's boutique. Still, I couldn't shake the idea. I opened my mouth to speak, but all that emitted was the screech of a fire alarm.

I winced at the siren. As if the afternoon wasn't hectic enough, someone walked through the fire exit just hours before. The fire department had already been out, using their universal key to shut off the sound but decided to stay. Even they were waiting for Alex, hoping to snag a photo before heading back to the station. I couldn't help but think the alarm was on purpose, signaling our time to leave the tent.

"Shall we?" He asked, making his way to the exit. I followed close by, my ears still rang as the alarm suddenly shut off, conveniently ending as we left the

tent. Staff members clapped as we emerged, not from
sarcasm, but genuine excitement to be working on the
shoot. Alex subtly waved, approaching the set that still
missed portions of black roses. On a table at the center
of the backdrop sat a green bottle of Drip, glistening
with artificial dew which was just sprayed on.

I stood in the back as the photographer, Richard,
made an announcement. "Welcome everyone, we have
lots to do! I just want to start by saying how thrilled I am
to be here, to be working with each of you… It's just…"

"I'm ready," Alex interrupted. His pinky scratched
his brow as he stared down at the bottle. "We start
now."

Richard hesitated, caught in a thought before
clapping his hands together. "Then… let's start!" He
announced, pulling out his camera, queuing a
soundtrack to be played over the speakers. Alex winced,
as if being disturbed from a deep sleep. "Ok, Alex, go
ahead and open the bottle for me." Richard instructed,
but Alex was already ahead of him, the cap twisted off
with a loud fizzy pop.

He looked up at me as I stood in the back,
hovering near a monitor as it displayed all the photos.
Richard was shouting instructions, but Alex kept his
eyes on me, not once sipping the drink. He didn't look
amused, or like he even wanted to be here, but once
our eyes met, they softened. I was still frustrated by
him, by the way he spoke to me, and the compelling
nature of his voice. I wasn't a child, but the way he
provoked the idea made me feel as though he
challenged me, daring me to prove him otherwise. I

could prove him wrong; I could be completely professional and nothing more.

"Aren't you thirsty?" Richard asked, still testing the lighting on Alex.

"Very." He replied, as if talking to me.

"Go ahead and give me a look." Richard requested, but Alex continued to stare in my direction. I turned away, pulling out my phone to see Parker's text.

Parker: Another late night, sorry Butterfly. Just wanted to give you a heads up.

Parker had been working so hard, spending night after night on this case. How could one man be so dedicated to his job, yet the other—Alex—be so careless and show up late? It was as if he didn't care, and if he cared about anything, then I was unsure of what it was. I looked over at the shoot, Alex's gaze no longer locked on me, but rather my phone. He scowled.

"Go ahead and give me something extra." Richard asked, "You know, something south of the border!"

My brow scrunched at his request, witnessing the projected box Alex assumed his role to be. A man with brown skin, expected to play a part that Richard presumed. Alex's eyes, switched from my phone over to Richard, staring in his direction for the first time.

"And how would that look?" He asked, his voice calm but charged with a low rumble. "Turn off the music," he snipped, shooting a look over to a man who turned down the dial. He placed the bottle back down on the table, the cap fell loose onto the floor. "I asked you something…" He repeated, "How would that look?"

Richard fumbled, accidentally taking another photo. He frowned, confronted with the reality of what he was asking, and the provoked tone that sprang from Alex. He hesitated, which almost sounded like a nervous giggle. "Well… I don't know." He confessed. "Something spicy?" His vague request warranted enlarged eyes from the staff, mine included. I wanted to crawl out of my skin, physically uncomfortable by the suffocating energy in the room.

"Hmm," Alex groaned, "spicy."

"I don't know what to say."

"I think you've said enough." Alex responded, stepping closer to Richard, his height imposing a response in itself.

"Mr. Rivers."

"You asked so confidently, I figured you knew what you wanted." Alex pressed patiently.

"I just… never mind."

"No, you had an idea, so share it. I'm curious."

Richard massaged his thumb along his own fingers, contemplating the thought he undoubtedly already had. "Maybe you could grab the bottle… I don't know, possibly dance with it? Can you do the Salsa?"

"Salsa?" Alex grinned, but this was anything but exciting for him. No, I knew it. He was pissed.

"Well, yeah, you know, like the Mexican dance?"

"Salsa is Cuban." He replied flatly.

"I didn't know…"

"I'm sure you didn't… You just want something

spicy… isn't that right?" He asked, "Or maybe dangerous? If it's a stereotype you want, you better clarify which one it is you need. There's a lot of them to choose from, and I think I'll pick one for myself. Maybe I can toss you from an overpass, just like the cartel in Zacatecas? Let you rot on a piece of rope like the pig you are." Alex gloated, delighted by the idea.

"You're fine as you are." Richard mumbled, his silent voice still audible amongst the quiet room.

"I know I am. Now take my picture." Richard held up the camera, the flash emitting a pop of light as Alex stared into the lens. Alex looked up at me, then down at my phone, announcing a final decision. "We're done here."

My blood ran cold at his calm response, his eyes set on mine as he approached.

"Wait. We barely started." Richard shouted as Nevia got on the phone, dialing a number with frantic fingers. We waited here for hours, and after a few shots, Alex was completely done. One provocation was all it took. Sure, it was wild of Richard to ask, but did it warrant Alex abandoning the entire set? I wasn't sure but also realized it could have been worse for Richard, and probably something he deserved, such as the man with the busted nose. Was it justified or an overreaction? The truth felt somewhere in between, but right now, it seemed fair.

Alex unbuttoned his shirt as he headed in the direction of the tent. "Are we really done?" I asked, "Don't you have a contract?" He handed me the black and gold shirt, quickly pulling over his own to leave.

"Lots of contracts, but little patience." He lifted his jacket from the chair, slipping it over his arms. "I promised you it'd be quick, and I delivered."

"This wasn't for me."

"No, but I would have done it regardless. He was wrong, and you know it."

"Yes, but..." I began.

"What are you doing right now?" He yanked the cuff of his sleeve, his strength correcting its place along his wrist. The commotion outside of the tent did not subside, as I could hear Nevia talk to the representatives of Drip.

"Cleaning up, I guess."

"No." He shook his head, "I can have that taken care of. So, tell me, what are you doing?"

I looked up puzzled at his question, reminding myself of my promise to meet his challenge. I'd be professional, even if he couldn't. There were already plenty of people in my life that left when things got tough, I didn't need him to do the same, not to me.

"I'm going home."

"No." His accent purred, drawing me to stare at his lips. "It's past lunch as you said and closer to dinner. You look hungry. I'm taking you to eat." He looked down at me, appearing as if he could lift me up and take me away.

"No, you're not. I have plans."

"Then this Friday."

"Are you booking me?" I asked, maintaining my unshakable position.

"Is that what it takes to see you?"

"If it's not business, then it's not happening. Besides, I have plans this Friday."

"Like what?" He pressed, patiently but not desperately.

"I'm seeing a play. *Phantom of the Opera.*" I shrugged, not knowing why I felt the urge to answer, maybe I wanted to deter him. "I'm going with my best friend." I added.

"What's her name?"

"*His* name is none of your business."

As soon as I said this, the whites of his teeth revealed themselves in a brilliant snarl. It almost stole my breath. In reality, it wasn't his business, and he didn't need to know who Parker was or how he was related to his case. Not that it mattered, Alex seemed completely detached from the consequences of his actions or anything to do with the aspect of lawsuits.

Regardless, I felt vulnerable, and I wasn't sure if I liked it, mostly because I had no control of how he made me squirm. "Why are you doing this?" I asked, not sure if I really wanted an answer, so I corrected. "Why were you at Bushwick last night? There is nothing to do out there. Nothing for you at least." I questioned, but his expression didn't budge.

"I wanted to see it for myself. I'm looking for something familiar, something I saw the day I met you." What could he see there that had to do with me? I spent my life trying to get away from Bushwick and from Claire. I hated how that place made me feel, but who could ever truly understand? Not a Hollywood celebrity, that was for sure.

"And what would that be?" I asked, watching as Alex dug into the pocket of his leather jacket. Clenched between the tips of his finger was a cookie, a Marcello Galletas, from the bodegas in Bushwick. He placed it between his lips, snapping it in half.

"For something just like me." His confession irked me; my ears burned from the comparison. I was not like him, not my character, not my life. He knew nothing about me, but he sought to find everything, and from what? A hunch that we were somehow the same?

I laughed. "You've mistaken me for someone else, Mr. Rivers. I'm not like you, and I hope to never be. Sorry you wasted your time traveling to Bushwick, but I hope you enjoy the cookies." I placed his shirt on the rack. He absorbed my words as some odd invitation.

"Every bite." He replied, watching as I left.

The firemen were still outside, waiting for me to leave so they could meet the arrogant Alex Rivers. I was ready to go, realizing he was right about one thing, that I was indeed hungry. My stomach growled as I left the set, my face still blushed from Alex's words. How could he get so under my skin? He didn't know me, and I didn't want him to know me, especially my personal life.

My phone buzzed for an extended moment, signaling a call as it vibrated in my purse. I expected it to be Parker, relieved to share about my day. He knew how frustrating Alex could be, but perhaps his perception was more intense than mine. Alex was abrupt, yes, but today with Richard he had a reason to be. Maybe this was true for other moments.

I pulled out my phone, exiting the building onto a

busy street. I went to answer, but instead I stopped. Immediately, I was sick, gutted by the name that appeared on my phone. No matter how much I wanted to run, she was always there, if not literally, then mentally. The person I tried to avoid, the fear I ignored, the mother I never really had.

Claire.

Chapter 7

I t had been a few weeks since I heard her voice, and honestly I was afraid to answer the phone. I always needed to prepare—both mentally and physically—equipping myself with the mindset to see a conversation through. I walked out onto the street as the sun began to set, while the phone still buzzed in my hand. I let it ring longer, anticipating it'd disappear and for the screen to go black. I guess I was just exhausted, already emotionally spent as a child, unable to help any further as an adult. I waited one more second, hoping I could care less than I really did, but couldn't. The role of an eager daughter meant nothing to me now. I just had to make sure that this woman in Bushwick was safe, both from others and herself.

"Claire?" I answered, my tone inquired a multitude of things: what's wrong, what now? I couldn't have expected the moan in her voice, though I should have, the almost dreaded rasp was what I heard anytime her words echoed in my head.

"I guess you thought I wouldn't figure it out, but I did. I always do." She sighed, "You know nothing gets by me, especially things like this." The explosions of an apparent action movie played loudly in the background of her call. She had left it on, almost as if Dad would come back home to his favorite film. I hated it, the sound of shots and explosions, the insufferable backdrop to their screaming arguments. I didn't watch them, in fact I avoided them, probably why I barely knew who Alex Rivers was.

"What are you talking about?" I asked, shuffling in a crowd with a finger propped in my ear.

She laughed to herself. "You've moved in with Parker. Tell me I'm wrong." The pitch in her voice was an anxious hiss. An accusation. Of course, no how are you, or I miss you. I wasn't surprised, this was our relationship, straight to the point.

"How'd you find out?" I sighed, more deflated. I kept this from her on purpose; I didn't need her voice in my head appearing in real life. I felt it enough, her own stinging warnings and fear.

"I didn't know for sure, but now I do. Thanks for confirming." Her voice was muffled, wrapped around what I assumed was another cigarette. I knew it wasn't cherry scented, it was yucky and oily, the smell that burned my throat. "A letter I sent to you got sent back, apparently you don't live at your old home anymore. I would have asked you, but what would be the point? You hid it from me on purpose."

"Because you worry too much."

"No. Because I know better." She sucked in a drag of her cigarette. "Your landlord described Parker to a tee. A tall and built man, dirty gold hair and green eyes, helping you move boxes into a truck. I only assumed correctly."

"Well, it's only temporary."

"I would hope so. Now tell me, what happened?"

She pressed, but I wouldn't give her anything. She didn't need to know about my job, how I lost everything and my business, and she especially didn't need to know about Alex. How would she react to a celebrity, a man who'd leave on a dime, much like her husband had? I couldn't afford another provoked meltdown.

"Nothing happened. I found a better place, and my rent was up. I'll move out soon enough." I answered quickly, brushing away her questions.

"I don't like it."

"Like what? There is nothing that needs your opinion."

"You and Parker together, it's not smart, and you should know better."

"And you do? What have you taught me that I didn't learn myself?"

"Everything on what to avoid, unless you want to end up like me, of course." She coughed into the phone, pausing into a silent rest. To be like her would be everything I feared. I only knew her as two people, a recluse or an overbearing extrovert, there was no in-between. Both versions were hard to handle, complete opposite spectrums. "I know, I'm not mother of the year, I know how you talk to me, and I you, but please… be civil."

"You love Parker," I finally responded. "So what's wrong?"

"I did love Parker," she barked, annoyed by our conversation. "I loved him as the sweet boy he was. But is he that anymore? I'm not so sure. He's a man, and we know what they're capable of."

"Not this, please." I scolded, "Not everyone is the same, Claire." I resisted the urge to mention Dad, but what I really wanted to say was not everyone was like him. I couldn't though, not for her feelings, but rather my own sanity. "Why do you think the world is out to get me?"

"Not you, but us! Always has been, always will be. Parker is supposed to protect you, but I don't think he can anymore. He's lost his innocence."

"Protect me?" I huffed, "Parker is my best friend, he's been there for me when I've needed him the most. And you?" I asked, biting my tongue. "Innocence is such a ridiculous thing to push onto someone. What do you know about that? Where were you to protect my innocence when I needed you the most? I was the parent, Claire, and still am in many ways." I pulled my finger out of my ear, pointing it to the ground as if she were below my feet. I couldn't finish the thought, how she failed as a mother, but especially as a protector. I never felt safe; I didn't feel what I did with the Joneses. They say you couldn't pick your family, but I say otherwise. I picked mine; it was Parker, Mama Meg, and Mr. Jones, they took care of me during the summers, the happiest time of year away from home.

"I did the best I could, and you know that. You had it rough, but now you're stronger because of it, Gemma." She defended.

"Not because of it, but in spite of it. And if I'm so strong, then let me make my own decisions." My curt tone expressed the impatience that came with her calls. Had this not been New York, people would have stared, but given the chaotic after work crowd, people were eager to get home and mind their own business. I needed to let her know I was ok; I didn't need her to worry. Worrying led to obsessive thinking, which led to doubt and fear. The last thing I needed her to do was lock herself in her room and fall into another spell. I remembered those moments too well, Claire had called them her 'cloudy days,' but for me, they were storms.

"Don't be mad at me." She said.

I refrained from replying, soaking in her words. I wanted nothing to do with her, and that thought made me sad. I wanted to love my mom, and in moments I did, but was never sure why. Perhaps it was an obligation of my heart, and though it was cold to admit, I could no longer compete with the exhaustion of our history. If I could stop caring, I would, but the truth was, I didn't want her to suffer. I just wanted us to be free, both from each other, both from the trauma we'd lived.

I turned the corner of a busy sidewalk, tucking myself in the nook of a brick wall. The smell of hot pizza caught my attention, reminding myself of the hunger I felt earlier. Was Claire taking care of herself? Was she hungry? "Are you eating?" I asked flatly, ignoring her request to not be mad.

"Yes." She sighed, "Erin is here, and I made your favorite… mac and cheese." I cringed. She had no idea what my favorite food was. Mac and cheese was what I ate because it was all I could teach myself at the time. I glanced down at a small burn that resided on my wrist, evidence of the little girl who was learning to boil water but ended up getting hurt. I wasn't even sad anymore, that'd require energy.

"How's Erin?" I changed the subject, checking on the only friend Claire had, the Puerto Rican neighbor who lived alone and visited often to watch TV with her. Erin's soft voice said hi on the other end of the phone, causing Claire to snort.

"Erin is Erin, she brought over some wine. We're about to have a few glasses and watch *Family Feud*." She confirmed, but I furrowed my brow.

"Are you still taking your pills? You shouldn't mix alcohol with those."

"It's a few glasses, Gemma, calm down." She exhaled, but I was quick to her annoyance. This wasn't a passive idea, this was a necessity, something that would keep me up at night. Without her medication, things went wrong. The thought alone made me feel like a little girl again, but not in a good way. Scared.

"Don't just disregard what I'm saying. Your depression needs to be managed, and I've seen enough of what it does untreated. You understand?" A not so gentle reminder of Claire's behavior, of the disorder which ruined both her life and mine. Depression took my mom away, and the mellowed version I was speaking to now was only thanks to new medication.

"You've seen enough of what it does untreated? How about living with it?"

"I have, with you. I'm just checking."

"Don't bring up the past. You have no idea what it was like. When your father left, it took everything from me." Her voice was almost in a tremble.

My patience was at its end with her, and I couldn't help but snap, "Well it almost took everything from me too. Please don't bring him up." I avoided talking about Dad, I couldn't chance her being stuck on this carousel, not now, not before wine.

"Don't do this." She groaned.

"Do what?"

"Run from this discussion, about how awful your father was."

"Not now, Claire." I tried to swallow, but my neck felt tight. I hated these moments, where I reached up and soothed my throat. I could smell the cigarette over the phone, the pungent rasp of her voice.

"When will you forgive me for that night?" She whispered. I heard the scoot of her steel chair along the linoleum floor, as if to tuck herself away from Erin's ears.

"I've got to go."

She sighed audibly, "Just like your father, when the going gets tough, the weak get going."

"I'm not like him, I'm not like you. I have my reasons." My voice cracked, but she persisted. I couldn't manage the things she was saying, the things she'd done, how every conversation led back to Dad and the night he left. Because of this, I felt far away, and amongst other things, it made it difficult to breathe. I felt this at times, but was always saved by one man, the person whose face I caught now, standing in line for pizza as an electric jolt sprang through my belly.

It was Parker, his gaze fixated on his phone, scrolling through the screen with his thumb. Without knowing it, he was there for me, his thick hair in a slick wave, combed back tightly like his fitted suit.

Maybe Claire was right, maybe I was running away, but after all that happened, didn't I deserve a break? Parker was my constant, one I fought to protect from the ugliness of my life. He knew enough about Claire, but he didn't know everything, and that was how I wanted it to be, partly from the fear Claire instilled, but mostly because I wanted to keep this life—here with Parker—untouched by the things of my past.

"I have to go, Claire." I said flatly, interrupting the middle of her sentence.

"Gemma, don't be a fool," her words fell short, lost in the abrupt disconnect of my phone. Maybe I was a fool, believing in a fantasy, believing Parker and I had a future, but it was the fantasy that kept me afloat at times, so I chased it, as I did now, walking into the shop to see him.

Chapter 8

"Hey, oyster boy!" I shouted, garnering the attention of every customer of the pizza shop. Parker's head shot up, instantly smiling as he saw me standing in the back. His eyes were soft, almost tender from the day, glancing as if relieved to see me.

"Gem?" Parker cocked his head. I waved, suddenly shy from my shout but eager to be by his side, even if it was just as my best friend. Parker scooted his way to the back, allowing others to pass ahead. The musk of his worn cologne was a sensory comfort, and after the day I had, its cedar wood spice was both sensual and profoundly relieving. "Why am I not surprised to see you here?"

"Intuition," I joked. "How do I always remember your creamer at Benee's?

"And I, your Tabasco?" He added, "A good team." He loosened his tie, his fitted grey suit more relaxed as he unbuttoned the top. "Did you get my text?"

"Another late night," I confirmed. "Glad you're eating though. Real food that is," I added, partly teasing.

"As opposed to ocean slime?" He asked. "Not as bad as you think, but not as great as others make it either." Parker motioned to the cashier, flashing two fingers before pointing down to the pepperoni slices. "I'm trying," he confirmed, "and it looks like you are too." He looked into my eyes, his emerald stare studious like an astute lawyer. "Are you ok? You look like you just got bad news." I was unaware of my expression but figured the lingering effects of Claire's call still persisted.

"Oh yeah. Uh, I just got off the phone with Claire." I admitted, leaving nothing else to be said. Parker studied me but rarely lingered on the topic.

"She still taking care of herself?" He narrowed his eyes, almost hesitant to ask.

I once scared Parker when we were kids. I came home to see him waiting for me, talking to my mom. Parker came to check on me, but I was terrified of what she'd say to him. Claire wasn't in the right state of mind, she would've said too much, even to little Parker who didn't know much about my past. The fact that Claire could have told him what happened the night my father left, sent me into a panic. So I yelled at him, literally pulled him out of the house and locked the door. I still felt bad about it, recalling how wide his eyes grew when I shouted, but it was necessary. I would do anything to keep him away from Claire's cancerous energy.

Parker was good at checking in though, asking only a few questions, but never enough to warrant another scolding. I was sure he wanted to know more, but he didn't pry. That was my fault, I wasn't sure if I could say the things I needed, especially after the rejection that college night. Had we been together, grown closer, maybe I would have opened up more, but who was to say what could have been?

"Yeah. She's doing great actually." I lied, easing my

own tension. I couldn't tell him everything she said, especially the part about how Parker lost his innocence. That'd be too weird. I picked at my pink nail polish, suddenly feeling uncomfortable with the subject in general. "I'll get drinks and a booth for us." I mumbled, swiping the red soda cups off the counter. I wasted no time in creating distance, allowing the conversation to pass. Parker paid as I filled our cups, nabbing a small booth in the corner. He sat down and passed me a jar of parmesan cheese.

"Big day today?" He unwrapped a straw, slipping it into my soda, "Tell me about your shoot." His request read more as a command, but the gleam in his eyes made me melt.

"Long for some. Not so much for others." I kept it vague, knowing the interest Parker had on certain details. "Someone was late." I added, knowing he'd fully understand who.

The waiter stopped by, placing round metal plates of hot pizza on the table. Parker folded his slice down the middle and took a few bites, keeping his eyes on me as I dabbed a napkin around the greasy edge of my pizza.

"I'm not surprised." He laughed, "Tell me, how's working with Alex Rivers?"

"You work enough hours on that man, don't you want to enjoy your dinner?" I asked, dousing more parmesan cheese than I needed.

"How late was he?"

"Well over two, almost three hours. Pretty much what you said. You've met him, you know how he is."

"Not really, just from word of mouth." He returned,

pulling a piece of pepperoni off his slice and placing it on mine. Parker mostly ate cheese but ordered the topping to share with me.

"Wait I thought you two met already?"

"I would if he came to any of the meetings. I've only heard from word of mouth. Some of the associates have told me stories, about him being late, about him storming off when things get tough."

"So you've never actually witnessed it?" My voice pitched higher.

"No, but I can imagine."

Our knees bumped under the table. The booth was so small, and Parker was so tall, his legs consumed mine with the graze of his fitted slacks. Unintentionally, I rubbed mine against his as I lifted my leg to be crossed. The feeling churned my insides, swirling like a hot pool.

"People assume a lot of things. Gossip papers like *New York Prestige* just want to get a story. Can't all be true." I mused, jabbing at the magazine Camilla worked at. I felt silly for doing so, having no reason to say what I did, other than to discredit the woman's profession.

"And are they wrong?" He asked, "How'd the rest of the shoot go then?" His voice deepened. I knew he wouldn't ask again because this time he expected an answer.

"Well, actually… he left early."

"Why?"

I stalled, chewing my food longer than necessary. I knew the truth confirmed everything he said, further solidifying other rumors that may have been told, even in *New York Prestige*. "He was upset."

"Sure." He drummed his fingers on the table, leaning back into his chair, "Of course."

"But he had a good reason for it." I defended.

"Still, he runs when things get bad, how can you trust someone like that?" His words echoed Claire's, but I knew that wasn't his intention. The idea someone could run away from a problem and simultaneously be untrustworthy gutted me. Sure, I ran from my past, but did that make me a bad person, or Alex for that reason? I wasn't my father, abandoning a family, leaving a little girl to fend for herself.

"Sometimes people have a good reason to leave, Park. You can't just assume what people say is true, and if you do, then take my word for it too."

Parker raised his eyebrows at my stance. "Are you actually defending this guy? You know he just beat up some DJ out in Brooklyn, right?"

"Yeah, I know…" I shook my head, "and no I'm not defending the guy. I'm not even sure if I like him as a person. Sure, he's rough around the edges, a little brash, but at least he apologized for being late. He has yet to be rude to me." I took a bite of my pizza. "Unlike Camilla," I added.

Parker twisted his lips, placing his slice back down on the plate. "Gem, Mila is nothing like Alex, trust me."

"It's more than that, Parker. I just don't need to be lectured about Alex, if you're going to turn a blind eye to Camilla. You know all this stuff about him, but it's either word of mouth or court hearings. You have an insight to his life, but what do you know about

Camilla?" I asked, shrugging my shoulders. "How long have you even known her?"

He was slow to respond, leaving me unsure if he wanted to answer. "Almost three weeks. It's casual, and if anything… harmless." He returned to his pizza, "I just wanted to show you what you wanted. That living with me could be normal and that you don't need to rush off."

"Well, whatever that was, it wasn't…" I wanted to say enough but couldn't. I was lying to Parker now, at the expense of my own comfort. He couldn't know the real reason I wanted to leave, and I couldn't admit that my mother, whose words I despised, still affected my life. I was afraid of rejection, afraid of becoming her. "Camilla may not be like Alex Rivers, but if you get to worry about me, then I get to worry about you too." I looked down at my pizza, solemn at the confession. "And that'll never change."

The entrance rang with a bell, people chattered softly, and plates clinked as a quiet moment passed between us. The noise was all a backdrop to the tension we shared, my tug of war of wants and needs.

"It's been a hectic few months." He sighed, "I'm happy just having you home. Honestly, all I wanted to do was make you feel better, but I'm afraid I made you feel worse." He glanced up, chewing the inside of his cheek, reaching across the table to touch my hand but stopped just before doing so. "I'm sorry if I messed up. Not just here but before. I'm trying to be the thing you need me to be, what I need to be, but that can be challenging." I was unsure what he meant, but the sweetness in his eyes showed he was genuine.

"I just need you to be you." I nodded, "That's all I ever needed."

"That's not enough." He replied, "You also need an apology. I'm sorry for the oyster bar, I'm sorry for Mila. I've made assurances on her behavior. No one talks to you like that, not even her."

He reached out finally, closing the distance to grab my hand. He squeezed it, an affirmation of his apology embodied in the tenderness of his touch. I knew I pushed him to this moment, and I couldn't help but feel partially responsible for how disastrous our communication was on this topic. I wished it were simpler, that none of this were the case. I supposed that was why it was a fantasy, and not something real.

My phone buzzed at the table, sounding like an alarm at our touching hands. I pulled away, observing a calendar request for an upcoming meeting.

...

CASSOWARY HOTEL *Fitting for Alex Rivers*.
Prep for exclusive interview. Tomorrow 8:00 P.M.- Penthouse.
(Details to follow.)
-Ivanna

...

It was a booking from Alex's assistant. I wasn't familiar with the location, and the time seemed later than expected.

"Have you been to the Cassowary?" I asked Parker, who suspiciously eyed my phone.

"What makes you ask that?" He replied, not giving me a yes or no. "That's where Alex Rivers is staying. He can't go back to The Pierre, not after what happened." He dabbed his face with a napkin, pushing his plate to the side.

"Because of the lawsuit?" I asked.

"Yes. And he's lucky to still be in the city, or even that any hotel will take him." Parker didn't want to go into detail, not for the same reasons I held secrets, but because he was more professional than most.

"I have a fitting there tomorrow." I revealed, gauging the reaction of his tightening lips.

"When?"

"At night… eight o'clock."

"Unbelievable." He shook his head, "Not you, Gem. It's just… it's just what I expect from this guy."

"He's busy, I'm sure it's the only time he had available." I said it, though I didn't believe it. Alex knew he couldn't see me unless he booked me, yet he was adamant about taking me out. This was different though, this wasn't dinner, this was possibly the sexy penthouse of a posh hotel.

"Has he touched you?" Parker asked, the urgency in his voice was almost as surprising as the question.

"Touch me? Parker, why would he touch me?"

"Don't tell me he hasn't pressed you yet? He can be persuasive; I know he'll try. He's a womanizer. Have you seen how many models he's been photographed with over the years?"

"He hasn't. Even if he tried, he wouldn't get anywhere with me. I can't date my boss, and the womanizer isn't my type anyway." I admitted, but didn't he get close? What had he done so far? He'd been persistent, yes, but also patient. The way he said things with such conviction, such ambiguous sexual lure, left me unsure if it was for me specifically, or for everyone he met. I could sit here and excuse his behavior on personality alone, but it didn't explain everything. He went to Bushwick, a place where no one wanted to go. Did he visit the hometown of everyone he met? That seemed unlikely, but he had done this, not just for anyone, but for me.

"I'm looking for something familiar, something I saw the day I met you." Those were his words when I asked why he went, and when I inquired for what he saw, his response gave me chills, *"Something just like me."* How could he feel that way, just by looking at me, by what little we'd shared thus far?

"I'm not convinced," Parker replied. "I know when you're hiding from me, Butterfly. I don't pry, but it doesn't mean I don't care. I'll let this go because I know that's what you want. But if he puts you in a situation I disagree with, I'll have no choice but to react. I won't let him hurt you, not once, not ever." Parker slipped another pepperoni onto my plate.

"Thank you." I said, not for the pepperoni, but for the apology earlier, for his commitment to be there, no matter what. I wanted to believe this because it fit with the fantasy I created, this little bubble of ours. There would be a day—if not tomorrow, or next week—where

Parker would fall in love and leave me behind. How would he look after me then? He wouldn't, and where would I be if I didn't take care of myself starting now? I reached for my phone, and his eyes locked on my hands as I confirmed the appointment with a text.

"I'm there if you need me, Gemma." He removed his eyes from my phone and back onto me, "No one gets hurt, unless it's him. I promise."

Chapter 9

I had no idea what to expect. Being around Alex amongst other people was difficult as it was, but alone, in his own private suite, how would he be? I straightened my posture, catching my reflective face in the elevator door. I'd be lying if I said I didn't prepare how I looked, wearing a tight, turquoise, high-necked mini dress with bellowed sleeves and covered cleavage. I kept my glam toned down to neutral golds and a rosy cheek, tightening my hair into a conservative bun. My message was crystal clear, spoken through fashion as I only knew how: I was a capable stylist and a total professional.

If Alex was as sly as Parker mentioned, I knew I had to be ready, to be astute to his movements and the things he'd do or say. I didn't want to be caught off guard, especially since he had managed to do so in every interaction thus far. I was never prepared for the things Alex said, how he rescued me from Gerard or how he scolded me like a child. I may not have had a father growing up, but the way he wielded his expectations made me imagine how it might've been. This was not to say he was the light of fatherhood, but rather, he was persistent, expectant, and held an authority that made many want to please, including myself, in the most professional sense of the way.

I wanted to be told I did a job *well* done.

The Cassowary itself was a pillar of glass and steel, a beacon for millionaires in Midtown, Manhattan. It made sense for Alex to be here, amongst the polished marble and crystal decanters, but not in Bushwick. That thought stuck in my chest like a loose and broken bone. I couldn't ignore it, especially since I had time to think, stuck in a speeding elevator that took forever to reach the top. His penthouse was on the last floor, the eighty-ninth to be exact. I smoothed out the sweat of my palms along the bottom of my dress as the elevator slowed down.

Be cool, Gemma, stay calm, stay professional. He's your boss, his interests go only as far as you let them.

The elevator jerked, softly stopping as the doors opened. My heart raced as I stepped out, instantly immersed in a massive foyer. At first, I was silent, startled as the elevator doors pinched from behind, my body still in its way. I listened for Alex, but only heard the faint melodic beats of soft music.

"Hello?" My voice echoed. No response. The steps of my clicking heels bounced down the hall as I entered the living room, intoxicated by the view of inferior skyscrapers. The tips of my fingers tingled at the sight, almost daring myself not to get too close. I faced away, as to not fall, redirected towards a large kitchen with sleek stone counters. It was hard to escape the surrounding glass walls, made not for an observer, but for a god to peer down, his garden being Central Park, manicured with dots of light and tiny people. It was both beautiful and consuming, fitted for a man like Alex.

He knew I was coming, but perhaps he was late, as often as he was. I expected him to appear at any moment, watching me like a lion in the dark. It was a thrilling thought, but also made me nervous. What would he see if he saw me now, a mystified girl, lost in his home? That alone made me vulnerable, but I assured myself I'd feel him soon enough, considering his devious eyes had a way of pricking at my skin.

A familiar box caught my attention, resting on a black table by my side. It was his pack of cigarettes, the name unbeknownst to me, burgundy and black, printed with a man in a headdress. I studied its label, almost metallic with a reflection, reading the unfamiliar Spanish word, *Tranquilo's*. I looked over my shoulder, then back at the pack, curious to smell the cherry scent as I had before.

I opened its top, removed a cigarette and placed it between my fingers. I tried to remember how he held it, mimicking its position, placing it near my lips, but not touching them. It allowed me to enjoy the scent that gave me chills and was different than Claire's. The fruity smell was unique, almost raising the hairs on my neck, a contrast to Alex's eyes which often put me on edge.

It was funny to think how he had such an effect on me, how he could be both, calming and scary, enjoyable and frustrating. I saw those traits in him, so how could he see himself in me? I wanted to understand it, and the clues around his house felt like a good place to start.

A slight shine glistened from the coffee table in the living room. I looked around, hoping to be quick enough to snoop and avoid being caught. Behind me was a large staircase, and its black railing stretched to the second floor, where I knew Alex surely was. I wanted to shout out again but also wanted this moment to sneak around, so I remained quiet. I inched closer to the table, looking down, lifting an unexpectedly heavy pair of handcuffs.

I swallowed, my mouth dried at their sight, what they implied. They felt so sturdy, so permanent, their clasp slipped into place, locked as if on my wrist. Who were these for, and what would they feel like secured around me?

"A prop." Alex's deep voice buzzed in my ear, startling me as I spun around. I screamed, simultaneously dropping the handcuffs and clutching my chest.

"Jesus, Alex!" I screeched already losing all professionalism, caught spying around the boss's house. I realized his cigarette was still clutched in my hand, so I hid it. I sheltered it in the ball of my fist, keeping it close to my waist. "I said hello, but you didn't answer."

"So you went searching for me?" He motioned towards the coffee table, "Maybe I was hiding under the cuffs?" His voice hummed with a tease. He could have scolded me, and I would have taken it, but his smirk let me off the hook. A small gesture of kindness I wasn't expecting.

"I was… just surprised." I replied, not answering his question. I was flustered, caught in the current state of Alex's shirtless body. Sweat dripped along his strong jaw and shoulders, tempted to be licked like salted caramel ice cream. Not an ounce of him was soft, each inch sculpted with careful intent; arms that could wrap around me, hands that could consume the entirety of my face. He was far sturdier and equipped, more so than my knees, which suddenly lost their stiffness.

"I'm either wearing these, or putting them on someone. Just depends if I'm the villain or not." Alex bent over, picking up the cuffs, catching the glance I stole. I was drawn to his chest, reminding myself of the womanizer he was. It was the angel wings, the ones of an assumed lover, whose initials twitched from the flex of his firm muscle.

"Which do you prefer?" I asked, mentally moaning at the stupid question. "I mean, in your movies, that is?" I hated being caught off guard, especially with Alex. I wanted to be as calm as he was, but I lacked the skill upon his surprise. It felt as if he enjoyed watching me squirm, forming me into this shy girl. I watched as he stretched, presenting the V-cut of rippled dark abs, their presence further implied, but lost in the trim of loose black sweats.

"I guess you'll find out." He tossed the cuffs onto the couch. "Thirsty?" He asked, walking into the kitchen. The question asked implied more than intended, and for that reason, I almost said yes. But I shook my head at the sudden thought, me in a compromised position, hopelessly pinned below his bare body. I rejected it.

"No, thank you, Mr. Rivers." I answered, following behind. His back puckered, drawn with renewed definition and sweat. He opened the fridge as I slipped the cigarette into my purse. My palm was damp from nervousness, and I was unable to put it back where I found it.

"No formalities, Gemma," he commanded softly, pulling out a pitcher of water. "It really is overdone." He tipped the pitcher over a glass, then raised it up to his lips. His gruff voice was tantalizing, his eyes stoic and dark.

"I'm not comfortable calling you by your first name." I maintained, setting a new precedent.

"Unless I scare you, then you call me Alex." He reminded, pointing out how I first addressed him when he startled me earlier.

"That was different."

"It was, and I liked it. Maybe I should scare you more often." He reached up with his hands, both of which were wrapped in white tape. I was reminded of his knuckles as he bit down on the strap, his pristine teeth clenched as he pulled it off.

"Are those bandages?" I asked softly.

"It's a wrap. It protects my hands."

"From?"

"Getting hurt while boxing." He gestured towards the stairs, "The bag is heavy, and I hit real hard. Can't let my strength get in the way of that." He took another sip of water, while his Adam's apple hypnotized me with a subtle bob.

"You have a gym in here too?"

"I have lots of things, but still adjusting to the new space." He admitted, reminding me this wasn't his first home in New York. He was no longer welcomed at The Pierre, the location of an apparent out of control party turned lawsuit. I wanted to ask but knew I shouldn't. That'd be a dangerous game, especially for someone as observant as Alex. I knew I couldn't ask questions if I wasn't willing to reciprocate, and I would be hard pressed to do so.

"Well, it's very lovely… Mr. Rivers." I asserted my stance once more.

"Call me that again, and I'll correct you." His tone was a warning, shooting shivers up my spine. He leaned over the counter as his hands gripped the edge. I followed his eyes which led to the couch, nodding at the cuffs as if they were a promise.

"I won't call you Alex, alone," I snipped. "I told you already, I'm not comfortable with that."

"Then call me by my name," he commanded. "Only for you, my *real* name. I want to hear you say it, for it to leave your lips." He took another sip as my arms stiffened, his request as simple as it was provocative. I didn't like his desire for me to say his name as if that would have any bearing or ownership over me, but mostly, I didn't like how it made me feel—tight, nervous, wet.

"And what would that be?" I asked but was met with a devilish smirk.

"Alejandro," he growled, his voice thick and soft all at once, "Alejandro Rivera-Marquez." I mouthed the name, *Alejandro,* denying his satisfaction to hear it out loud, but sacrificing my own pleasure in the process. He shifted his dark eyes from the floor towards me, staring through the fullness of his lashes.

I looked away, almost too self-aware of my body and

who was staring at it. Why did he look at me with such desire, such patient conviction? I was pressured by no one, but by the voice in my head, where I repeated a thought: *He wants you, and he'll take you.* I couldn't fixate on anything but his body, the sweat riddled tattoos and blood pumped veins. Maybe it was just him, maybe it was the penthouse, but now that we were alone, I found it more difficult to resist his stare, to stay professional as I promised.

"I expected something more Californian," I laughed, breaking my awkward silence. I held my breath, but I was unaware for how long, so my words came out with a deep inhale.

"As opposed to something more New York?"

"Well, we're different here."

"How?"

"More pushy, in your face, get what you want kind of people." My words were laughable at best, I was none of these things. Should I even call myself a New Yorker? I wasn't pushy nor did I enjoy oysters on the regular.

"Who says I don't do any of those things?" He asked, shifting his eyes from the floor and back to me. I concealed a whimper which twisted in my chest like a snake, wet and loose, slipping past my stomach and down my legs.

"Then you must fit in." I added quickly, "You must be enjoying New York."

"No," he corrected, "Not in the least."

"That can't be true." I scoffed. This was the world's greatest city, who wouldn't enjoy it?

"It is," he insisted, "It's too loud. The cars, the streets, the people. There's no place to think or to be alone."

"There's plenty." I hushed him, taking offense to the city I loved.

"Like?" He challenged, "Where do you go?" He was doing it again, studying me, rolling his tongue as he posed a question that seemed intentional.

"Nowhere in particular." That wasn't true, and he knew it. His body adjusted with a sigh; his shoulders expanded.

"Tell me." He repeated the demand, cocking his neck.

"Honestly," I admitted, "I have an annual pass to The Met. I mean, I *had* one. Money's been tight." I waved away.

"The Met?"

"Yes. I like art, I like expression, I like…"

"Fashion." He interrupted, scanning my outfit. His eyes moved down every curve of my body, deciphering it as if it were code. He was learning and quickly, my admission of expression being taken to heart.

"Amongst other things." I added, not letting him get too carried away. He ignored this though, staring along my hips and up to my chest. I figured he would gawk, but he didn't, he moved along, studying my neck and the bun in my hair. I wasn't sure how to interpret his eyes, both hungry and appreciative. "Shall we?" I motioned, "Alejandro?" Saying his name evoked a smile, introducing the pinch of his dimple, something I hadn't noticed outside the furrowed creases above his brow.

"Right this way." He gestured, walking past my body and into the living room. I dug my hand into my bag, grazing the stolen cigarette, reminding myself of what I'd done. I ignored it, pulling out a measuring tape and a notebook. I stood determined to get through the night— no more gawking, no more *stealing*. "Where would you like me to take your measurements?" I asked, thumbing out the tape.

"The bedroom." He replied, reaching for a towel that was laid over a chair. I thought of Parker, his looming voice in my head, scolding about Alejandro and the power of his sex. Was I just another link in a long chain of women? I assumed so, and though I played with the idea myself, I knew better.

"No." I assured.

"Is that so?"

"Yes. I take this job serious, and I expect you will as well." His intrigued dark brows raised as I continued, "I'm not going to just jump into bed with you, no matter how sexy or persistent you may be. Understood?" I poised my chin to meet the height of his chest, snipping at his pursuit.

Alejandro wrapped the towel over his shoulders, seemingly impressed. "You really are a good girl, aren't you?" He asked, leaving me no space to reply, causing me to feel little. "The bedroom has a trifold mirror, bright lights, and a stool. I got that ready for you, a space to do your job." He pointed around, "This room's dark, but you may prefer that now, considering how red your face is."

For a moment I looked out the window, assessing if

it would shatter easily if I were to jump to my death. I was mortified. Once again, I was on the defense, but I was flipped by his intentions. I was the fool, not him, and his standards were now matched with my expectations. Did I meet his?

"This'll do." I winced, ignoring how naive I felt. Alex posed below a descending light, his muscles contoured by the shadows it brought. I wanted to apologize but lacked the courage to do so, so instead I changed the topic. "This fitting is pretty exciting. Ivanna said this was for an exclusive interview in June, right?" I questioned, measuring his back.

"So I'm told. It's for the *Tonight Show*, promoting the movie," he added, almost bored, but then sighed in relief, "there's also an upcoming project of mine, something more personal."

"Like your upcoming boxing career?" I teased, but almost shuddered as he stuck his arms out. His knuckles were still bruised, healing from purple to green.

"That was different." He assured, knowing what I meant.

"The man in Bushwick was different? As opposed to what, other ones?"

"The man himself? No. Those men are the same. But what do you know about that?" He asked calmly, not once defensive, "What have you read?"

"Only that he's not pressing charges," I studied his hands, "which seems odd."

"Not odd at all. He's the one that got comfortable, felt the need to put his hands on someone else."

"On you?"

"No." He snapped his finger, his thumb alone a cracking whip, "A woman." I looked away, understanding the extent of the fight, the cause that even *New York Prestige* failed to notice. Sure, he was violent, and violence was always wrong, but in the defense of another person, was it truly?

"That was brave of you…" I added, feeling sorry for bringing it up.

"Not brave, but impulsive. I see men like him, and I lose control." He looked away. I could tell he regretted sharing, his normal confident stare now unsure. It was difficult imaging what losing control looked like for him, considering he was so dominant in every aspect of his life. I guess losing control equated to violence, or maybe to the correction of another being.

"Guess it's not a topic you want to bring up in the interview."

"Better than others I guess. It's always the same pattern, the same boring questions. People believe what they read, not what they're told, at least for me that is."

"Well, that's not fair." I immediately quipped.

"No, but it is what it is. It's the price you pay for being famous."

"I'm sure you're not just a tabloid, look at what you've accomplished." I motioned across the room, as if it were a trophy he'd earned. "What does *Alejandro* want to share with the world?" I asked, garnering a dark but curious raise of his brows.

"Alejandro?" He laughed softly, "They're not interested in him, only in Alex Rivers." The veins of his hand popped tightly, curled by the casual clench of his outreached fist.

I may not have understood, but I knew enough to see his frustration, not towards me, but the idea in itself.

"I am." My loose confession fell out, relaxed unlike the tape in my hand which wrapped tightly around his firm chest. I was so close, smelling the familiar cherry scent rise from his golden skin. I knew so little about him, about his bold tattoos, the angel wings, and his past. Alex was for the people, but he already said, Alejandro was for me, a name he shared for my lips to speak. It was worth the question, worth the time to understand. "Why do they call you Alex Rivers?" I asked, monitoring his reaction.

"The name Alejandro never paid the bills. They thought it would cost them money. Too long for credits, too Hispanic for their audience."

"Too Hispanic?" I asked, finding the thought a little absurd. In the fashion world, I was used to foreign names being the charm of many established designers. I never thought twice about their names, about how it could cost them money. I didn't understand.

"I was type casted. I was always a secondary role, a Mexican mobster, a construction worker, a tool to support some menacing cartel man, but never a lead. I changed my name; I changed their perception. I was no longer just Hispanic, I was relatable, a name people could speak quickly and recognize on a billboard." He looked up at the ceiling and scoffed, "They wanted me, they just didn't want my culture."

I hesitated to speak, feeling somehow privileged to

hear his perspective. It was a personal thing to admit, and I wondered what—if anything—I could do to recognize what he was sharing. This man had everything, but what did it cost him? His identity? His name, the very one he gave me to say out loud.

"Well, I like your name," I confessed. I wasn't sure if it was enough to say, but it may have made him happy regardless. Everyone had an opinion on him, but who really knew him? Even Parker saw Alejandro from one aspect of his life, nothing beyond a history of lawsuits. "You're more than what others think, we all are."

"Is that so? You make it sound so simple."

"Well, maybe not simple, but it's true, I guess it just takes time to see it." I struggled to believe the things I said myself. I was the culmination of other's perspectives. Gerard saw me as a piece of garbage, and Claire saw me as the failed daughter who never called. I knew I was more than these things, but at times it was impossible to accept, if not completely reject. Maybe the same was true for Alejandro, for the assumptions people made. "I wouldn't hide your name, it's not just for me to speak, but for people to know. Especially now." I looked back at his bruised hands, at the notion he actually defended someone. That was honorable, wouldn't that person want to know the real Alex Rivers? "People love you, and you can't deny that. I'm sure your fans want to know who it is that they admire. People unlike Richard that is," I reminded from the Drip campaign. "I hope he learned his lesson. The way he spoke to you was wrong, and I'm glad you left the shoot actually. That took courage… I'm not sure if I could do that, but you did."

"You think the whole world could accept the truth of who I am?" He asked, not curious but pointing out the naivety of my sentiment. Maybe I felt to close to the idea of being defined by others, having been labeled all the awful things I wished to erase, a sister included.

"I think there is more to share than just what's written about you. Maybe it's time people listen."

"Or maybe, just one person." He added firmly, leaving little room to think that he meant anyone other than me. I hushed my words, accepting the silence that fell between us. I wasn't sure if it was the cherry scent or not, perhaps it was his stare, no longer putting me on edge, but relaxing my nerves. If I allowed myself to admit it, I'd say it was nice, calming even.

"Thank you." He craned his neck, slowly peering down.

"For?" I asked unsure.

"For what you said about Richard. I don't need the validation, but the recognition is nice. Maybe you should be my agent instead." He joked, but it was sweet. "And what about you, Gemma?" He asked, "Who accepts you for who you are?" His question was strange, but not in the context from his experience. He seemed to have this perception of me, that my authentic self was still in hiding. He was wrong though, my past was separate, something I kept away from who I was. I was honest, at least for most of the time, and what was shared was only with Parker. No one else.

"I have someone," I mumbled, shrugging.

"A boyfriend?"

"Yes." Without thought I replied, as if it were true

all along, but shook my head, "Well, he's my friend, and he's a boy... but it's more." I slid down to my knees, running the tape along his leg, "It's complicated." I hated to talk about it, I hated opening up, and Alejandro could sense that.

"I like complicated," he affirmed. "Complicated is interesting." It was hard to stare up while down on my knees, his legs spread, and his stature towering. I tried not to look but couldn't resist as my hand accidentally grazed over the large package that bulged down his thigh. I squeezed the muscles in my tummy, braced for the clammy wave that rushed to my hands. "The best friend?"

"I'd rather not say." Doing my best just to avoid it all together. I had already made a fool of myself tonight, and now I felt as though it were happening again.

"What's wrong?" he asked. "Be a brave girl for me, and share." He slipped his words down from his lips. I followed them along, past the cooled sweaty muscles and towards his crotch. My knees started to sting, pressed into the wood floor in a position that he'd probably seen plenty of women in. Was he thinking the same, and how could I stop him if he did? Had he tugged the bun in my hair and forced himself between my lips, I'd be helpless, enslaved to blow him like the subordinate I was. This made me blush, and I hated that it did. "You tell me more, and I'll tell you a secret of my own."

A secret? What could he possibly share? I was sure he was filled with them, his age and experience alone had years on me. He was older, maybe the age my father was when he left, but nothing like that man. He was assertive, he was present, he was the cherry smoke that defied what I knew about yucky cigarettes. I flicked my tongue against the inside of my cheek, considering the payoff.

"You promise?" I asked, almost like a child unsure of his word. He crossed his heart, his long finger traced along the dark wings of his chest. This was a game, one I was tempted to join.

Show me yours, and I'll show you mine.

"I swear it." He said, snarling with an emphasis on the word *swear*. I really contemplated his offer, unsure for a moment before sighing out loud.

"Ok, it's complicated because he's my best friend, but now he has a girlfriend and…"

"Stop." Alejandro raised his finger, shushing my words. He was adamant to control the conversation, to lead the questions.

"What is it?" I asked.

"This isn't complicated."

"Yes, it is." I maintained, but he persisted.

"Have you two fucked?" He asked callously.

"I'm sorry?"

"I asked you, have you two fucked?" He spoke more clearly, my body still down on my knees, looking up at his height.

"No…"

"Has he ever tried?" He asked, going through a mental checklist, a criteria. Of course he hadn't, he never made a move; it was only me, always was. I thought of that embarrassing night, back in college, the moment I confessed and puked on his shoes.

"I'm still waiting." I answered, sounding pathetic.

"How do you know he likes you then?"

"I don't know. Sometimes I think so, but…" I was stuck, but Alejandro didn't wait. He bent over, and his strong hand cradled my chin. My breath hitched, with his first true touch, an example of something I knew nothing about, especially with Parker.

"Stand up." He commanded, his gruff voice radiated in my ears. My hesitation was met with his assertion, "Do as you're told." He ordered with all the promise and certainty of a loaded gun, dangerous and ready to pop. I felt uneasy, almost sick and joyed at once. I lifted from my position, coaxed by the strength of his impatient hand that touched my chin. He raised me to the creased brow of his smoldered expression. I was closer than I had ever been before, even while measuring, the space between us only big enough for a whisper.

"Like this?" I asked, making sure I understood. Every delicious, toned muscle was flexed for my eyes, designed to suck me into his world.

"Just like that." He confirmed, the fangs of his pearly white teeth appeared with confidence. "Tell me, Gemma," he whispered, "does he look at you like this?" Alejandro tilted my chin, guiding me to his gaze. My body grew weak, hypnotized even, as his forehead leaned against mine. His scent seeped into my skin, consumed in the subtle sweetness of cherry flavored breath. Every cell in my body exploded, rocked by the throbbing rush of blood that quivered in my veins. For this moment, encapsulated within his hands, I was entombed with warm euphoria.

"Well?" He pulled me in closer, his hips pressed tightly against me, overwhelming every risen hair on my body.

"Well?" I responded, my brain in a fog.

"Does he look at you like that?" He asked, peeking down, reaching for my hand. I dropped the measuring tape as he lifted it up.

"Well, he isn't a movie star, so no." It was the best I could say, and my words fell like dribble.

"Star or not, if he doesn't make you feel like you're his whole world, then your answer will always be no." His attention lowered to the silver butterfly around my finger. I bit my lip as he noticed, assessing the reaction it caused. "Is this from him?"

"Yes…" I moaned, helpless to the enjoyment he got from watching me squirm.

"Of course he doesn't fuck you. He thinks you're a butterfly, he thinks you're fragile. But I don't. You're a good girl, but good girls are meant to be broken." He purred so softly, his meaning unclear. Did he break hearts or break innocence? I felt the truth both in my chest and between my legs. "He wouldn't know what to do with you, anyways… not like me that is. When I fuck, it's to make you scream." Alejandro let go of my hand, resuming his position to be measured.

His words made my hands tremble, surged with a strange adrenaline as I got closer, pulling the tape around his neck. I was still rattled by that moment, by the sense that he could fuck me so hard that I'd undoubtedly scream. It swirled in my stomach, something I begged the universe for, but with Parker, yet here it was, mocked so clearly with Alejandro; or was it Alex Rivers who fed the line? It was hard to know who that man was, the actor, or the person. It had been built into my mind already, Alex was not to be trusted; he was a wild, womanizing, bad-boy. But maybe there were two sides, one for the papers, the other for me, behind closed doors.

"And you?" I asked, ignoring the clear effect his words had between my legs. "You owe me a secret."

His eyes shifted, almost pretending to search his mind for what was already on his lips. "Hmmm," he hummed. "The secret is I'm no longer hiring you as my stylist."

I scrunched my face, shooting a panicked glance. Was this all a trick to lure me in, to get me closer to him? I felt defensive, once again snapping into reality.

"Then why am I here?" The tape slipped out of my loose grip. Alejandro stepped closer and tucked a loose strand of hair behind my ear, delighted in my mystified state.

"I'm going to make the world see you, Gemma. You're not going to style me; you're going to design for me." He stepped back toward the table for his glass of water. The unexpected assignment left me speechless, but more so than that, terrified at the prospect that my dream could actually come true. I refuted without wanting to.

"Styling and designing are totally different, Alejandro." I shook my head.

"I'm aware." He took a sip from his glass, "I saw your portfolio, I know what you're capable of." He arched his eyebrow, "This isn't charity, this is an expectation. This is your dream, isn't it?"

"Yes, of course, but…"

"But nothing. I want you to do as you're told. You have two months." He shot a look that dared me to protest, but rather than suffering the consequence, I looked away.

"A suit, I'm assuming?" I asked quickly, flipping the pages of my notebook. "What style would you…" Alejandro cut me off.

"I'm not interested in that question." He walked closer, "These are your choices." He appeared over me as the bright city lights glistened behind him, confirming what I knew was true; he was the king of this castle. "You said it yourself. I'm a sexy celebrity, now show me what that looks like."

"By design?" I reminded myself of the words he used the day of the shoot. He wanted to see how I saw him, and that idea still continued.

Alejandro walked me to the elevator, pressing the sleek silver button on his panel. The door slid open, dinging in the air as my queue to exit. I stepped inside, but as I turned around, I noticed that Alejandro leaned against the opening, blocking the automated doors with his cherry scented body. He stared at me, just as he had in the past, just as he had moments ago with my chin in his hand.

"What is it?" I wiped my lip, self-conscious something was wrong.

"I lied to you earlier. About New York. I wasn't enjoying myself, but now I am. It's different now. You did so good today." He exhaled a gentle praise, affirming my job.

"Then why are you staring?" I asked again, with complete hesitancy.

"I'm just reminding you, how a man should stare when he's interested." I was unable to leave, shackled by his expression, "*Piedra preciosa.*" He said those words again, the ones I knew nothing about but wanted to hear. I wanted to know, I wanted to ask, but he only allowed me a moment, a quick glance of his eyes, scowling and dark, charged with a promise, that the doors were better shut than left open another second.

Chapter 10

On the corner of Forty-fourth and Eighth, drops of cool rain fell along my bare shoulders. Of all the nights for it rain, it had to be now, dotting along my pastel mint dress, the floral spring pattern picked just for Parker. Despite the promise of a storm, I remained completely excited. Tonight was our night, a chance to get away, to remember the moment we met as kids.

Edging closer to the marquee, I sheltered my damp hair under the glowing theatre's header. It was thirty minutes until the play, and I began to worry. I checked my purse once again, securing both our tickets. They were here, but where was Parker? We agreed to meeting in front of the Majestic because of his late shift today.

He'd been completely consumed by this case, by Alejandro, staying all night at the office for most of the week. But he knew tonight was different, it was important in a different way. It was uniquely us, a tradition we never missed as adults, something I spent my last bit of money on.

I looked up at the sky, observing the source of low rumbling thunder. The whole thing made me anxious. The crowds entered the lobby of the theatre as I pulled out my phone, unable to resist sending him a quick text.

Gemma*:* Park, I got the tickets, but you may want to bring an umbrella, especially if we walk to dinner after.

I turned around to look in the window, correcting my frizzy hair from the rain. Even if we weren't together and even if I were meant to move on, I wanted to look good, not just for him, but for me. It wasn't a date, but it always felt like one, the single moment I waited for each year. My phone buzzed, two quick messages came in at once.

Parker*:* Tickets?
Parker*:* Oh shit, Gemma!

I laughed, unintentionally snorting at the messages. It was a joke, so odd that I couldn't even respond before his next message came through.

Parker*:* I'm on my way.
Gemma*:* Lol! Very funny. I know you wouldn't forget about Phantom of the Opera. I'm all dressed, hurry up, I'm standing in the rain!
Parker*:* No, I fucked up! Seriously, have them hold my ticket at box! But go inside, stay warm for me.
Gemma*:* Wait… are you serious?
Parker*:* I wish I wasn't.

I laughed to myself, shaking my head, this had to be a prank. The reply dots appeared on my screen, only to disappear again. He was probably thinking of something funny to say.

Gemma: Ok, seriously, where are you?

Parker: Far, but racing over. There's traffic though.

Gemma: Of course there's traffic, it's New York. You on the Upper East Side?

Parker: Further. Mila needed me to pick her up, but she surprised me with her family instead. I had no idea.

I was gutted. This wasn't a joke. I caught a glimpse of myself in the window, and the wind softly swung my earrings. I looked like a fool, my reflection a mocking reminder of how much I cared, completely dressed with makeup to match. I tried to convince myself as I did earlier that it was all for me, but it wasn't, I did it for him. The familiar and unsettling sound of thunder rumbled from above, causing me to coil closer to the brick wall as I made myself smaller.

Gemma: Where did you pick her up at?

I asked, but worried at the answer. The bubble to his message coming and going. I read it like a sigh, the defeat in his own voice.

Parker: JFK. I swear this was a mistake. I told them I can't stay, I'm dropping them off, I'll be there for you.

There was no way. JFK was in Queens, way past Bushwick, way past anything. He wouldn't make it, it would be at least a couple hours to fight the traffic, if not more. It was Friday, and I was alone, and I wasn't sure why. I reminded him, even during breakfast about our plans. The more I looked at myself, the sillier I felt. The frizz in my hair still not corrected but took low priority to tears that threatened my mascara. My phone buzzed loudly, signaling a call from Parker.

I wanted to answer, I wanted to hear his voice. I knew he was probably panicked and assuring him would help lessen his stress. I could have done that for him, but I wouldn't, not with the lump in my throat; he'd hear that, and once again, I wanted to shelter him from the ugly I felt. I ignored his call, clicking the button pained me, so I sent a text.

Gemma: It's really loud right now, can't talk.
Parker: I'm still coming.
Gemma: No, Park, please. It's totally fine! Honestly.
Parker: I don't care, I'm coming.
Gemma: Well I do. This is an exciting time, meeting the parents already. I want to hear how it goes, so go hang out. Remember, I want you to live a normal life.

I sent the message, doubling down on this belief of a normal life, the one I tried to convince myself of. It had already gone this far, so why not continue? When the phone buzzed back, I didn't check it. I didn't want to see what he said, I only wanted to know how I left it. Maybe it was what I needed. Parker may not be in love, he may not be anything with Camilla, but I knew someday he would be, and he wouldn't be there for me like he said he would. This was my reminder again, walking alone amongst the wet pavement, that dependency wasn't Parker's job, but instead my own.

I pulled out a single ticket, taking my place amongst the chattering crowd. Many people were couples, some were not. A few looked in my direction and I them, a silent connection of solitude that didn't go unnoticed. People did this all the time, *things* alone, it was fine to do, but my excitement fell flat as the usher tore my ticket. This wasn't meant to be alone; this was meant to be shared.

Parker wouldn't be here tonight, and his replacement became clear as I heard the sudden pop of uncorked wine near the concession. I was guided by the glow of an illuminated candy display as I sat on a stool, placing my purse on a golden hook near my knees.

"Red wine, and a large buttered popcorn," I requested, not proud of the combination, but desperate for it nonetheless. The lady smiled, placing a napkin by my side as she left.

At first I was tempted to check Parker's message, reminded by a bag of peach gummy rings in the glowing display case. Had he been here, would he have bought them, and if so, would he have placed one on my finger just like old times, or did having a girlfriend mean our entire relationship would change? This wasn't the first time he had a girlfriend, but something felt different with her. I contemplated buying a pack, its flavor as soothing as my new appreciation for cherry cigarettes, but I couldn't think about anything else, except the idea of Parker with Camilla.

I pulled out my phone along with an envelope holding Parker's loose ticket. The bartender came by, dropping off my plastic cup of wine, but stopped as I reached out. "Would you give this to the front booth?" I asked, slipping her the single ticket. "They can give it away if they want, it doesn't matter." She twisted her lips, her pity something more uncomfortable than what I wanted, so I turned my attention towards my phone.

Parker was never one for social media, but I imagined Camilla was active enough for the both of them. It wasn't a good look, snooping around, but the habit was new, beginning with Alejandro the night I found his pair of heavy handcuffs. What other surprises would I find, starting with the new woman in Parker's life? Being a gossip columnist for *New York Prestige* was no tame indication, and her feed confirmed this. She was quite the socialite, every other photo being at an event, an extravagant party with wild cocktails and designer dresses.

I was surprised to see Parker, the freshly posted picture of his face welcoming her page. I wanted to cry. His expression was timid, almost lost in the candid photo of Camilla and her family. Parker wasn't one for parties or large gatherings, which Camilla clearly enjoyed. Even in college, we spent our time alone on the roof, versus the actual frat parties themselves. I read the caption below the photo: *Perfect night with my perfect man.* In it, Camilla kissed his cheek, her long lashes on display, squinted and proud.

What she wrote was true, Parker was perfect and, in reality, so was she. It was no wonder why he liked her, and maybe that was my clue. I was just a sister to Parker, the opposite of Camilla, who was a voluptuous, dark haired, chocolate eyed beauty.

Maybe she had an energy to her that he craved, one I couldn't produce. Confidence? She was compelling after all, her alluring stare was almost reminiscent of Alejandro, but only in color, not in effect. His were a synopsis of a powerful man or perhaps a delicate facade. Handsome and possibly dangerous, it was difficult to tell if his eyes revealed the truth, or mirrored a perception the world viewed him as, a Hollywood bad boy. The term itself made me laugh, he was anything but a *boy*, but instead an older and more assertive star. He wasn't Parker, who was more considerate and kinder, who himself wasn't a boy, but whose childhood intertwined with mine. If I didn't stop him, Parker would've come tonight, even if he missed it. I was sure Alejandro would never do something like that for anyone. Parker was different, he was sweet, but that notion alone didn't make me feel better about him not being here tonight.

Suddenly, my thumb slipped, liking the photo of Parker and Camilla, the woman whose page I wasn't even following. I panicked, but soon became startled as the crowds behind me grew louder. I was lost in the noise, the once quiet chatter more static now, met with the bright flashes of clicking camera phones. A group of suited large men walked in, shielding the view of a single man.

I was mortified.

I couldn't believe who had arrived.

Alejandro.

Chapter 11

He kept his head down, his dark eyes squinted from the flashes, attempting a cooled wave of the hand nonetheless. He looked up, much taller than his own security, making eyes in my direction. Quickly, I spun around, twisting the cocktail napkin in my hand. Why was he here, why did he come? I knew the answer already, it was because I told him where I'd be. I rejected his invite to dinner during the Drip photo shoot, and now he was here at the Majestic, looking for me. I reached for my wine, raising it to my lips, trying my best to go unnoticed.

He wouldn't dare come over here; he was in the spotlight, his reputation and all. I kept my head down, studying the playbill, rereading the same sentence over and over again. Mentally I wasn't ready, already wrecked from tonight, the damp evidence of rain still on my dress and hair.

The woman at the counter dropped off my popcorn, her eyes trying to assess the commotion behind me. "Can I get you anything else?" She asked, half listening, half distracted. I dug my hand into the bucket and stuffed my mouth, nervously eating without enjoyment. I tasted nothing.

"I'm good." I hushed, but knew it was too late. Her soft eyes widened into round empty plates. Alejandro's presence was palpable, thick like a fog that hung in the air. The flavor of gummy peach rings was no longer on my mind, but rather displaced with the scent of cherry tobacco. I didn't appreciate how this sweet smell alone could shove my thoughts aside.

"Manhattan, Four Roses Bourbon, please." The familiar deep voice announced itself, requesting a drink with silk-like clarity. The bartender was startled and so was I. It took everything in my power not to turn around, but my resistance was challenged, his deep welcoming voice earning a peek of my eyes, "Gemma." He grinned.

I clenched my jaw, "What are you doing here?" I asked, not once looking his direction. His leather clad arm brushed against my body as he leaned against the counter.

"Here for the popcorn," he took a piece, tossing it into his mouth, "clearly." I peered behind him, staring at his security who blocked off the crowd. People stared with amazement, snapping pictures of him and me.

"I see you brought your friends. They should be able to keep you company."

"They're here for me, I'm not here for them. It's a necessary displeasure to get what I want."

"And what would that be?"

"More time with you." He lifted his drink to his lips.

I scoffed. "Don't do that." I warned him, looking away, as people were escorted to their seats.

"And what am I doing?"

"Pretending like I'm some mystery needing to be solved. It's not true, so you can go and see the play now." I picked up my wine to leave, but he took it from my hands, placing it back down.

"I'm not pretending, and I could care less for your perception on that." He looked over his shoulder, his furrowed brow creased with an olive glow, "Where is your friend? The boy?"

"He's coming soon," I lied, "So, you should probably leave." I warned, but not even this bothered Alejandro.

"Then let him come." He placed the caramel-colored liquor down on the table studying its hue. He made no attempt to hide his physique, his toned arms tight in a new leather jacket. The constricted noise caused by its creased movements felt almost sexual, as if the pressure of his large biceps could snap near my ear like a sturdy belt.

"He won't like you." I sneered.

"Why is that?"

"Because I don't like you." I stated sharply, frustrated by his persistence. Now was not the night, not with my damp hair, not with Parker letting me down. The truth was, I didn't like Alejandro, not only because he frustrated me, but because he made me feel at odds. The way his eyes coiled my insides, turned my stomach into knots, twisted below as if springs were tightening between my legs. I wanted to scream, I wanted to push him, I wanted to do a lot of things I couldn't acknowledge.

"You're lying." He leaned closer, his cherry scent posed like a signal.

"What?"

"You do like me, I can tell. If you didn't, I'd see it in your eyes. Say whatever you want about that, but unless you prove me wrong, I'll think otherwise."

"You're ridiculous." I laughed, amazed at his audacity. There was nothing to see, nothing to prove, my eyes said nothing. I refused to admit anything I felt.

"And you're being coy. What did I tell you about acting like a child?" His clear warning sent shivers down my back, the glow on my cheeks no longer from the wine, but from his words.

"And what? You want to somehow correct that?" I hissed, challenging his tempered scowl that made me sweat. He licked the corner of his lips, the collectiveness of his attitude morphed into frustration.

"I'm dying to," he replied. "Give me another reason to, and I will."

"You wouldn't," I laughed, calling his bluff, but his intended glare said different. He was serious, and I knew it. He'd carry me over his shoulders if I said another word and teach me the consequences of my actions. He'd show me what his version of a good girl was, and that alone made me cross my legs.

"I'll ask you again, where is your friend?" He returned my wine, nodding for me to take a drink. I did, but only to quench the dryness of my tongue, not because he demanded. I wouldn't yield to his requests. If he could see the truth in my eyes, then that scared me most of all. I hated attention, especially as spectators watched while being escorted away. I spent my life building barriers to keep people away, and if he could see beyond that, what would that mean?

"He couldn't make it." I confessed.

"You'll watch it with me then." He pointed his chin to a set of stairs, "I've got the best view in the house, and I don't want it to go to waste."

"And how would you know it's the best view?"

"Because I'm looking at it." His absolute conviction almost made me laugh, but only to soothe how nervous he made me. I knew I would've squirmed, but now I couldn't move, almost paralyzed by the weight of his words. "I'm here, he's not. It's not safe to leave a butterfly unprotected, unless you're with a wolf." He assured, looking down at my ring. I curled my finger into a fist, hiding Parker's gift from his sinful eyes.

"I don't need protection." I pulled my purse towards my shoulder, finally finding the strength to rise from my seat.

"I know this, but does he?" He asked, truly playing games with my head. Parker knew this, didn't he? Regardless of how he felt about Alejandro and about me working with him, the warnings he gave were purely with good intentions. Unless, of course, I was the little sister, needing to be saved. I couldn't sit here any longer, I couldn't let him look me in the eyes and see my truth.

"Enjoy your view." I pushed him aside, making my way back through the busy lobby. The crowd shouted, their attention back on Alejandro as I pushed my way through the thick wall of people. I hoped it'd kept him away, and I wasn't sure how much more I could take. As much as I was curious to join him, I was nervous of how it'd go. It was better to leave, to find the seats Parker and I had when we were kids.

I hurried along the steps, entering the theatre encased with gold trimming and red drapes. Immediately, I noticed someone new was in Parker's spot, that the free ticket was actually given away. It was a large man, consuming the seat with a box of sour cherry bombs. Not the man of my dreams, but someone just as lonely. He glanced at me with his pale face, adjusting the position of his glasses on the rim of his nose. I'd take anyone over Alejandro, over the risk he gave with his prying inquisition.

Tonight was already a mess, between Parker's absence and Alejandro's less than subtle approach. He was muddying the boundaries, challenging the border between professional and personal. I suppose we were outside of work, but that didn't mean I should have been any less frustrated. What did he expect me to do? People were taking my picture tonight, and I was certain it would end up online. I could imagine the headlines already, *Gemma Harrison, celebrity stylist who fucked her way to the top.*

Unbelievable.

The lights slowly dimmed, and finally I felt safe. Alone in the dark, I knew I couldn't be seen or bothered, or so I thought. The red curtain rose, as audience members clapped, but all I could hear was the distant mumbles of a man's voice. It persisted, sucking my attention to the neighbor on my left. I glared while my eyes adjusted to the dark figure by his side.

Alejandro.

We caught each other in observation, then back down at the man in Parker's spot.

"How much for your seat?" Alejandro asked, his thick voice still stout enough for everyone's ears. The pale man looked annoyed, ignoring Alejandro, but I shushed him. Alejandro pulled out a wad of money, flipping the bills in his hands. "Five thousand cash, along with my VIP seat. I won't take no for an answer." He warned as the man sighed, lifting from his seat. They switched as Alejandro pulled the box of sour cherry bombs from the man's hands. "The candy stays too." He bargained, finally allowing the man to leave. He sat by my side.

"Am I supposed to be impressed?" I scoffed, annoyed I wouldn't be enjoying my favorite play tonight. I knew people were watching us, star-obsessed fans who devoured the privacy of my moment.

"You don't need to be anything, just by my side is all," he said, but it irked me. I couldn't be by his side; I wasn't even sure I could make it through the play with all his distractions.

"Don't do that." I warned.

"Do what?"

"Flirt." I shook my head.

"Does it make you uncomfortable?" He asked fishing out a red candy ball. I didn't answer him, because I wasn't sure what it made me feel. Strange was the word that came to mind, but not negative, more compelling.

"You certainly have a favorite flavor." I looked down at the candy.

"You've noticed," he delighted, "and you?"

"I prefer peach rings." I asserted, its meaning only held by me. I prefer Parker, I prefer comfort and stability. As Parker would say, simple was a luxury, and the man knew what he was talking about. Alejandro was anything but.

"You prefer what you know, but you haven't seen anything yet." He placed a cherry ball in my hand. "Eat it." He commanded, but sweetly. I slipped it between my lips, chewing the almost sour but sweet ball that puckered my cheeks. It was good, maybe just as much as peach rings, but I wouldn't admit that.

"Do you even like this play?" I asked, puzzled as to why he was by my side. "It's not worth whatever obsession you have to suffer through this. It's my favorite, so I won't let you spoil it for me."

"Don't fool yourself. You should know by now, if I want something, I take it. Unlike your friend, I have no hesitations."

I rolled my eyes at his mention of Parker. "Fine, whatever you think. Just be quiet during the play."

"Not yet. I'm not done." The rasp of his voice carried the scent of cherries once again. I wanted another candy but didn't want to ask. It was as if he could read my mind, slipping another cherry ball into my hand, knowing what I wanted from perception alone.

"What now?" I almost shouted, closing my hand around the candy as I sunk into my seat.

"I'm taking you out after this."

"Not a good idea." I mouthed.

"Why not?" Alejandro grew louder, garnering a collective shush from the people behind us. I felt so uncomfortable, like a complete disturbance.

"You're my boss. It's not appropriate." I tried so hard to resist, but he smelled blood. Somehow, he knew how to bend me, how to make me snap.

"I told you I have expectations. I've hired you to make me a suit, haven't I?"

"Yes… I started the sketches a week ago when we did the fitting."

"That's not good enough. I told you it needs to come from your vision, the one you have of me."

"And it will."

"But how can it? You still don't know me. According to you, my perception is all wrong. Therefore, you owe me clarity, that is, if you want to do a good job." He warned, but the calming coax of his voice made me want to melt.

"I do…" I promised.

"And I know you will, that's why you'll let me take you out. Unless of course, more persuasion is in order." I looked around at our neighbors with their annoyed expressions. He would talk until I said yes, and he wouldn't stop.

"Ok..." I spat.

"Ok?"

"I said ok!" My lowered voice came out more as a shout, setting off another chain of loud shushes. I shot Alejandro my best attempt at an evil eye, but it only brought him devilish delight. His expectations were clear, and I was determined on succeeding at my task. I didn't know why I needed it, but I wanted what he promised, an opportunity to be told I did a good job. But why did it have to come from him, and why did it make me feel so weird? I hated how he caused me to cross my legs, that somehow he burrowed his words into the core of my gut. There was something about him, but I just didn't know it, and I needed to find out in order to do well on the suit.

I figured it was his touch, his scent, the way his voice slithered over my ears. He was compelling, and my body reacted. I convinced myself it was nothing more than some primal instinct, but that in itself was a challenge. What he asked was no simple task, leaving me to face the reality of what was to come. I knew tonight carried the possibility of either being heaven or hell, but what I didn't know was who he expected me to be, an angel or a devil.

Chapter 12

"**I**s this how it always is?" I asked, slamming the car door shut. I felt out of breath, having trudged our way through the theatre of screaming fans. I could still see the flashing photos outside, muted by the black tinted windows.

"Tonight was a good night," Alejandro observed. "Wait until my movie comes out." He reached through the seats, tapping the shoulder of his driver. "We're set, Charles." He commanded. The large, pepper-haired man behind the wheel pulled out into the street, chased by following fans. I couldn't believe my eyes, watching as people ran along the car till we merged with traffic.

"Well I'd hate to see it on a bad night…"

"Let's hope you do." He rolled his shoulders.

"And why is that?" I asked confused.

"Seeing the bad night means you're seeing it with me, and that means I've stolen you for even longer than you expected." He exhaled a cooled breath, "And I'll take that…"

The mere suggestion of being taken settled in my gut like the first sip of hot tea. He really was a megastar, and his unbridled approach only magnified how truly startling it was to be by his side. The truth was I was in the car with a celebrity, but for me, he was just my boss, an acquaintance at most. I reminded myself of this, combating the awkwardness of his suggestive eyes, which not only observed my body, but possibly dared it to be naked.

Alejandro's expectations were clear; I was to know him, and he was to know me. Challenging the belief that he had some ability to figure me out only made things worse. This excuse to take me away, the purpose being to benefit the suit, seemed like a front. Did he just want me alone? I wasn't sure what to say, so instead, I focused on adjusting in my seat. I was comfortable but anxious, my hands cupped in the palm of my lap.

"So," I started, the volume of my voice louder than expected. I cracked my knuckles, not realizing how hard I was squeezing my own hands, "Where are we going?"

He didn't answer, at least not right away. A brief moment of light leaked through the window, catching a glimpse of Alejandro in the shadows.

"That's a secret." He concealed, his face and golden skin illuminated in the hot red flame of his lighter. He cupped his hand around a cigarette, taking a calculated and purposeful drag. I could tell he savored it by the way he exuded a sweetened cloud from his angular unhitched jaw.

"I imagine you're full of those." I commented. "Getting to know you feels like a difficult task, probably why others resort to the gossip column."

He laughed to himself, soaking in the idea. "I could only imagine what they would write about you. But it may not be long before we find out."

"That wouldn't happen."

"Keep telling yourself that." He continued calmly,

taking another puff of his cigarette. He made it a purpose to watch my movements, the ones I tried to conceal, but not even my wayward eyes were safe. He followed my stare, the sly one I trailed along his body and up to the glowing cigarette. He pinched it, concentrating his eyes onto my breasts, as if imaging how hard he could squeeze them until I squirmed.

"Your cheeks are red." He grinned, pointing it out as if I weren't aware. The truth being, I felt them burn ever since he sat next to me in the theatre, but now, they were especially pronounced on my porcelain skin.

"Because of the crowds," I lied, "guess it was a lot to take in." I collected my poise.

"Have you ever smoked before?" He asked, the tip of his ring finger rested at the bottom of his lip.

"No," I answered quickly, but looked away, "I don't like it or the way it smells." The urge to correct what I said slipped from my mouth, as if not to be insulting, "But not yours. Yours are sweet, contrary to your perception."

"They are sweet," he replied, "and soft." I was left unsure of the topic, if it still remained on cigarettes, or rather, the lip he chewed. I took a moment to adjust, assuming the former.

"And why do you smoke?"

"Many reasons."

"Well, give me one because I can't think of any."

"To stop my cheeks from turning red." He toyed, playing on my comment about the crowds and how they got me flustered.

"So it's relaxing?"

"More than that. Yes, I enjoy it, but it helps."

"Helps with?"

"Stress mostly, but also, nervousness." He admitted, an unlikely candidness that took me by surprise. Despite his words, he didn't look nervous, in fact, the opposite. His impenetrable stare was a challenge, as if looking too long would catch me on fire. This was not a nervous man.

"You get nervous?" I mused, easing the tension.

"Of course, but I'm good at hiding my emotions, almost as good as you." I thought of the times I'd seen him smoking, once at the photoshoot when we were alone, another possibly being the night of his fitting. Though I didn't see him smoke at the penthouse, the sweet smell was still on his skin, as if he had one before coming downstairs to surprise me.

"Well you smoke around me, so I must stress you out." I welcomed his eyes now, "That or I make you nervous." I pushed this narrative, doing my best to be like Alejandro. Quick, presumptive, and observant.

"You don't stress me out. If it were that bad, I'd leave." He didn't comment on the nervousness but provoked another feeling, leaving when things get bad.

"So I've heard. It's not a good look though, not for everything at least." Such as the meetings I heard about him and his lawyers, that's what I wanted to say, but didn't.

"If it's not necessary, sure, but what's wrong with leaving when something is bad?"

"It reminds me of someone, and I don't like it." I snipped, clearly reminiscent of my father, how he essentially abandoned us, causing Claire's depression to worsen.

"Reminds you of someone? Is this related to the cigarettes as well?"

"Close, but no. Running away from problems lacks character, it makes things worse than what they are." I said it so baselessly, as if I weren't guilty of this myself. Avoiding my mother wasn't the same, or at least I believed so. She wasn't an uncomfortable meeting with lawyers like Parker described for Alejandro, she was a lifetime of exhaustion.

"Everyone runs from something, even you at times. You've avoided enough of my questions to reveal something in itself.

"And what would that be?"

"That doing so comes easy to you. It's in your nature, but I know better."

I scoffed, his continued ideas both irked me and made me laugh. "You think you see meaning in everything, and that's just not true. People do and say things every day without giving a message."

"Is that so?"

"Yes, and avoiding a topic is not a testament to my nature, but rather, the nature of *us*, our relationship. You're my boss, you're entitled to nothing other than a job well done."

"I'm entitled to the truth, and it begins with admitting that you're a purposeful woman."

"And what is that supposed to mean?"

"Simple." He twisted the butt of his cigarette to be extinguished, "You think you're clever, and in many ways you are. You dare not speak the truth, but the truth is written everywhere. It's what you wear, it's how you look, how your body responds, the way you cross your legs and hide your cheeks."

"Meaningless." I snipped, clenching my teeth. The fact he'd seen that, that he noticed that particular movement with my legs made me burn. "That means nothing."

"Is that so? I can tell you one thing for certain. You're in love."

"That's not true!" My tone was already an apparent give away. His confidence was far too staggering, even for my defensive screech.

"I knew it the moment I saw you tonight. Give yourself more credit."

"Sitting at a bar with popcorn and wine doesn't indicate love."

"No, but gardenias do. That's not just a floral dress you're wearing, it's a message." He looked down at me, scanning my bare shoulders, studying each marking and imperfection. Everything was vulnerable, the freckles I'd earned from the Hamptons' sun, the tiny dark mole along my collarbone. He wasn't just looking at me, he was remembering me, for what, I wasn't sure. I placed my hands together, digging them into my lap, resisting the urge to cross my legs once more.

"Gardenias?" I asked, but it was a bluff. Of course I knew what they meant, of course I wore them on purpose. But admitting this confirmed everything Alejandro said was true, and I wasn't ready to acknowledge that, nor him.

"They mean secret love, and it's no coincidence you were meeting your best friend, the one who's relationship you call 'complicated'."

"And it is."

"I thought I cleared that up for you." Alejandro shifted in his seat, pulling himself closer where we were shoulder to shoulder, but his lean into me felt threateningly close. "If he doesn't stare at you like I do, then you're missing the point." His tempered eyes left my insides sticky, glued together like a dirty paper doll. I gripped the seat below me, squeezing the leather, wondering if it was as smooth as his jacket.

"And what about your flowers?" I protested. He stared at my lips, the concept of him inching closer was just an illusion, or maybe an uncertain wish. I eyed the black rose on his hand, its vine curled into his cuff. "You're not the only one with hidden meanings. If you think we're so alike, then you're just as guilty."

"And what do you think it means?" He asked, running his thumb along the dark ink.

"I'm not interested in giving you my perception. And if it's my perception you want, then go ahead and read a *New York Prestige* article, because it's all I have." I let go of my seat.

His face melted into a more refined but serious stare. He looked away for the first time, finally down at the flower in question. He didn't smile, he didn't frown, he gave me no clues to how he felt other than with his silence, which suddenly became profoundly still.

"Death." He answered, the tail end of the word trickled like a stream of hourglass sand.

"And let me guess, you're a fan?" I scoffed, assuming it was some signature look he wished to portray. If his molten brown eyes and furrowed brow didn't say it enough, the ink reaffirmed an identity. *I'm a bad boy, get too close and get burned.* This felt true, not just because of Claire's warnings, but because the way his body made me feel inside.

"No. Not a fan."

"Is it for love then?"

"In a way."

"See, you avoid my questions too. You like to point your finger and accuse me of doing that, but you're just as much to blame." I spun his words on him, feeling like I had finally proven a point. "It must be in your nature."

"You're right. That's why we're more similar than you think." His reply caught me off guard. I laughed.

"We're nothing alike. I'll admit my dress has meaning, but I'm not sure all your tattoos do. I feel like some are superficial, a warning to keep people away. I think the ones you hide have the biggest meaning, but those aren't the ones people see. But what do they really mean?" He made it nearly impossible to get to know him, and wasn't that why I was here?

"And what makes you think that?"

"The angel wings on your chest." I quickly added. "People will question the tattoo on your hand, because it's visible. Either they can ask, or they can assume what it means. Either way there's a narrative. Hidden angel wings with initials, now that's specific, but you don't have to explain what people don't see."

"But you saw them." He challenged, hinting at a

possible vulnerability that I may have overlooked. Did he allow me to see them on purpose? For a moment I sat still, the sounds of beating rain persisted on the window. It was beginning to storm harder, much like the drops that fell before the play.

"I think it's a past lover," I confessed. "One you don't want to talk about." The car came to a stop, and I honestly hadn't realized how long we'd been driving for.

"You're right about one thing, it's certainly something I don't like to talk about."

A low roll of thunder tumbled above, giving me an uncomfortable chill I despised. As soon as I felt this, I was welcomed by a sudden warmth that sheltered my palm. It was Alejandro, his hand caressed mine, the black rose stared back up at me. I sucked in my lips, preventing them from parting, relishing the distraction from the man who I'd been arguing with for an entire car ride.

"You don't?" I asked, shy from his touch. As much as I hated to acknowledge it, he was good at reading my body and knew when to touch me. He must have seen a look in my eyes, one from the thunder, and knew what I needed.

"I don't, it's not easy sometimes saying the things we wish to hide. But it can be easier to express ourselves in different ways."

"That's true…" I agreed, tempted to touch the rose for myself, but resisted.

"You may think I'm wrong, but I saw that in you, I feel like you may agree, and that's why I brought you here." I followed his eyes, looking past the window at a familiar building.

"The Met?" I asked, confused. I was excited, and he could tell, relishing in his cleverness.

"A place to think, to be alone." He reminded me, repeating the words I mentioned the night of his fitting. He'd thought the city was too loud, he wanted to know where I'd go for silence, but really, he wanted to know where to take me. "Everything in there is an expression, but nothing is said out loud. Perfect for people like you and I."

"Like us." I agreed, looking back down at his hand, at the black rose. "Death?" I asked one last time, challenging how open he was truly willing to be.

"Mourning." He confirmed, his eyes sunk into mine as the driver opened my door.

Chapter 13

The Met stretched across our path, its uniformed steps welcomed an entrance of illuminated pillars. My silent appreciation was cut short as my dress became doused by the excessive rain. I'd forgotten an umbrella but made a point to remind Parker for one as I waited outside the theatre. I missed him, reminded by the wet drops on my cheek as I made my way towards the steps.

"Not that way." Alejandro corrected my direction, his voice lowered to my ear, heightening the awareness of how he made me flinch. His leather jacket lifted like a wing, tucking me inside. "You need to keep warm, I won't let you get sick."

"I won't," I said, almost in a promise. "I thought we were going inside." I didn't even need to duck my head, his tall figure and shelter were enough for me to walk comfortably along his side, still, I tucked my arms in, avoiding the rain as he pulled me flush against his body. His core was feverish, almost stinging hot, echoing a reflection of my own.

"We are, but it's not as simple as you think. Now, get closer." He commanded, knowing it would help with the rain. I conceded, my crossed arms, brushing his sides as I followed his lead. We avoided the stone steps, walking adjacent to the street and into a patch of shrubs.

I didn't think twice as we moved off the pavement even though my heels sunk into the wet grass. It was pitch dark as the light faded from our path. I wanted to ask more but was distracted as my knuckles grazed the side of his hard torso. Even with this, the slightest touch, I experienced the defined grooves of his chiseled obliques. I hunched my shoulders, tempted to pull away, but was saved as he released his jacket from above.

"This is us." He assured, stepping into the red illuminated enclave attached to the building. I twisted a loose strand of my wet hair, twirling it on my finger, my nervousness more apparent without the distraction of his body next to mine.

"They're closed!" I stated anxiously, "This isn't an entrance."

"It is for us."

"Don't you dare even try." I looked away from the door, surveying the darkness of Central Park. We were alone, but I didn't know for how long. I was certain it was locked from the outside, but I didn't want him to even touch the handle. The alarm would be deafening, just as it had at the Drip photoshoot. "I'll leave."

"Try, and I'll throw you over my shoulder."

I shook my head. "I'll scream."

"Swear?" He begged, overly joyed from my threats that seemed to excite him. I tensed, both from his words and the thought of getting caught.

"You're such a jerk."

"I'm honest, at least with what I want, and as much as I would enjoy hearing you scream, I'd prefer you save your voice. I have plans for it." He added, slipping something out from his jacket. "Tonight we enter for free." In his hand was a key, its shape far too unique to go unnoticed.

"You didn't?" I asked, assuming he'd stolen it from the firemen at the photo shoot.

"It was a gift," he replied. "An exchange for one hell of a photo." He slipped it into the lock, twisting it to the side. The click of the handle made me flinch, but no alarm was triggered.

"This is totally illegal." I warned.

"And?"

"And, it's not a good look," I defended, "not for me and especially, not for you."

"You my good girl?" He asked, an uninvited pressure to bend. I was a good girl, and though part of me was embarrassed to admit it, I kind of enjoyed hearing him say that. This time, I wasn't sure if he was teasing or if he meant it. His potent stare was interrupted by a drop of rain that fell from a loose strand of his hair. This was a contest to see who'd budge, either I would leave, or I would follow him, both my choice alone.

"Don't call me that." I insisted, pushing him aside. I pressed on the handle, popping the door open. It creaked, revealing a long dark hall with swooping cool air. I stood at the opening, less confident than I pretended to be. "You first." I requested, my hesitancy garnering a breathy laugh. He seemed brave, and if he wasn't, then he was as good of an actor as others had claimed. I followed as he stepped inside, allowing the door to shut, to encapsulate us in the dark.

"I knew you'd come, I also knew you'd enjoy this." He stated, the sound of his boots as thick as his voice.

"Save your confidence. You're lucky I haven't been here in a while, and I'm desperate enough to see it again."

"I know all about being desperate to see something again." He replied, his presence close behind, noticeable only through the scent of cherry smoke. He was talking about me. His unapologetic pursuit typically made me shy, but in the dark, we were invisible, which helped. He couldn't read me, and I couldn't read him. It was safer in the shadows, a realization I knew early as a child.

"This isn't the only bad thing I've done." I announced, attempting some form of credibility.

"I don't believe that." He suppressed a laugh.

"It's true. You may have a reputation, but that's only because people know you. I've been wild, I've broken the law." It sounded as lame out loud as it did in my head, but Alejandro entertained it.

"What could you have possibly done?" He questioned as we left the hall, entering an expansive room of marbled statues.

"In eighth grade I found a box of pants in the school auditorium. They were just sitting there, folded neatly, completely unattended."

"And what did you do?" He asked, stopping below the windowed dome above our heads. The pouring rain tapped along the glass, twisting the moonlight that fell upon his handsome face. I stared at him, contemplating how he made me feel. I wasn't certain if it was good or bad, I just knew it was different.

"I took them." I confessed.

"So you're a thief?"

"Yes, well at least I think so. Are you still a thief if you bring them back?"

"I don't know, I'd say not," he replied, amused and not the slightest bit convinced. "Why did you bring them back?"

"I didn't realize until I was home that the box was for our marching band. I had thirty pairs of pinstripe pants, all with the school logo on them." It was a shameful confession, especially for what I needed at the time. Outside of Parker, no one knew I grew up poor. That fact alone I wasn't embarrassed by, but the fact I was forced to wear the same clothes for three consecutive grades made me self-conscious. Not only did the clothes grow out of style, but I grew out of them. It hurt to wear the things I had, but I had no choice, which is why I stole the box. "I was so embarrassed I couldn't even carry them back to the auditorium, so instead, I left them on the football field. It got even worse when maintenance accidentally mowed over them, shredding them into pieces. Principal Sanders held a school assembly about how awful we all were, but really it was just me." Alejandro dug his teeth into his bottom lip, horribly attempting to conceal the humor he found in my story. "Are you laughing?" I asked.

"No." He corrected, "Just second guessing bringing the pants thief to an invaluable museum."

"Don't even." I scoffed as if I would leave with a painting in hand.

"There's a difference from feeling bad and being

bad. I would know." He lowered his voice, almost reassuring me.

"Have you ever stolen anything?" I asked, stepping along his side, touring the empty halls.

"Of course. Just like you."

"I doubt you stole a box of pants."

"No, but something still of value, something I needed to survive. When you grow up with nothing, you'll fight to have anything. I'm sure you could relate?" He questioned me, extending a bridge for me to cross. I related, especially with the notion of growing up with nothing. I pondered my response, if it was safe to admit to him or not.

Safe was an odd word to consider, but appropriate. I looked around, comforted by the idea of walking in the dark. At home, when the fights got bad and the screaming began, I'd run to my closet and lock myself in. It was bittersweet, a feeling reminiscent of childhood, of terror and comfort. It was there in the dark, with my fingers in my ear, where I could finally feel free. I wasn't Gemma, I wasn't anyone, I was merely in space, floating away. It was true what Alejandro said, *when you grow up with nothing, you'll fight to have anything*, and for me as a child, that included a way to cope. I gathered now was no different, realizing safety was a perception rather than a guarantee. If the darkness in the closet was safe, then maybe so was The Met.

"You're not wrong. You've seen Bushwick. I'm sure you could imagine."

"Don't need to. I've lived it." He said with certainty, following me as I lead the way into an exhibit hall. "You haven't been here for a while, but you still know your way around."

"I do."

"And where you taking me?" He asked, snapping me from my haze. I hadn't realized till he asked, that I was heading somewhere on purpose.

"I want to see if something is still here." I replied, turning the corner to a hall entitled "Generations."

"An old friend?" Alejandro asked, once again assuming the truth. What I wanted was here, displayed at the end by a small leather bench. I took my time to approach it, observing its face with silhouetted moonlight above. "You could say that." I finally answered, "It's my favorite painting. I'd come look at it any chance I got," I added, "that is, while I had my annual pass. I think it's leaving soon, so it's nice to say goodbye."

Alejandro grew considerably quiet, focused in a moment of complete contemplation. The darting dark pupils of his eyes shifted side to side, assessing the entirety of the painting I loved. He appeared speechless, but that would imply an inability to form a thought. I knew this wasn't true as he hummed, calculating some conclusion before opening his mouth.

"*Latchkey Rose*," he finally read out loud, its title printed on a small silver plaque. "Nice to meet you." The growl in his voice was suggestive, as if he discovered another meaning to who I was. He wouldn't be wrong, and his salutation appeared less for the painting, and more for the person I supposedly was beneath—a scared little girl.

The pale painting featured a child, the wisps of her hair lost in a fog. Her smile was weak, almost forced with the acrylics slabbed along her body, painted in thick mountainous stokes. At her neck was a rose, but not just a rose, a wound in disguise. Without thought, I reached for my throat, massaging it from the strange nervousness it made me feel. Alejandro was staring, observing once again, both the painting and me.

I considered my feelings for a moment, carefully picking my words. I wanted to say something, but I didn't know how. If I couldn't share this with Parker, then how could I with anyone else? The only one that could relate wasn't even real, she was in the painting, stuck in a frame from an artist who was dead.

"Sometimes," Alejandro started, "we cover the things that hurt us with something more beautiful. It could be fashion, it could be music, or art," he pointed to the painting, "it could be a rose... but at the end of the day, it's all just a shield for what's really beneath," he added as his unwavering stare fell into mine.

"Pain?" I asked, questioning it myself. I knew the answer and begged for him to agree, but all he did was stare.

It was his turn to speak, to share, but if we were as similar as he said, then I wasn't sure if he would. He opened his mouth, but only bit his lip, the hitch of his voice signaling a word resisted in a groan. I turned to look away, but instead I screamed, frightened by the sudden crash of thunder that fell from above. It quaked the walls around us, pinching my heart into a shakable flutter. Without hesitation I dug my head into

Alejandro's chest, who was much closer to me than I realized. I plugged my ears, wincing at the low boom of fleeting thunder.

"Are you scared?" His voice hummed from his chest. The fold of his leather jacket creased with a noise, as his arms wrapped around my body. He secured my spot, allowing my ear to rest on the thick wall of muscle that pulled me close. My throat tightened, both from the painting and the thunder that reminded me of home.

"It reminds me of arguing." I admitted, realizing despite the shadows, Alejandro and his leather jacket were the darkest things here. I gravitated to that, and in that safety, slipped out a truth. The dark had a way of doing that, just as it did when I climbed the stairs of the frat house with Parker long ago. Back then, it made it easier to confess my love, but it also got me in trouble. I should have known better. I was vulnerable once again, especially in an exhibit dedicated to families, a subject I specifically avoided. "My *neighbors* would always argue," I lied, feeling a new sense of shame. "Any loud noises take me back to that time. I don't like it." I wasn't sure if he would believe me, but I wanted to say it regardless.

"Hmmm," he hummed. "Neighbors." The tone of his voice was comforting, letting me know my answer was accepted, whether if it were true or not.

I was consumed with the rich scent of his cherry smoke, a soothing antithesis to what I grew up with. I wanted to tell him that, but I wasn't sure how it would sound, considering I was cowering in his arms.

"Why cherries?" I asked, innocently inviting the distraction.

"Why Marcello's Galletas?" He questioned, reminding me of my cookies. "The flavor is a comfort, a specific one at that."

"Did someone you know smoke them too?" I shifted topics quickly, knowing he was closer to my truths than I was to his.

"Smoke? No. But they remind me of my mother, and I suppose that's what I like about them." He responded. The mention of a mother was never good, and I feared he'd ask me about mine. I wanted to pull away, but instead I shut my eyes, steadying myself in his embrace, preparing for another roll of thunder.

"Tell me about that." I asked. "The memory?"

The hesitancy in his voice appeared but not before he sighed. "Fresno isn't known for their cherries, but there was man who grew them regardless. He would hire my mom to pick them in the spring, and I'd help her."

"Like the agave?" I asked.

"Different," he affirmed, "but in a good way, only because it was with her. She took extra shifts for the money, even if it was raining."

"Like it is now?"

"Yes, even worse. But she put me through school, she encouraged me to be an actor, even if I wasn't sure I could be. She did a lot for me," he paused, "for us."

I craned my neck to meet his face, my hands held in a prayer, tucked along his abs.

"Us? So you have siblings?"

"A brother." He said swiftly, "Younger."

"What's he like?"

"A lot like you," he pointed with his chin. "I see something in your eyes that I've seen before."

"Like what?" I asked, pulling up closer. Suddenly I felt so small, lost in his hands, frightened that if he let go a coldness would replace his touch.

"We used to have *neighbors* too…" He said softly, using my encoded word with gentle consideration.

"Would they fight?"

"All the time, and it would scare him. I hated to see him like that though, so I would go find him."

"Find him?"

"Yes, he'd hide under the bed, but I'd join too, not out of fear, but worry. I'd hold him and tell him that he'd always be protected, so long as I was around."

"And you see that in me?"

"I saw it a long time ago, in the moments where you touched your neck, the look you gave Gerard when he mentioned your mother. It was all the same. I knew it when I saw you, you're reliving the same fear that I saw in my brother."

My lip twitched from his story, the comparison of me to his brother. It felt familiar, and though I shouldn't have cared, it still hurt to be seen this way. Was this all I was capable of conveying? "So I'm like a sibling to you?" I asked.

"A sibling?" he growled, his grip tightened along my back. "What a fucking thing to say." My folded hands dug into his chest causing me to gasp as he pulled me in. "Ask me that again, and I'll show you what you are to me." I blinked at his words, their stinging promise a key to my parted lips. I hated it, the control he had over my body, separate from my mind which begged me to stop. I wanted to scream but couldn't, I could only feel the slick warmth slipping between my legs.

"Why are you so persistent?" I pulled away from his grip, knowing if I continued to get close, I'd lose myself in his touch, and I just couldn't risk that.

"Persistent as you are stubborn," he said with a deep rumble from his chest. "You still can't see it?"

"Stop acting like you know me! Just because…" I couldn't even say it out loud, the words I knew were true; our pasts were probably similar, they were most likely fucked up and messy, yet talking about them felt nearly impossible.

"Say it," he commanded. "That is, if you have the courage."

"Sorry I'm not brave like you," I hissed. "But I don't need a protector, I'm not your brother."

"Fuck protection. You're a mouthy good girl who gets under my skin, but maybe that's what I want. I was brave because he needed me to be, I was a better person because of what he saw."

"Is that why I'm out here, is that why you need me to know you?" I laughed, "Tell me what you want me to see, but I can't make you be a better person from that alone."

"I don't know what you'll make me, probably fucking crazy, but I'm here to find out." His slithered accent licked around my ears. "Fuck what it costs me, I know what I want and what I see."

"And what do you see in me?" I challenged, unable

to fathom what set me apart from all the possible women that surely plagued his life.

"My past and my future!" He shouted, yanking me close. The sweet mint from his lips matched the cherry scent I quivered to taste. Alejandro's frustrated exhale came out in a groan, manifested in his resistance to do god knows what. Take me? Fuck me? I would never allow it.

"Don't put that on me. I'm not bonded over my past; I'm running from it. You and *no one else* needs to know about that part of my life. I've already told you, we're not the same. What do you know about a troubled home anyway? You had both your parents, not even I had that." I pushed him aside, but he followed close.

"Both my parents?" he asked. "And you think that's better?"

"I wouldn't know! I have no father! And what could you say about that? You probably couldn't be as honest as you think. It's hard for people like us, and if you think we're so similar then neither of us are getting answers."

"You want to know what I think?" he seethed. "On what a father is, on what it's like to have one in the house?" He turned to a large portrait, a black and white photo of a family eating dinner. He grimaced at the photo, observing a man at the head of the table, a patriarchal figure whose face warped into a frown.

"Alejandro?" I hesitated, his intense stare not once shaken.

"Not everything can be said at once, but what I have is how I show it. I can grow though; I can learn from you, from us." The swish and clink of a switchblade alerted my attention as Alejandro took one out of his pocket. His eyes boiled with a redness that scared me, almost glowing amongst the dark. I jumped, petrified as he swung at the photo. He slit it in half, cracking the glass, shattering millions of fragments onto the floor.

"Alejandro!" I screamed, my mouth covered as an alarm blared through the halls. "What did you just do?" I shrilled, unable to fully process what I just witnessed.

"I fixed it." He snapped. I looked up at the alarms, at the flashing white lights that strobed through the pitch-dark halls.

"We need to leave!" The panic in my voice felt unmatched to his collected expression. Without words, he gently guided my elbow towards an adjacent fire exit.

"What's another alarm going to hurt?" He asked shoving it open, triggering a new chirping siren. I wanted to run, but that made me feel more guilty, so instead I quickened my pace. My brisk strides weren't quite a jog, but short of just that, as we entered the street.

"What the hell was that back there?" I pulled my hand away from his, moving away from the electric chaos that was now The Met. "Why would you do that, Alejandro?" The pounding rain continued to pour on us, this time, without the shelter of his jacket.

"Why are you so defiant?" he questioned. "Did that frustrate you?"

"Yes!" I shouted. "It pissed me off!"

"Good. Now you know what it's like to try and break through your walls." He reached for my hand, but I pulled away. I felt foolish, letting him inside my mind, being vulnerable to such a sporadic man. He was so spontaneous, so jarring, I was shaking with adrenaline.

"No. That's not the same! You can't go around acting like the world is your playground." I shoved passed his large body. "Famous or not, you have no right."

"Just stop already!" He shouted, following close. I scoffed at his command, seeking shelter under a nearby canopy.

"What do you want from me?" I screamed.

"You." He groaned loudly, a noise that emitted from his core, short of a shout. "I did what I did, it was compulsive and raw, and I don't regret it. You may think you're clever, hiding behind your mask, but I see past that, and it's that person, the one beneath I'm trying to catch."

He stood in front of me, his hair dripping, slicked back from the rain. He felt like a dream, or maybe a nightmare. He was a bastard, he was persistent, but most of all, my body was hopelessly addicted.

I couldn't accept such an idea, that we were alike, but I had seen those eyes before, the same he had while staring at that photo. They were mine, a similar expression he described, the very thing he saw in me: sad, messy, and fucked up. Is this truly what he wanted?

"I'm sorry, but you're wrong." I took a step forward, raising my hand to hail a cab. I was stopped by a firm but gentle pressure wrapped around my wrist, squeezing me securely. Alejandro spun me around, pinning me against the wall as he raised my arms above my head. My stomach caved in on itself, sucked from the force of air as his forehead pressed against mine.

"Gemma, you don't know what you do to me." His chest rose with a rhythm, a frustrating pace desperate for air that we both fought to take. He leaned further, the strength of his toned body firmly pressed against mine. "Why is this so fucking hard to see that there is room to grow, a chance for us?"

His lips hovered right above mine, seeking approval. The lines were blurred, my urges clearly begged me to lean in, to taste the nectar of his full lips, but the thought scared me. I was the girl in *Latchkey Rose*, but I was also my mother's daughter. I was afraid of what letting him in would do, of what a man like him could do to someone like me. His palm grazed my wet cheek, pulling me closer, and as much as my blood burned and stomach dipped to be touched, I couldn't allow it.

"Let go of me," I huffed out, signaling the release of his grip. He listened, his eyes still stern as I walked away. "You've got the wrong girl." I reached out, singling a cab.

"Says you. I know who you are and what you're worth. Not even your friend sees that, but I promise you this, I'll show you what I see, and better yet, I'll make you feel it." He looked away, almost concerned, giving me a shot of those dark eyes for a silent goodbye.

I knew he meant it, the things he said, but to imagine their possibility was far too real. How would that feel, what would that be? It was a terrifying reality that he could see me, more than a sister, more than a facade.

This was all I needed to know, convinced if I didn't shut the cab door, he'd come take me away. I had no choice, not with my fears, and if I'd let him come any closer, he would do it immediately. All I had, all I needed was the urge to drive away.

Chapter 14

What would it take to get him out of my head? If only there was a pill or a wish, anything to rid Alejandro from my mind, I would take it or do it. The cab ride home was incredibly quiet, although the thoughts in my head were loud. I was practically screaming as I checked my phone, almost expecting an alert to warn me of my inevitable arrest. Honestly, I just wanted the night to end, to dissolve into the dark and sleep it away.

The cabbie pulled over, pointing at the meter for payment. I handed him cash, my hands still damp from the rain which continued to pour outside. I think he sensed my exhaustion, avoiding the smeared makeup casually running under my eyes. If only he had known the night I had.

I stepped out, still without my umbrella, unprotected by Alejandro's jacket. I didn't need a man to shield me from the rain, or to save my night, nor did I need one to watch a play or eat dinner with. I didn't need anyone, but I wanted someone, and there in lied the problem. My wants and my needs never aligned. I liked the idea, hell, I loved it, but it never worked out. Did I judge too much, were my expectations too high? Maybe I was the crazy one, not slashing gallery art or sucking down shellfish? But what I needed was a reset and quite possibly a bath.

I was already feeling better, slipping the key into the door, walking quietly inside Parker's apartment. It was dark, and I avoided the light, knowing if I saw my face in a mirror I'd probably scream.

I made my way inside, placing my purse on the counter, peeking down the hall. Parker's door was shut, probably asleep. A small victory, one less thing to worry about—him seeing me like a wet doll with stringy hair.

I opened the fridge, grabbing the nearest bottle of red wine. I didn't even get to enjoy that tonight, my merlot at the play was ruined the moment Alejandro stepped inside. To think he even took it from my hands, the audacity and command he had. I bit down on the loose cork, popping it out with my teeth, spitting it out into the sink. If he were here right now, I'd like to see him try again. I'd probably scream or maybe slap him in the face. That was probably what he deserved, especially after the scene he caused at The Met. I shuddered, making my way to the bathroom with the bottle tucked between my arms.

I pulled on the large silver handle of the egg-shaped tub, allowing instant hot water to pour out. I couldn't shake the sense of how crazy the night had been, but the running sound of the faucet was an assuring comfort. I turned around, removed my dress from my shoulders and allowed it to fall to the floor. It was a relief, each piece undone like wet saran wrap, my heels and all. It fell into a pile, as I stood completely nude, dripping a tiny drop of liquid bubbles into the stream of water.

I caught my reflection, my body bare and toned, reflecting the sight of my loose wild hair. I picked up the bottle of wine, my bath buddy, sipping it as I slipped into the warm water.

Instantly, it soothed the soreness of my feet, the relentless scurrying that ended the night was less than forgiving. I took another sip, almost groaning. I was not this person; I was not the girl Alejandro believed me to be. He was so convinced we were alike, but if that were true, then he would have never ruined that photo.

Running the water along my neck, I traced an invisible line down to my wrist. I still felt Alejandro's grip from when he pinned me against the wall, and maybe that was why I still thought of him. He was crazy both in the worst and best ways, a feeling that unnerved me inside. And who was he really? Alex Rivers the actor, or Alejandro the lover? If what he did was an act, then I was fooled. He seemed persistent to capture me, and as tempting as it was, his wildness was far from anything I ever had, especially compared to Parker.

But what did Alejandro see that Parker couldn't? Was Camilla really that much better? How could we be so close, so perfectly matched, yet so opposite in feelings? I popped a few bubbles, mindlessly poking, staring down at my smooth legs and perked breasts. I worked on my body, my style, and looks, not that it mattered, it was our bond that was beautiful, romantic even. Him and I were *simple*, which in his words was a *luxury*, and after tonight, simple was all I needed. Still, I found myself asking, *am I not enough*?

If it wasn't my looks, if not our bond, then what was

it? I sipped my wine, almost slurping, allowing the bottle to bob along my side as I let it go. I contemplated for a moment, biting my nail, considering Parker's reasoning to possibly be something more devastating.

Was Parker worried I'd end up like Claire? Depressed? Sick with a disorder that plagued her body and mind? He was there for me during those days, when her illness latched onto me, making life as a child excruciatingly difficult. Did he know too much, and despite all I tried to hide from him, should I have hid more? Then, I thought of Alejandro. That look he gave, the pain he saw in me also lived in him. Could he care for the thing I tried to suppress? Trauma?

This all could have been true, but maybe it was simpler. I wasn't Camilla. I could never be her, seemingly perfect, flawless in more ways than one. She seemed to come from a normal family and had a job and success. I had none of that, I was the little sister, the one who needed a place to crash. Whoever she was, whatever she had, he liked it.

The bubbles caressed my neck as my foot reached to shut the lever. The water stopped and finally all was silent. I sunk in slowly, allowing my lips to touch the fizz, to tickle my nose. I wish I could give Parker that same thing, I wish I could give him everything he wanted.

The sound of a quiet thud caught my attention, initially causing me to recoil further into the tub. I was startled, irrationally covering my body with the security of bubbles as if that were protection alone. It was the smallest of noises, possibly a neighbor, the creak of a spring, or the knock of a cabinet. I glanced back down, but not before I heard it again. I had the sense to call out, to say *hello* to whatever was there, but instead, I stayed quiet.

Thud, thud, thud.

My attention was diverted, focused by the muted moans that came from Parker's bedroom. It appeared once more, the almost sultry gasp, fostered only by the initial slow thrust of a man in a woman. I covered my mouth, shocked by the noise, realizing with envy it was Camilla whimpering Parker's name.

They must not have heard me come in, nor the slam of the fridge or the draw of my bath. I was a secret; a dirty little ghost, listening to their moans. Her voice suddenly grew louder, hitched with one brief scream. The strong thud of the bed was softened, blocked by the wall that felt so close. Between me and them was only a small barrier, leaving me practically there by their side. I'd never heard this side of Parker but imagined it time and time again. His broad hard chest, chiseled in shape, equipped with the tools to last, to ruin the subject beneath his body. Camilla confirmed this, her audible gasps indicative of each drive of his hips.

I slid into the tub, my ears muffled by the bubbles, unsure of what to do. Initially, I was jealous, instantly burdened with the sting to make it stop. But then I felt something else. Something odd. I poked my head back out, somewhat curious, almost indulging in the sound. If I were to admit it, I felt naughty, my legs slicked with soap, excited by the lure of rough sex next door.

But I could only pretend for so long that I wasn't interested in including myself somehow, each advance more teasing than the rest, the fantasy built in my mind. The distinct slap of flesh that carried between the rooms caused me to twist in the tub, a sound which I imagined only to be Parker's full weight against Camilla's round ass. Yes, I knew it from the sound alone, that Parker was taking her from behind, evident from the belt-like snap I just heard from the other side of the wall. Camilla's moan trailed into a screech. Parker just spanked her—hard—in what possibly was the most cheek reddening pop of a slap I'd ever heard. It was this noise in particular, alone too vibrant, too thick with temptation that I couldn't help but desire more, wanting specifically what Camilla was getting. I reached down only once, spreading my legs, wanting to touch myself but knowing it felt wrong. I could barely admit how their sounds turned me on, their noises more animal than not. They weren't just having sex, they were…

"Fucking." The deep voice rang in my head, finishing the thought to the word I was ashamed to say. "You like to hear them *fuck*, and that makes my good girl wet." Alejandro appeared so clearly from the corner of the room, flashing a devious but imaginary grin.

"It's not true," I lied, fighting the thought. "It's wrong to listen. I should leave."

"You'll do no such thing." He warned, raising his finger to his lips, shushing me to be quiet. "What did I tell you? Good girls are meant to be broken," he groaned, edging closer, his hair still dripping from the rain, "and I'm here to do just that."

"Get out of my head." I shut my eyes, forcing a

thought of Parker to appear, but it was useless against the rasp of Alejandro's interrupting voice.

"Make me, you're the one thinking of me."

"Only because of tonight, of what you put me through. Let me be clear… I'm sick of you."

"You're not sick of me," he burned. "You're sick *with* me. I'm in your blood, baby. I'm between your legs." He sat at the edge of the tub, tracing the loose bubbles by my knees with his thick and threatening finger. I clenched myself together.

"I told you. It's wrong."

"I heard, but don't tell me that again," he hissed. "Instead, tell me what you hear."

I listened for a moment, and my face burned at the arousing sounds next door. Camilla's erotic moan alone set me off, a moan so forced it could only come from gritted teeth. No. She was more than muted, possibly biting into a pillow. Alejandro wanted me to say it out loud, he wanted to lure me into his crass sense of sexual deviancy. I'd try as he wanted.

"Breathing." I whispered.

"What kind of breathing?"

"Panting? I'm not sure. Like she keeps missing a breath."

"And why is that?"

"Because… she's on her belly, and I think he's inside her. And maybe he's too big for her." I licked my lips.

"What's too big?" He placed his large hand on my knee, guiding my legs open with a soft pull.

"His…" I shied at the word, the idea itself could only be evoked by Alejandro.

"Don't be a child," he warned. "Say it like you fucking want it."

I sucked in my bottom lip, my legs spread from the force, tempted to mutter the filthy word I knew I wanted to say. "Cock," I choked out, taking a moment to swallow.

"That's my good girl." He slipped his hand along my wet, tingling thigh. "Now show me what you want, or I'll show you how I've been craving you in every way."

"I want…" The words escaped me as my finger ran past my navel and between my legs. I didn't tease myself, I merely hovered, knowing it was wrong to get off on this, on Parker's private moment.

"Everything I've ever said is true. I see you for who you are, and I know the things you want. It's *you* who can't admit it. But here I am, once again, telling you what I see."

"What?" I almost cried.

"A naughty little slut who wants to get fucked." He tilted my chin, raising my eyes to his, "Listen to them now, tell me you aren't wet from that, that you can't resist yourself any longer."

"I can't." The banging bed frame rattled the wall, and Camilla screamed again. It was too vivid, the scent of sex, the steam of wet bodies, the taste of cum.

"You can, and you will… now touch yourself."

I pressed down on the sensitive nub of my clit. "Like that?" I moaned.

"Yes. Now pull away." He replied, almost upset with the restraint he held. I listened and waited for his next command, "Now do it again." I continued playing this game, listening closely, feeling as if I was in the room watching them fuck.

"Am I doing ok?" I asked, the wet slickness on my knuckles much warmer than the water.

He caressed my chin, "You're doing so good." He praised, "Just like I knew you would."

"I am?" My core tightened with an intoxicating whirl, listening to the sensual words of praise I'd been begging to hear from his lips.

"Mmmm," he groaned, twisting the perked nub of my nipple with this large thumb, "so fucking good. Tell me you like it." He asserted. I felt absolutely guilty and impossibly dirty as my breasts rose from the bubbles and into the cool air. I just couldn't stop.

"It's so fucking good." I admitted.

"Then rub harder for me." He urged me to please his sight. I shut my eyes, rippling the water with each quick touch.

"Faster?" I asked, picking up my pace.

"As fast as your little cunt needs. I want to see what makes you come." He looked up intrigued, recognizing as Camilla shrilled Parker's name. "I saw them myself, fucking like dogs in the heat of a dark room. I bet you like to hear that though, don't you?"

"Yes…" I stuttered.

"I knew it. You'd watch them from the door if you could, touching yourself while your friend stretches out new pussy."

"That's wrong…"

"It is, but it doesn't make it feel any less good, now does it? I heard it myself, the sound of that dirty bitch getting railed from behind, slick like the sound of suckled pink taffy. That, Gemma, is how it sounded when he slipped himself inside her. Now answer me this… does that turn you on?" he asked, gripping my thigh with a pinch. "Hearing your friend fuck a whore?"

I squirmed. His words my own, vulgar and rough, just like him. "It makes me want to come," I finally confessed, imagining Parker being the one to ride me raw. I tried to focus, but Alejandro's imagined existence was as vibrant here as it was in the real world.

"You come when I tell you to." He demanded, "Are you thinking of him?" By the hitch of Camilla's voice, she sounded close, prompting my eagerness to join, to feel the final thrusts she endured.

"Yes." I inhaled, "I want to feel…" I gasped as my thighs vibrated, "I want to feel him so bad." I shuddered. Alejandro fixed a loose strand of my hair, placing it behind my burning ears.

"Show me what it does to you."

"What else could you possibly want from me?" I asked, still rubbing myself harder than ever before.

"Raise those fucking hips for me, I want to see that little pussy out of the water."

It was easy to comply, my feet planted in the tub, anchored to stop my orgasm. I pressed my back further, allowing my navel to rise from the bubbles as my ass dripped with soapy, hot suds. I continued to rub myself like the filthy showgirl he made me feel like.

"Now, spread yourself for me." He growled, "Pull those pretty lips apart and show me how swollen that little clit is."

"Stop…" I hissed, "You're so…"

"Filthy?" He grinned, "Yes, but just like you. Now you're being shy on purpose, and you know how that provokes me. Even if I don't say it, it makes me want to bend you over and fuck you rough. Now do as you're told, and spread yourself like the good girl I know you are."

I felt reluctant at first, but shutting my eyes helped. He wasn't wrong, and I hated it, knowing that he wanted to see me on display was a sickening and naughty pleasure. Slowly, I pulled myself open for him, allowing the cold air to hit the warm leaky spot he begged to fill. The stretch alone was euphoric, a blooming display that buzzed with the pulse of rushing blood. I could feel myself clench, my pussy tightening for him, squeezing a visible contraction that would hug the girth of his cock if he were to slip it in.

"You're so fucking tight, I could never fit myself inside you completely…" he warned, pressing my hips back down into the tub, "but that's my job now, my pleasure, and my property. No one fucks you, but me." He grunted through clenched teeth as the black rose above his knuckles disappeared beneath the water. His palm rubbed along my lips, teasing my opening with a promise of a plunging finger. "And no one makes you come but me." He slipped himself deep inside, causing the warm bath water to spill over the edge of the tub. I gasped, clenching my stomach, bracing for how tight I felt around him.

"Stop." I ordered, unable to control the building climax I felt. I wanted to come when Camilla did, I wanted to come with Parker, but Alejandro's finger made it difficult to do so. My body was already on edge.

"I don't stop till my good girl comes. Only when I lick it off my finger will I leave." The speedy strides of his fingers inside me, quickened into an impossible desire to release me in the dirtiest of ways. Camilla and Parker both moaned, his guttural voice thick and chilling, leaving me to squirm.

"I can't take it. I'm so fucking close it's driving me mad." I panted, biting my lip to silence my building release, the splash of my water far too loud, far too reckless and obvious. "Why do you want me?"

"I said it when we first met, you might not be what I want, but you're what I need. As if I had a choice. When I saw you, I had to fucking have you." He slipped another finger inside, stretching me further than I ever felt before.

Why did he make me feel so dirty? The way he made me feel was complex, something I wasn't able to pinpoint, especially now distracted only by the tingling knots that filled my core. He made me hot, angry, and sometimes—the worst of all—seen.

"Breathe with me," he commanded. "I'll count you down like my good girl, then you can come." The rasp in his voice made me leak, my insides screaming, ready to burst. "Three."

"I don't know if I can wait." I begged.

"Don't you dare. Ride with me. Listen to your friend come, and know it's me instead." His face was so clear, so ripped with aggression. I could even smell the sweet cherry smoke from his skin, "Two."

The pounding slaps next door increased, our speeds matched as the bed pounded against the wall. I bit my lip, each scream, each turgid thrust was Parker's, but also Alejandro's. He was inside me, stretching me, filling me up. "I can't."

"One," he spat. "You're almost there. Now suck your filthy fingers for me, show me how you'd suck my cock." I did as I was told, sticking my free finger into my mouth, sucking hard, desperate to feel the imagined cum spilling down into my throat. I winced at the screams that made me want to fuck, arching my back, buckled with the pressure that tightened below my stomach. It was the inevitable crashing decent of a colossal orgasm.

"Faster, I can't wait any longer..." I pulled my finger out of my mouth for a breath. I had to bury my face into my arm, clutching onto the rim of the tub, holding on as I stretched my legs. I couldn't stop myself, reaching the peak with Camilla, indulgent of the thick hot cum that Parker likely spilled all over her stomach.

"Alejandro..." I whined.

"Come..." He demanded, his finger deep inside, curving into a naughty hook that sent me over the edge. "Fuck..." I cried, my legs pinched from the pressure, a mess that threatened to shoot out like a squirt of relief. I screamed into my arm, biting it till it burned. My insides were wrecked, completely exploded with hot cum that slipped passed my fingers and into the tub like a jetted cloud. I shivered, wet and loose like the little slut that Alejandro dared me to be. The good girl, the good whore.

"Say my name, make me proud." He cooed.

"Alejandro…" I oozed again, feeling the depth of his fingers escape my body. He reached up, his fingers wet from my insides, slipping the taste of me between his lips. He sucked them.

"That's my girl." He hummed, "Coming when you're told. My good listener." He winked and did as promised, fading away into the dark like swirling cherry smoke. My lungs burned as if running away, and in a way I tried. I wanted to escape Alejandro and his infuriating persistence. He was everything Claire warned me of, and yet, I was the one he wanted. I knew better, but my body didn't. It frustrated me, and I couldn't explain it.

There was so much to consider about tonight, but none of that was important as I soon began to scream.

It was Parker, he was here…

Immediately my ears rang, alerted as I looked up at the swinging door. "What the fuck, Park!" I shrilled, covering my body with bubbles. His hard muscles tensed at the sight of me, startled by the screech of my voice. He was caught off guard, and for a moment he stared.

"Fuck!" He shouted, the shock of my nude presence alerted his hands. He slammed the door shut, but it was too late. I saw all of Parker, his toned abs and flexing arms. He was dripping in sweat, with veins that popped from the work he just did. It was burned in my mind, the length of his cock, curved and erect. It glistened in a tight condom, Camilla's wetness still visible at the tip which sat filled with white cum. He'd drained himself completely, almost bursting it at the brim.

"I'm sorry, Gem!" Parker shouted from the other end of the door. "I didn't know you were home!" I heard the panic in his deep voice. How much did he see of me, besides my empty floating bottle of red merlot? He was flustered, almost stuttering into nonsense, "Good night!" He shouted, shuffling back to the room rather quickly, before slamming the door. I crossed my chest, still covering my erect nipples from the pulsing orgasm that tingled on the tip of my clit.

"Goodnight!" I finally coughed, still partially covering my mouth. I leaned back into the tub, allowing the silence to settle. What the hell just happened, and why the hell was Alejandro invading my thoughts! I sunk into the water, hued with burgundy, muddied by my spilled merlot. Just when I thought the night couldn't get crazier, I had to take a bath.

Chapter 15

Mornings were determined by a few things, quality of sleep, and the type of hair you wake up with. Today, I knew both would be bad. Last night was odd to say the least, but my dreams were pure chaos. I was exhausted, physically worn from running in a nightmare, chased in The Met by Parker's big penis. I was awakened though, startled by the clicking heels of Parker's leather dress shoes.

Immediately, I was rushed with a sense of fatigue, knowing I'd have to see him in the light. He sounded busy out there, playing jazz on a speaker, clanking in the kitchen. Was I blowing this out of proportion? We were both adults, contrary to the glittered stars on my purple robe. I hadn't truly thought of last night, what I heard Parker do, or why Alejandro invaded my mind.

Tightening my robe, I slipped my head out the door. I hadn't figured what I would say or do, but I left regardless, patting the frizzy rats' nest that appeared on my head. Maybe if I pretended to be extra sleepy, I'd enhance that whole I-don't-care-that-I-saw-you-naked-vibe. I shuffled down the hall, squinting my eyes, committing to this awful new plan. It wasn't much, but it was all I had as I entered the living room.

Parker leaned against the counter, hair mussed back neatly, eyes fixed down on a plate. His manicured face and tailored grey suit stood in opposition to my robe, reinforcing the idea that rushing out to confront him was a bad decision. He seemed so focused until hearing the soft shuffles of my fuzzy slippers.

"Good morning, sunshine!" He practically chirped, or tried to, given how thick his voice was.

I panicked, sticking too confidently to my sleepy persona. "Yo." I embarrassingly half-waved, my eyes squinted. I cringed internally. Yo? I didn't look sleepy, I looked stoned. Parker shot an odd look, unfamiliar with this hip, sleepy Gemma.

"Umm…" he laughed, nodding toward the dining room, "have a seat." Parker gestured to the dark table, motioning to my mug filled with tea. "I steeped it for you. Four drops of honey, no sugar."

"You know me so well," I chuckled, taking my seat. This wasn't bad at all, despite my minor turbulence, I think I could actually pull this off. Parker came back around as I took a sip, quietly burning my mouth.

"Something to say sorry." He announced, placing a plate in front of me with a large bagel.

"It's just a penis, Parker. I've seen plenty before. We're adults." I waved him off. He hesitated to respond, still standing by my side. His package was literally in my face, teasing me not to look. I stretched my neck, avoiding a curious peek.

"Umm… this was for missing the play," he adjusted the weight on his feet, unsure of my assumption, "not… for the penis."

I took another sip of tea, pretending I didn't hear, "Well, it looks delicious," I added, but clarified, "the bagel that is, not the penis." *Fuck*. "That was rude. I mean the penis was great, but I was talking about the bagel." *Somebody please stop me*. I reached down, taking a massive bite. A part of me hoped I'd choke, at least it'd stop me from opening my big mouth again. I chewed as Parker sat down in front of me, "I forgive you." I said mid-bite, looking down at my plate. Parker smiled at my timid response.

"I didn't hear you come in last night." Parker, being Parker, saved me again, avoiding the obvious blunder of my words.

"It was late. I thought you were asleep." I replied. He certainly wasn't asleep, if anything it was the opposite. "Is Camilla still here?" I asked, realizing I just admitted to knowing she spent the night.

"Camilla?" He scratched his brow with a sturdy finger, "You knew she was here?" For the first time in a long time, I saw him wince, clearly not proud of the idea of being caught. I owed him the courtesy he'd given me, so I spared him.

"Oh! I only guessed. I thought I heard her voice this morning. I assumed she dropped by before work." I shrugged, hoping it helped. I stared a little longer, noticing a red line along his neck, small but visible. A scratch mark from Camilla?

"What else did you hear?" He asked, his tone prying like a lawyer to sniff me out. That was a big question, one I wasn't going to answer honestly. I heard everything, the bed against the wall, the screaming orgasm Camilla cried. Even Parker, his deep moans and grunts, were a stifling roar. I never heard anything like that before, and I certainly never made those noises myself.

The last time I had sex was with David Myers, a rather unassuming tax accountant from Midtown West. He was a sweet guy, but texted in all caps, a habit I didn't much care for. While we were together—though brief—I never had an orgasm, and in reality, it never felt good. The saving grace of our relationship was his hair, a lot of which reminded me of Parker's, the color and style. Even before David, I wasn't with many other men, and maybe Parker knew this. I wasn't Camilla, the vixen sinking her claws into him.

Suddenly, this made me feel more self-conscious than it should have. Last night I listed the possible reasons why Parker and I weren't together, but never once assumed it was because I was some inexperienced little girl. Is this how he saw me, his butterfly? My awkward morning turned into a sad one, once again feeling like a non-sexual being, a sister to the man I loved. He probably couldn't imagine sex with me, or *fucking*, a word I rarely used, unless apparently with the aid of Alejandro. Why was I thinking of him again? I didn't appreciate his presence last night, in my mind, playing along with my dirty fantasy. He called me a good girl, but not like how I imagined Parker saw me. He was delighted by it, and in a lot of ways, wanted to break me from it, to mold me into his own girl.

"Besides the barging door?" I replied. "I heard nothing. You took me by surprise." I widened my smile, hoping to cover the disappointment I felt. "I hope you didn't see anything." I added, distancing myself further.

"And what if I did?" he asked confidently, even quietly like a secret. "Like you said, we're adults. I can handle it."

I hid the obvious lick of my lips, dabbing them with a napkin. Though unintentional, his question gave me the blood pumping surge of sexual joy. I only wished I felt sexy. Instead, I was dressed like a child on Christmas morning, unmatched to his dapper display. He took a sip from his beige mug, a gift I'd gotten him that read, 'This coffee's too hot, I'm suing.'

"Yes, we're adults." I agreed, attempting to correct the perception I had of myself. Parker was right, but how honest was he in his ability to handle adult things? Adults did a lot, such as sleep with their girlfriend and not try to hide it. Did he sleep with Camilla because he thought I wasn't here? And if I had been here, would he have resisted?

"Well, I was thinking of you." He replied, as if the meaning extended all the way into the sheets of his bed.

"Sorry?" I asked.

"Last night, Mila took me by surprise. I thought it was just a favor, picking up her parents, but when I dropped them off, it was for a party."

"Your favorite."

"Yours, too." He laughed, knowing damn well our preference for quiet settings. "I tried to get away, but how would that look? I know you told me to enjoy myself, but it was hard knowing where you were."

"The play was the same, nothing new."

"And our seats?" He asked, "You keep them warm

for us, Butterfly?" His low voice inquired with an expectation.

"I kept them safe." I lied, knowing that mentioning Alejandro would be a nightmare. Though Alejandro could care less about Parker and his involvement in the case, Parker was different. How could I tell him that *Alex Rivers* sat in his seat and that afterwards, took me out? That would be enough for him to grit his teeth, considering the obvious dislike he already had for the man. Immediately I panicked, realizing that there were worse things for him to figure out than Alejandro just taking his seat. What if someone saw us at The Met? What if I was in trouble? I changed the subject, "So how was it meeting the parents?"

"They're really nice." He shrugged, "Very huggable, love to dance, pretty friendly. Just a normal family." *Normal family*, of course, not that I knew the meaning. The way he threw the term around reminded me I was outside of that, not that it was his intention. Another benefit to Camilla's reputation, outside of her gorgeous looks. "I met about twelve of her cousins. There was a lot of people."

"Any tequila?" I joked, reminding him of the New Year's Eve that once ruined his night.

"Gemma…" He set his mug back down on the table. "Even the word… I can't." He raised his chin to the ceiling. "I brought back tons of food though. There is a bag of *tim-hollies* in the fridge."

"Tamales." I corrected, "Please tell me you didn't pronounce it like that." Though Bushwick was home to predominantly Puerto Rican families, I still knew what a tamale was. The neighborhood wasn't just limited to Puerto Ricans, but home to Dominicans, Mexicans, and even some Columbians. Food was interchangeable, mixed and enjoyed by everyone. Even I, the pale white girl from Brooklyn, had my fair share of tamales, but usually only during holidays. It was an unfortunate truth I refused to admit, that its corn husk was the only thing I typically unwrapped on Christmas morning.

"I tried my best." He shrugged, "It wasn't *The Phantom of the Opera* with my Butterfly, but I survived." He took a bite of his bagel, chewing for a moment before realizing something. "Speaking of family, Mom wants me to remind you that the Hamptons trip is coming up."

"That time already?"

"Sneaks up on you. First week of June."

"A month away? Yeah, I think I can go…" I sighed, chewing my lip.

"Think? What's there to think about? Don't you want to help make the famous potato salad?"

"Don't you dare," I scolded playfully. "It's my favorite thing ever. Oh, and the Spuddington story." Parker groaned, but I loved it.

"She'll be sure to tell it, with or without mimosas." He added.

"Always with, and like she says, it's full of fruit, so doctor approved."

"So why not then?" He pressed but stopped as a thud hit the door. The morning paper, delivered on time. Parker stood as I swallowed another bite of bagel, collecting my response.

"You know, work is kind of weird right now…" I refrained from saying more, thinking of the possibility of Alejandro calling me in for another meeting. Would I even agree to that, and after last night, would I even work on his suit? Suddenly it felt too messy, the fantasy I had, the actions he took. I wasn't sure if I could see him again, not out of anger, but fear. There was something in his eyes I hated to admit, a chance of being similar despite my complete resistance. It was better to ignore it, and in fact, in this moment, I considered myself jobless. Parker returned with the paper, removing a thin framed set of glasses from the pocket of his jacket.

"Weird?" He arched an eyebrow, "How so?" I swallowed a hot sip of tea, recognizing the tone change in Parker's voice. The question was less about the oddities and more about Alejandro. I knew better.

"Oh, you know, just really busy." I replied. Finally, I was more convincing than my previous persona of Sleepy Gemma. But Parker wasn't done. He adjusted the frames on his eyes, their round, silver shape a compliment to his angular jaw.

"And *that* guy is behaving?" He asked, not even mentioning his name. "Keeping his hands to himself?"

"Parker?" I laughed, my eggshell confidence already cracking, "Of course. It's a business relationship, and that's always been the expectation." He folded the newspaper on the table, his green eyes peering back through his lenses.

"How was your night last night?" He asked calmly, ignoring the toasted bagel on his plate. I twisted a strand of my own loose hair, unprepared to answer. I had focused more on how to avoid talking about his penis, I hadn't even planned on discussing where I was. Surely someone would find out, a shattered work of art at The Met wouldn't go unnoticed.

"It was fine," I answered quickly. "Calm night." *Calm?* I didn't know why I added that, or why his eyes always made me buckle. This was an effect of his, but not exclusive; Alejandro appeared to have a similar gift.

"And after the play, did you eat dinner?" His finger toyed with the bottom of his lip.

"Yes."

"Where?"

"Joe's Pizza." I lied, defaulting to my favorite.

"Makes sense, then home, right?"

"Yes, sir," I snipped. "Why does this feel more like a cross examination?"

"I want to know where my client was last night."

"Your client?" I asked, genuinely confused. "Me?"

"Yes. You, Gemma."

"I'm not your client." I said confused, but the chilled feeling around my neck sent shivers down my back. What the hell was he implying?

"You might be, and if push comes to shove, I'll be here for you, just like always." He pulled his glasses off, "Gemma…" he tensed, sliding the newspaper across the table, causing me to jump, "What the hell is this?" He scolded as I clutched my robe, staring down at the front page.

"Oh my god." I gasped, "It's me!" I shouted, lifting the paper into my hands. The headline was printed with thick black letters, reading: *Bad Boy, Alex Rivers, Spotted*

With a Sexy Accomplice Near Last Night's Museum Vandalism.
Below was a photo of Alejandro and I, not at the met,
but below the canopy, his hands wrapped around my
wrists, lifted in the air.

"Gem, what the actual fuck?" Parker pulled the
paper from my hand, reading the caption below out
loud, "*Forty-year-old playboy, Alex Rivers, is still looking like a
work of art, seen near The Met last night, accompanied by his yet
to be known mystery date.*" Parker's eyes widen as he read
the lines, raising his voice. "*Police reported finding a
photograph tattered to pieces at one of the exhibits. There is no
evidence at this time to place Alex Rivers as the art murderer.*"

"Park, I can explain." I stuttered, not from fear, but
complete shock.

"Explain what? How this piece of shit is going to get
you into trouble? Am I going to have to you bail you out
of the fucking precinct?" Parker shut his eyes as his
fingers massaged the bridge of his nose with utter
distaste. "Goddamn it, do you know how many lawsuits
this guy has, how much trouble he's in? The guy can't
even fucking act like an adult, instead he's dragged you
into his shit. Gemma, this is not ok. It's going to catch
up to him; I'll make sure of it." Parker raked his hair
back, his voice fuming. "Were you at The Met? Yes
or no."

"Yes, I was, but I thought everything was ok, he
made it sound like it was taken care of."

"Of course, he did, he's a liar. He can't even take
care of himself. How dare he!"

"But I can!" I defended.

"Can you? You can't even be honest with me." He

pointed to the photo, "This is not him *keeping* his hands to himself." He reached out so quickly, with gentle ease that took my breath away. He snatched my hand, observing my wrists, "Did he fucking hurt you?" His large thumb grazed my palm. This move alone, paired with his aggressive protection, made my nipples pebble. He gripped harder than Alejandro did, as if I'd slip through and disappear. No one's touch could make me feel more like the center of the universe, than the security of Parker's alone. This was the lawyer, my Rattlesnake, his fangs exposed when provoked. I clutched my robe, concealing his effect.

"I am honest. I just didn't want you to worry, and if you're asking if he hurt me, then no. He certainly didn't scratch my neck, at least." I tossed my hand into the air, but Parker ignored the quip, the acknowledgment that I knew of his sexual prowess.

"He's dangerous, and not just because of the guy he beat up in Bushwick."

"That doesn't count. That man was hurting a girl. Alejandro defended her."

"Alejandro?" He asked, his accent perfect this time, unlike with the tamales. "You call him Alejandro now?"

"Well it's his name! Celebrities do it all the time, and actually it's really upsetting why he had change it. It's not all black and white, Parker." I wasn't sure if I was defending Alejandro or my decision-making skills, but both felt close together. "He was at the theatre last night, honestly, one thing lead to another. The Met was for an assignment, to better understand him for the suit I'm designing." It sounded weird coming out of my mouth, but not as weird as how Parker's face turned.

"The theatre?" He questioned, his voice almost lost, confused but not angry. "Are you dating this guy?" His accusation made me squint. Why would he even ask such a ridiculous thing? Yes, last night was fucked up, and yes, I was upset about it, but Alejandro wasn't everything the papers wanted him to be. As much as I hated his reaction at The Met, I knew there was something more to him, something complicated, and just because we were photographed together in the way we were didn't mean we were somehow a couple. Regardless, I hated that Parker even asked, considering he shouldn't even care who I did or didn't date.

"Why would that even matter to you?" I asked. "You're not my dad, you're not my lawyer, and you're certainly far from a boyfriend. I don't need to explain my personal life to you or the assumptions you have!"

As fast as the words spilled out of my mouth, Parker replied. "You're right," he scoffed. "I'm none of those, I'm more than that. Don't think for a second I'm not the person who would lay his life down for you. This is me, my role, the thing I feel called to be. And by the way, fuck him, if he cared about you, he would protect you, not compromise you."

"If he cared? Well if *you* cared you would have been at the theatre with me!" I shouted. His otherwise beautiful lips frowned, soured not by oysters or salmon, but the taste of my own words. He possibly hated this more, and his eyes proved it with the shimmer of disappointment. I regretted it as soon as I said it. It wasn't fair to put that on Parker, regardless of how hurt it made me feel. He tried to still come to the theater, and despite his willingness, I assured him it was ok.

Parker stepped closer, "This guy is all wrong for you, and I'm not just talking about business anymore. You can do so much better, and I won't let him hurt you."

"He won't! And honestly, maybe he's not as bad as you think, just complicated."

"Why, Gemma?"

"Why what?"

"Why did you have to go and choose him?" He asked.

Choose? The question was as strange as the implication. But more so than that, it was a question so open to interpretation that I didn't know where to start. *Why? Because you rejected me, because I laid out my truth and it cost me my heart. I picked you, and for some reason I'm your little sister.* I felt completely foolish, scolded while wearing my childish robe.

"I didn't choose anyone," I shouted, poking his chest. "You don't get to pick and choose people in my life, Parker, and you certainly don't get to lecture me about bad company." I turned away, adjusting my robe, "You don't see me yelling at you for hanging out with Camila. Who—by the way—is totally wrong for you."

"I just want to protect you, Gem!" He shouted, "Don't you see that?"

"Well, don't!" I squeezed my voice out from the tip of my chest, "I don't need that from you, Park. What I need is for you to…" I shuddered. His gorgeous eyes were soft, looking at me for some answer, some permission to what, I wasn't sure.

"Be patient?" he interrupted, completing my thought. "Is that what you need? I am, more than you realize. I know there are things you don't want to talk about, things you hide, but that doesn't stop me from being there for you. I wish you knew, god knows how much I fucking care."

"I do…" I tried to convince.

"You think you do, but you have no idea, and what it costs is patience. I practice it every day, but this guy tests it like never before. Try and stop me from caring, it won't happen, Gem." Parker lifted his coat, slinging it over his large shoulders as he walked past the door.

"Where you going?" I asked, as if it weren't obvious.

"I have to go to work, and thank Christ, because I'm going to get rid of this guy." His lowered voice felt like a promise, but before he left, he turned and looked me in the eyes. "He compromises you again, and I'll fucking end him. Not in court, but wherever he stands, goddamn it." He left, not slamming the door but securing it shut with a quick click of the lock.

I curled my hands into a fist, not out of anger, but frustration. As infuriating as Parker was, I could see his intentions were pure. Be that as it may, was it still fair for him to judge Alejandro? In some ways maybe, but even I had to rethink everything Alejandro did, an action not to be confused with excusing his behavior.

I went back to my room, completely shaken over the conversation. I couldn't concentrate on anything, pulling the chair out from my small desk, sitting down to think.

What would happen next? Yes, I considered myself jobless, and no, I didn't expect to hear from Alejandro, especially after last night. Needing to focus, I flipped open my book of sketches, sorting through the possible designs and fabrics I selected for Alejandro. I bit my nail, contemplating everything I'd done, somehow questioning my own judgment. Even if I were to make a suit, it would have to be something different, something new to the side I saw in him. But what was that side, and was it accurate?

If Parker couldn't see how awful Camilla was, could the same be true for me? Was I seeing Alejandro through the same distorted glasses? This was a curse, one Claire suffered from herself. She saw the best things in the worst men, and I couldn't help but feel worried about that thought.

The front buzzer rang with a chime, signaling a request from the lobby door. I closed my book to answer the call.

"Jones residence?" I presented, unintentionally sighing into the speaker. Not a moment passed as a static voice clicked through.

"Gemma Harrison?" The winded tone seemed annoyed, causing my prompt reply.

"Yes, can I help you?"

"We have a package that requires your signature." I leaned my head against the wall, racking my brain for anything I could have ordered. Fabric swatches, thread? I squinted, pressing the switch once again.

"Come on up!" I shouted, pressing the button to unlock the door. I waited close by, still unsure of what was to come. I looked back at the bag of bagels resting on the counter, the ones Parker got up early to get. It was funny that something so simple could make me feel so guilty. There was something about that bag, sitting there quietly undisturbed, it reminded me of all Parker had always done for me. Was I wrong to yell? Maybe he saw me as his sister, but I didn't want to be made to feel that way, no matter how sweet the intention was. I fixed my robe once again, surprised at how fast the knock came at the door.

"Ms. Harrison?" The thin, mustached man questioned as I opened the door, handing me a shipping slip.

"Yes!" I nodded cheerfully, as if I weren't just shouting at my best friend, "Do you know what it is?" I asked, figuring there was some label he read. He stepped to the side, pulling the large package up.

"Don't know ma'am, but it's fragile." He placed it in my arms after I signed for it.

"That's odd, I don't remember ordering anything." I was ignored as the man turned to walk away. He was less interested than I was, but regardless I hurried in. Leaning against the wall, I shut the door with my foot, tilting from side to side in a walk. I was truly puzzled, my brain in a fog from the morning as I sat on the couch, admiring the size of the package. It was wrapped in brown paper and topped with a cream envelope. I peeled it off, removing the tiny card held inside.

Gemma,

This is a token for last night. What you saw was real, the good and the bad. Just know, I wish to see you as honestly as you saw me. Anything outside of this, I'm truly sorry for.
Take this time to work on the suit, and I will be back for you in the coming weeks.

Be a good girl, mi pierdra preciocsa,
- Alejandro

A good girl? I wasn't sure which it was, Alejandro's insistent label or Parker's dominate need to protect, but suddenly I felt the urge to pinch my thighs together. If either of them were here, would they comment on me doing so? I wasn't sure, I only knew Parker was determined on keeping me safe, and Alejandro was sending me mysterious packages.

I looked back up at the wrapping, bending the corner of the card with my thumb. What could it be? His note felt so honest, causing me to question his intentions. Was he truly sorry?

I peeled back the corner of the brown paper, tearing it down through its center. It was a wooden box, adorned with a handle and two metal clips.

"What did you do?" I murmured to myself, removing the lid to see what was inside. Not a moment passed when suddenly I was caught off guard.

I froze.

My eyes widened, staring at the sight of what lied within.

Slowly, I reached inside, carefully pulling out the large canvas from the case.

It was *Latchkey Rose*, from The Met. The real, honest to god painting in my hands. I had forgotten how to breathe, slowly placing it back in the box, as I was certain my shaking hands would drop it. Of all the things to do, of all the gestures to make, this was the one he did. I couldn't even imagine the price he paid, the steps he took in such a short time to make this happen. It was too much; it was beyond my comprehension, leaving me scared to even touch the box alone.

Covering my mouth, I looked out the window, staring at the bright skyscrapers across the street, focusing on anything that could ground me back to the world I was in. The buildings outside were so clear and visible, unlike the murky waters Alejandro and I found ourselves in.

We could never align, not perfectly anyways. This was my belief. But there was something we shared, a lack in the ability of being open that I couldn't ignore. Our expression was code, leaking fragments of truths for others to perceive. How could I be mad now, just because he was clever enough to see my signs? He wanted what I wanted, a way to show the world who we were. For him, he was not Alex Rivers, but Alejandro Rivera-Marquez. That's why I was here, that's why I was supposed to make his suit. If words couldn't do it, then I could, and maybe he saw that in me, not just the good girl, but the woman I knew myself to be.

Chapter 16

An entire block was gated off, home to curious fans attempting to peek over the production's guarded rails. This was the mysterious yet magnetic effect of Alex Rivers. I made my way through the crowd, flashing my badge to security at the entrance.

Everyone was so excited, buzzing with the hope to catch a glimpse of the star himself. I was not. I was the opposite, completely and hopelessly nervous. It had been more than a couple weeks since I'd seen Alejandro, and when Ivanna called to schedule this appointment, a lot had already happened.

The hotel party that landed Alejandro into a lawsuit had been getting more media attention than I expected, leaving me to believe his absence for the past couple weeks were more than just movie related. Still, Parker wouldn't share much about what was happening, as non-disclosures were in the works along with the speculated settlement to come. I just knew Parker wasn't pleased and that he wanted to take him to court, to air out the dirty details of whatever happened at The Pierre Hotel.

On top of this, despite gifting me an already invaluable piece of art, Alejandro also paid for the services I provided thus far. This was an expectation, yet the amount was not. Fifteen thousand dollars was transferred into my account, whose routing number was never even shared with Ivanna nor Alejandro. That was a question on its own, but the amount delivered raised my concerns. Despite the cost of materials, and the effort I had already put into the suit, fifteen thousand felt less like a salary and more like a payment to spend time alone. I couldn't accept it, which is why I'd written a check, returning a significant portion of ten thousand dollars. I knew it would be tough giving up that money, but I had to, along with the painting that still sat in my closet.

I second guessed my choice in coming, or even bringing the check, considering I was still unsure about how things from The Met would transpire. I'd probably need the cash, but Parker insisted he'd take care of anything that came my way. His need to secure my safety extended far past my body and included my future out of jail. Oddly enough, despite his extensive outreach, Parker wasn't able to find any acknowledgement that the photo at the museum was even damaged, not from Alejandro's attorney nor The Met itself. Besides the one mention in the paper, it was as if that night never happened. I wanted answers but was unsure of the cost, given the gatekeeper, the man who haunted my thoughts that night in the bath.

I approached Alejandro's trailer, a metal bus painted black and silver. I expected him to be inside, waiting on a throne, beckoning me to my knees with the hither of his finger. He gave me that impression, and I figured he could wield it on most women, possibly even the girl whose initials I assumed were tattooed on his chest. I climbed up the steps, unlatching the door.

"Hello?" I croaked, already forgetting how to use my voice.

"Alex?" A feminine rasp echoed along the chrome kitchen, questioning my arrival. I stepped up, relieved I wasn't alone.

"No, sorry." I replied, turning the corner. A rather tall and glowing woman sat on a lounger, her legs crossed in the slacks of a red designer power suit. She looked up from her phone, her eyes big and dark, shining like the sleek bobbed bangs that hovered above her brows. I clutched my book of sketches to my chest.

"Don't tell me." She smiled, her hoarse voice familiar, "The one and only Gemma?" She crinkled her nose, her freckles creased with a delighted grin.

"Please don't tell me I have a reputation." I joked, attempting to ease the nerves in my stomach.

"A big one, babe, but I'm a fan." Her eyes nodded to the coffee table. Sitting on top was the paper of Alejandro and I, my arms pinned above my head. It was so embarrassing to see.

"At least I have one, I guess." I murmured, noticing as the woman extended a greeting.

"Ivanna Cortez," she reached for my hand, giving it a firm but gentle shake.

"The woman behind the magic!" I replied.

"Finally, someone recognizes it." She laughed, motioning to the counter, "Coffee?"

"I'm good, thanks."

"Trust me on this." She persisted, "It's my brew,

Colombian and strong." *Just like me,* I expected her to say. She was gorgeous, and I wasn't the least surprised Alejandro had a vixen for an assistant. She was dressed as I should have been—professional, confident. Her breasts were hidden along the notched lapel of her suit, and mine through the thin orange fabric of a turtleneck. Alejandro was so perceptive, I had no choice but to minimize how I expressed myself. I wore jeans and white sneakers; shoes more fitting to run in, given how things went down at The Met.

"Thank you." I replied, as she handed me a mug. I took a sip as she watched, waiting for my approval. It was sweet, not overbearing as I had in the past, almost chocolatey.

"Well?" She asked.

"Actually… pretty good," I admitted, "and I don't really drink coffee, so that's impressive." She seemed satisfied and took a long sip.

"Good coffee for Alejandro's good girl." She winked. Immediately I winced, unsure of what Alejandro may have said, or what she knew.

"I'm not his girl." I laughed, feigning interest as I stared into my dark coffee.

"He's a private man, Gemma, but nothing gets past me." She stirred more creamer into her mug, her gaze not once leaving my direction, "I'll admit, I took a peek at the card he wrote you. I couldn't resist, especially with this spell you have on him."

"Spell?" I asked, baffled at how she described our relationship.

"Big time, babe." Her eyes got larger, which I didn't

know was possible. Her accent peeked when she pronounced *big*, similar in the way Alejandro would have. Her curves and assertiveness reminded me of Camilla, though Ivanna was actually friendly.

"I think you've got it wrong," I dispelled, setting my mug down on the counter. "I'm sure he's this way with everyone. It's an act, it has to be, right?"

"An act?" She almost snorted, tilting her head back.

"Yes! The way he looks, those eyes and stare. It's down to a science, right? Tell me, how many women has he had in this very trailer alone?"

"Women?" she asked. "One, and you're looking at her." She walked over to the couch, crossing her long legs as she took a seat.

"What about all the articles and photographs of women over the years? It's all over *New York Prestige*…"

Ivanna's reaction was collected, yet sarcastic. "Those tabloids, they will tell you anything for a good story. If Alejandro needs to be photographed with a woman for publicity, it'll be done to appease the appearance they want to portray, but it doesn't mean he's with them. Besides, Alejandro doesn't have anyone, and he certainly can't tolerate people."

"What star can't tolerate people?" I laughed.

"The biggest one of all. Why do you think he's late all the time? The man is practically begging for Hollywood to get rid of him, but they love him. Regardless, he doesn't walk away." Her calm but sobering words reminded me of the conversation I had with Alejandro at his fitting. Other than his name, what else did he sacrifice to get where he was, and was it worth it? Still, if he wanted to leave, why wouldn't he just do it? It seemed odd for his personality, especially with how assertive he was.

"Why do it then?" I asked, unable to think of a good answer.

Ivanna shrugged. "A distraction maybe? Just like this new personal project of his." She nodded at my sketchbook, "Are those your designs?"

"A work in progress." I answered, but was distracted by what she said, "What personal project does he have?" I recalled, familiar with the vague mention he made while I measured his body.

"Tequila. The man has been working tirelessly on it. He certainly isn't shy about his preference for physical labor, or its rewards. If that wasn't apparent by his ripped shoulders, then it is by his tan." Of course, immediately I thought of his hands, both rough and large, yet delicate to my skin. How could they be both, harvesters of agave and evokers of tingling nerves? The way he had pinned my arms that night, he could have just as easily lifted me up and raised me to his lips. I took a sip of coffee again, just to feel something other than the frustrating thrill of that memory.

"Seems like a big distraction." I imagined.

"Maybe a temporary one, that is, until he finds something more permanent." Ivanna tipped her nose in my direction, as if I were the solution to his problems. I couldn't help but twist my lips.

"That's a silly thought." I protested, embarrassed she'd even suggest the idea.

"Not from my point of view. I know the man. He neither cares for or seeks out other people."

"I don't believe that."

"It doesn't matter what you believe. I know the truth, and I get the sense that he's determined to show you that too."

"Well, he has a funny way of showing it sometimes."

"He's complicated," she admitted with a sigh. "But growth isn't always a pretty process."

"That makes me sound more like an opportunity than a person." I stated.

"That's a shame. You make it sound as if growth is exclusive to him, rather than inclusive to you." She sipped her coffee, "Maybe he has his hands full with you, rather than the reverse." She added, pointing out my apparent walls.

"So, no women in his life?" I asked, still in disbelief. Alejandro could have any woman he wanted, yet I was the object of his incisive focus. There had to be some cruel joke in there. I wasn't worth the time or the effort and agreed with Ivanna to an extent. Maybe I was the difficult one. Regardless, Ivanna's conviction felt unshakable, leaving me to regret even asking the question.

"Besides me," she pointed to her freckled cheek, "no one." She was quick to add, clearing any misunderstanding, "But Alejandro and I are more similar. Not romantic if that's what you're thinking."

"I wasn't sure…" I mumbled, not willing to admit the idea crossed my mind. I wouldn't be jealous, that'd imply some entitlement I couldn't face.

"Our tastes are more similar." She inhaled.

"How?" I asked sheepishly.

"We both enjoy the company of a *good* girl." She lingered her eyes into mine, "But I'm not willing to spend eighty thousand dollars on a painting like he did."

The price that slipped out of her mouth made me choke on my coffee, causing it to fall from my lips and onto my turtleneck. I coughed, but Ivanna laughed, handing me a wad of napkins. I gawked at what she said, the outrageous amount Alejandro spent. All that for me, all that for an apology, on top of the salary? It was too much to fathom, an amount of money I never knew I'd possess. Knowing that the painting was just lying in my closet, made me sick; it belonged in a museum, or possibly a safe.

"Why would he do that?" I asked out loud, wiping coffee off my lips.

"Ask him yourself." She motioned to the door, "He's finally here."

Chapter 17

The swing of the door startled me, but not as much as the thud of heavy boots. I tried to cover the blotch of coffee on my shirt but panicked when I smeared loose pieces of tissues along my chest.

"You have five minutes!" An older man with thin white hair entered, following closely behind Alejandro, "I can't pay for you to be late every day!" The man shouted, taking a swig of pink Pepto. Alejandro came in with a scowl, creasing the lines of a permanent stern expression. They softened, but only for a moment as his eyes locked on mine.

"Gemma." He greeted, ignoring the man behind him. While I hadn't seen him in weeks, I wasn't prepared for the presence of his weighted steps or the gravity of my name spoken from his lips. I'd forgotten how to say hello, my mouth opened, but shut as I dropped the napkin onto the floor. *He* was presentable, unlike myself, fitted in a black button down shirt and tapered black slacks. Had he dressed for me, a chic mafioso style, absent of the leather jacket I was accustomed to?

"Good morning." I replied softly as I kneeled for my napkin. There was something in my shyness I knew he enjoyed but knowing that made me even more shy. It was as if he wanted to punish me for it or, instead, praise me for it. I wasn't sure. Even now, my timid voice provoked the twitch of his lip, a signal that the resistance he showed was slipping. Calmly he took his seat.

"You have four minutes, now!" The man barked, looking at Ivanna, "Get your client under control."

"I'm his assistant," she corrected, "and he's a big boy, he can control himself."

"Enough is enough! We are wrapping up in June, and we have these final scenes that need to be worked out."

"And you'll have them," Alejandro argued, his eyes fixated on mine, "when I say so."

"It doesn't work like that."

"Then get rid of me, or better yet, I'll leave." Alejandro threatened, his expression for once alleviated. It was as if he invited the words, the approval to be shut out and closed off. This is what Parker mentioned, the stressed man who leaves when things get tough. I wasn't sure how true that was anymore, given the insight Ivanna shared. He seemed less in control, and more like he was just existing. Maybe he didn't know what he wanted, but when his eyes met mine, that question didn't exist.

"Don't be an asshole," the man barked. "It's not you the studio will fire, it's me!" Alejandro sighed, checking the expression of an unamused Ivanna. She jutted her chin, giving some hidden message to make things better. Alejandro seemed to understand, shutting his eyes with a deep breath as he shoved his hands through his hair.

"It's me, baby, deal with it." He groaned, replying

with the familiar words I first read in a billboard weeks ago. A catchphrase of sorts, not Alejandro's, but rather Alex Rivers'. Those six little words melted both Ivanna and the director's face into a smile, as if the words, *"Come on down,"* were just announced on The Price is Right.

"Fuck, he's good." The man conceded, "Don't you agree?" He turned to ask me, but Alejandro interrupted.

"Don't talk to her," he barked, rolling his eyes up to the man. "Now leave, before I do." The room fell flat with a buzz, a strange energy suddenly cut by Ivanna's loud slurp of coffee. The director mumbled some obscenity as he left, and Ivanna snickered.

"Who's hungry?" She chirped, flipping through her phone as if to make an order. "Gemma?"

"Nothing for me."

"I'll take the usual," Alejandro answered sharply, "and be sure to bring Gemma the same. Along with a new dress." He studied my body, noticing my stain.

"That won't be necessary." I replied.

"It is if I say so." He looked at Ivanna, "Put it on the card and go to Saks."

"Anything in particular?" She asked, looking at me, but instead, Alejandro answered.

"Something spring, something with flowers." He gestured with a sudden realization, "Daises, if possible."

"If possible." Ivanna repeated, almost in a question.

"At any cost." He asserted, shooting a look that boosted Ivanna's urgency. She quickly got up and parted with a smile. The snap of the door latch was loud, highlighting the new sense of silence that filled the room.

Finally, against my better wishes, we were alone, and my dread returned. I still didn't know what to say. The last time we saw each other was ugly, yet impactful. I felt a lot of things, but mostly confused, leaving me with no balanced opinion; I was both frustrated and curious. Yes, The Met was terrible, but his brutal honesty was refreshing in a way. I'd wanted that for myself, or at least to try, the problem was I just didn't know how. Maybe that was what Ivanna meant by growth, a mutual exchange of people learning through experiences.

"I don't need a new dress." I started, unable to think of anything else.

"A turtleneck and jeans?" He questioned, slowly rolling up his sleeves, "Now you're really trying to throw me off."

"It's just a shirt."

"It's never just a shirt, not with you."

Fuck, he was right, and clearly his choice of buying me a floral dress was an indication of who he saw me as. *Daisies* were another flower of love, a symbol of innocence, patience, things he must have seen in those quiet moments where he studied me. He was clever, but also purposeful. It wasn't just a dress, it was a message, *I know you better than you think, so why even try?*

"I don't need to be taken care of, but thank you." I raised my chin.

"Still, I'll do as I please. Just like at The Met. Which, by the way, my lawyers have cleared your name from. I'll always make sure you're protected."

"Even from you?" I asked. Would I eventually be guilty by association? I was now a subtext to another one of his events, something he paid to have erased. The Met ignored it, and the law seemed to ignore it. Was he really that powerful? Maybe in a way he was, keeping his lawsuit from the public's eyes with unprecedented ability. We all had our secrets, myself included, but what really happened with him at The Pierre?

"There may be a few bumps, but I'm more pleasure than pain." His rough voice was as alluring as the tattoos on his arm. I straightened my posture, composing myself with an attempt to act unimpressed.

"Still, I had to seek legal counsel. What you did was very compromising."

"Maybe, but I fixed it, as I always do." He grabbed my coffee mug, the one *my* lips touched and took a sip. "Who's the lawyer? I'll pay the bill."

"That won't be necessary, I wasn't charged."

"Free?" he asked. "Must be a terrible lawyer."

"Actually, one of the best lawyers, and also my friend." I defended, enticing an inquisitive glance from Alejandro's face.

"*The* best friend?" He asked, almost amused.

"Yes, *him*." I snipped.

"A lawyer?" He sighed, giving me a devilish grin, "I thought I hated him, but now I know it."

"You don't know him." I replied, unsure if he actually did. Yes, Parker was hellbent on ruining him in court, but I was still certain Alejandro didn't even know the difference. He seemed to care less about the trouble he was in and more about me.

"I do know him," he maintained. "Maybe not specifically, but all lawyers are the same, and nothing is free," he warned, implying Parker's guidance was more nefarious than expected, but that wasn't the case. If I called him now, he'd be here within minutes, and if Alejandro was as bad as he thought, he'd probably kill him.

"You're right, nothing is free." I reached in my back pocket, pulling out the check I wrote earlier. "This is yours." I insisted, placing it in his hands. He studied it for a moment, then placed it down on the counter.

"You don't want to be paid for your services?" He questioned.

"Yes, but not that much. It's ridiculous, along with the painting, which I can't accept." I clutched my sketchbook to my chest, guarding myself from his eyes.

"You said it yourself, that painting was leaving soon. Now you don't need to worry about that or an annual pass."

"That's a wild way to look at it. You can't just stop things from leaving with money." I figured the same was true for me.

"Well then, didn't I just prove you wrong?" He grinned, "Doing the thing you said can't be done. So what now, Gemma?"

"So now I'll return it."

"Go ahead," he looked away. "Do as you please, the painting isn't mine, it's yours."

"It's not mine, it's a payoff."

"Payoff?" He asked, more curious than not. He reached across the counter, removing a loose cigarette from a pack of *Tranquilo's*. "What am I paying you off for exactly?" He glanced down, lighting up with the flick of his gold lighter. He took a long drag, then emitted a scented stream of smoke through his nose. He looked like a bull, the firm muscles of his shoulders barely confined in designer cotton.

"I don't know, as an apology? Maybe for something else?" I half confessed, tiptoeing around the possibility that it was all an attempt to pay for sex. No… that would be ridiculous, like he'd ever pay for such a thing, but still. It was for something more, and by the sinister glee of his handsome face, I assumed it was for an eternity of my damned soul.

"Are you unhappy, Gemma?" He asked swiftly.

"No…" I replied.

"Do you want to make this suit?"

"Well, yes."

"Then what's the problem exactly?" He evoked an urge for me to shout.

"You!" I huffed, annoyed again at how he made me feel. I hated how I noticed the subtleties of his body, the crease of his smirk, the twitch of his lip, the appreciation of his Adam's apple which bobbed after the long drag of a cherry cigarette. I hated the intuitive stares, the questions, and the arousing praise that caused me to squirm.

"If I'm such a problem, then keep both the money and the painting. Consider it your severance."

"That's not what I want." I protested immediately.

"Then speak now, or I'll make you scream it," he warned. "You have a chance to leave, to start your own

248 | LAWSUIT AND LEATHER

business with what you have. So if that's what you want, then go." He challenged me, truly questioning my intentions. He wanted to know why I thought *he* was the problem, but the honest truth would reveal more than I cared to confess. What would I say, if not the truth, how I masturbated to the thought of him while taking a bath? How I'd secretly been attracted to him, while fighting off any stolen moments we had together?

Fuck.

"I'm not a quitter," I quickly retorted, "I won't run away like you do."

"Won't, or can't? I'm giving you a chance to leave, but if you stay, then all bets are off."

"What the hell is that supposed to mean? You can't just throw money at me or force me into ultimatums! I didn't ask for any of this, especially the painting!" I shouted, triggering a sudden leap from his chair.

"You've assigned value to that, not me! Say and do what you want, but don't ever think I'm not here to get what I need. Paintings cost me nothing," he gritted. "It's your time that's priceless, it's what I crave. And yes, if you stay, I'm not holding back anymore." He shook the floor with each step he took toward me.

"Like what? What could you ever do?" I shivered, stunned by the swiftness of his approach. What would he do once he lost control? Bite me? Lick me? Destroy me?

"Find you!" He hissed, interrupting my thoughts with how dangerously close he felt. "I'll find you in the dark, the real you, just like that night at The Met. And once I do, I'm taking that girl as mine." My lip quivered at his sight, leaving me with the odd sensation to cry. I wasn't scared, nor sad, but rather, thrilled.

"You're too persistent." I spat, enthralled by the leathered spice of his designer cologne.

"And you're too resistant." He added, "That boy thinks you're a fragile butterfly, and it pisses me off." He tilted his head, allowing gravity to pull a loose strand of mussed hair away from his face. "If you were my butterfly, I'd pin you to the fucking wall. I'd pluck those pretty wings right off your body, and make you see you're meant to be more."

The vision of ever being pinned by him trickled from my mind and down to my arms. I shivered, the tone of his accent like liquid sex to my tongue as he extinguished his cigarette on top of my ten-thousand-dollar check. He filled the room with a final puff of sweet cherry smoke. *What made him light one in the first place?* I thought, remembering what he said before.

"Do I make you nervous, or stressed?" I asked, my breathy words lost as he reached for my chin. His body brushed my knuckles, whose color turned white from gripping my book. He was close enough to touch, begging to be felt, flexed effortlessly just for my eyes.

"Fucking stressed," he growled. "Frustrated by how little you value your worth." He caressed my jaw, gritting his teeth with restraint.

"I can't help it." I stuttered.

"Well, I can." He promised, "I'll correct you and those little thoughts. Give me a reason I shouldn't bend you over and spank that fucking ass like the good girl you are."

I shook with a release, gutted by the delight of such a wicked idea. The good girl spanked, the good girl corrected. I pinched my thighs, savoring the threat of his large promising hands on my chin. His head lowered onto mine, hovering his lips as if to steal my soul with a kiss. I wanted to scream.

"No…" I begged, my unconvincing plea not even a request. My mind wanted to run, but my body melted into his secure grip. Had he chosen to spank me, I feared what he'd see, what he'd feel. Surely the renewed wetness leaking between my legs would slip along his palm. He'd see my lies as blatant walls from my mouth, all being attempts to keep him at bay. In his eyes alone I was transparent, and why would now be any different?

He grasped the nape of my neck. "Fuck, *'no'*." He moaned, "Let your lips say *'no'* again, and I'll stop them with mine."

Alejandro pressed himself against me, his growing erection warmed at my hip. My body begged for it, the permission I needed; *give in, allow it.* Not soon after this conviction did I know how truly weak my will was. I was no longer here to bend, but rather break. At the cost of my own personal disappointment, I needed to feel him; if not now, then at least once before leaving. "No…" I whimpered, embracing as he leaned further, my lips parted for his.

As soon as I shut my eyes, a loud bang pounded at the trailer door. I was startled, jumping as a man shouted outside, for Alejandro. I blinked, seemingly lost, awoken from the hold his eyes still had on me.

"*Piedra preciosa,*" he cooed, rubbing his thumb along

the bottom of my lip. "Wait here and *don't* leave," he ordered. "We have unfinished business." His eyes took a moment to study the sketchbook that gripped in my hands. I practically froze at his touch, his order to wait emboldened a need to please.

"I will." I replied quietly.

"If you need anything, you come find me. I'm taking care of you *now*." He said with some form of deep satisfaction, as if he had been waiting to admit it. He pulled away, yanking a suit jacket off a rack, slipping it over his tightened shoulders as he left. I hadn't fully realized if he was still in the room or not, I only recognized my sudden collapse onto the couch.

Chapter 18

"**F**uck!" I screamed into to the palm of my hand, biting it with the nip of my teeth. "*What* the fuck did I just do?" I asked aloud. Nothing happened, but if it had, I would have lost it all: my credibility, my professionalism, my standards.

I didn't try to stop him, his words or vulgar imagination. He wanted to bend me over, he wanted to discipline me with a stinging spank. My jeans suddenly felt tight, my legs twisted in a pinch. Would he prefer the clap of denim on his palms, or rather the tight flesh of my bare ass? I imagined the latter but imagining was part of the problem. I'd done that enough already, and perhaps that had been the reason I was so compromised.

I had a hard time thinking clearly in his presence. I always found myself caught off guard, tempted by a stare that was equal parts lust and longing. But what did he see when he saw me? What did my eyes convey, fear or excitement? Both similar, but possibly one more distinguished by the burn in my cheeks.

I'll find you in the dark, the real you, just like that night at The Met. His haunting words finally settled in my stomach, the one that turned with a sickness. I felt as though I'd just come off a roller coaster, my limbs still tingled with adrenaline. *Find* me in the dark? Is that where we were? Two stubborn people in the shadows, seeking some sense of similarity?

I couldn't shake the sense, or rather the fear, I was meant to be hurt. He had the chance to kiss me, and clearly I presented myself to receive it. Had there been no knock, would he have done it, or would he have still pulled away? To him I was possibly just the thrill of a chase, a drug to the junkie who enjoyed conquering women just as he had conquered Hollywood. Could my resistance be just that? My shyness a tease, the good girl who he said was *'meant to be broken'*.

My eyes went back to the newspaper, the one with the photo of us. His face was blocked, but mine wasn't, giving the honest view of my expression. I knew I was pissed, completely infuriated by what he'd done that night. Not only did Alejandro destroy a piece of art, but he compromised my identity, along with the legitimacy of my business. Despite that anger, despite my complete frustration, I saw something different in the front-page photo. I looked neither angry or frustrated, my wide eyes the totality of one single word: captivated.

Is this what Parker saw? A look that sparked the question of if Alejandro and I were dating. I knew he was protective over me, but was there anything to really fear? Did he really want to kiss just now, or was the torment he caused prize enough? I couldn't know without the discomfort of being vulnerable, but if the newspaper was any clue, then there was one thing I knew for certain. Despite there being a stack of newly published magazines, it was the old tabloid of him and I that sat at the top, a place to be grabbed both quickly and frequently. Was this the sign I needed to see, finally using my skills of perception to look beyond the mask of Alejandro?

My phone buzzed loudly, rattling along the keys in my purse. I figured it was Parker, sensing I was somehow thinking of him, or instead, sensing I was somehow in trouble. Neither was true, but the name that popped up on my phone was a telling warning in itself: Claire.

If I had any thoughts of what to do, she would be the one to dispel them. Had she known what just happened, she'd advise me to run, to flee at the real possibility of a broken heart. I would never let it get that far; it was a blessing and a curse, one I owed to her. I shook my head, my anxiety worse from her name alone than what I felt with Alejandro.

"Claire?" I greeted. I wasn't friendly, but I wasn't cold either, just professional, something I apparently no longer was around Alejandro.

"Gemma?" A spry yet stressed accent whispered on the phone, a familiar voice that seemed less cheerful than I remembered. "Honey, it's Erin." Though not visible, I heard her hand hovering near the receiver. Claire's friend and neighbor had a way with being discreet, and it was something I both appreciated and feared to hear.

"Erin? What's wrong?" I asked, already lifting myself off the couch and grabbing my sketches.

"It's just… I don't know, Gemma, you know these things better than me." She almost whined, not out of annoyance, but anxiousness. I felt my throat wrapping in on itself.

"What happened?" I asked, unlatching the door to the trailer.

"Your mother's not doing well. I think something happened. I didn't know who to call, and I didn't want someone to come *take* her away."

"No, you called the right person," I rattled, stepping down the steel steps and onto the street of the set. "Where is she?"

"The kitchen?" She seemed unsure, "I just don't know. We were here cleaning out some cupboards, but then she screamed and…" Erin seemed panicked. "Gemma, she's crying, and she won't even look at me."

"Crying?" I looked around for help, as if someone knew what to do, but no one ever did, especially not me.

"I think you need to come home." She stated, seemingly more worried. *Home?* The word felt far away and removed. That was not my home, that was a cruel reminder of everything I ever hated, everything I ran from. I had compassion for Claire, but at what cost? People who knew my mother knew she was depressed, and as sad as it was, they had an expectation for her to be in pain. What was their expectation for me, if not to be there to help? But no one knew how I suffered, the self-dependent child who grew up too quick. I wouldn't put that burden on anyone, not like how it was put on me, which is why I kept it a secret.

"I'm fine." I replied to myself, forgetting that Erin was on the phone.

"I'm sorry, dear?" She asked, but I didn't know how to reply. If I went back, what would that mean? Would I get stuck again, weeks at a time? It happened before, a similar situation while working for Gerard, and he threw it back in my face. What if it happened again? What would Alejandro say if I couldn't complete his suit because of my ill mother? I didn't know what choice I had. The duty I had as a child carried over to me as an adult. It was all mine to bear—the responsibility, the dread, the trauma.

"Don't leave her alone." I panicked, "I'm coming now." Before Erin could reply, I hung up the phone, squeezing it with a tight and anguished grip. I needed a taxi, but had to leave the lot. As much as I wanted to call Parker, I couldn't let this life bleed into his. Despite what Erin said, that wasn't my *home*, Parker was, and I was still determined to keep that separated. Quickly I turned around, biting the nail of my thumb as I tried to swallow.

For a moment I felt lost, unsure of the proper exit or which way I came from. I wasn't even sure if I should tell anyone where I was going, or even if it mattered. Alejandro ordered me to stay in the trailer, and I knew I wasn't supposed to leave. But I had to. I just couldn't get caught, not with his perception, not with his insistent nature. I turned around again, quickly this time but not quick enough.

"What's wrong?" Alejandro's deep voice startled me, but not as much as his body did when I ran into it.

"Nothing." I pushed him aside, "I have to go."

"Don't give me that." He gently stopped me with the palm of his large hand.

"Give you what?" I asked, stroking my neck,

soothing myself the only way I knew how. I didn't want him to see, but I couldn't help it.

"You're doing it again." He nodded, "Who hurt you?"

"No one. I'm just stressed."

"What did I tell you? You need anything, you come find me."

"This doesn't concern you." I stammered, unsure if I was going to cry. I didn't want to go back; I didn't want to see Claire. In that home, I felt small, like a child again, but not in a good way, not like how Alejandro did. He was older, more confident, and his approval came when others didn't. Was that wrong? Earlier I compared his conquests to a junkie, but was I just the same, seeking something I never had? Maybe I craved it, maybe that's why I didn't leave with his so called 'severance'.

"I told you." He cooed, "*I* take care of you now." He reached for my wrist, lowering my hand from my neck, "And I'll be fucked if you try and take that away from me."

Chapter 19

My body sat stiff against the soft leather seat. I burrowed myself into the corner by the door, staring out the tinted window, looking at nothing but thinking of everything. Although I was grateful for Alejandro and amazed by his willingness to help, I was scared. This was so personal, so intimate, so beyond what I normally shared, even with Parker.

Outside along the chain-link fence and stuffed, steel trashcans sat a unmanicured mural of the Virgin of Guadalupe. There must have been a party not too long ago, the evidence detailed by the half-melted candles and scattered squares of paper confetti. Those were colorful and filled with life, unlike the brown and grey buildings lining the street where we parked.

Alejandro quickly glanced down at his phone which buzzed in his hand. He clicked it off, ignoring a call.

"You can answer that." My voice cracked, used for the first time since getting in the car.

"It's my lawyers. I already told them where I'm at and what I'm doing." He shook his head.

"And the movie set?" I sighed, knowing he cancelled the whole production for me. After all the money they probably spent, the time and permits acquired, I was the cause for it to go to waste. "I just feel like a burden."

"I'm the burden," Alejandro confessed, "and in many ways selfish. I didn't want you to be alone, I didn't want you to think anything other than the truth."

"And that would be?" I asked, still looking out the window.

"That whatever it is you fear, it'll never be bigger than the support I'll give." His uninterrupted words were a welcomed feeling, but their security only lasting a moment. "How do you feel?" He asked.

"I don't know." I was still unsure of what word to use. *Sick? Scared?* It was a combination of things, all associated to Bushwick itself. "How do you feel?" I asked, not knowing why, but curious nonetheless.

"Feels familiar." He lowered his voice, "It may not be the same, but I grew up *here*," he added, "not physically of course, but this energy."

"Energy?" I questioned.

"Mmhmm," he hummed, looking out my window, "the energy of the street, the painted walls and vendors. I've read this story, I've lived it. Especially this," he gestured, motioning to the seat between us, "the energy inside this car." His calm voice implied the clear and anxious tension I hopelessly emitted. He knew it, he felt it, but most of all, he seemed to relate to it.

There was probably a part of him that understood the problems of my past, but could he understand the pain I felt now? The truth was, on top of trauma and fear, I felt guilt. How could anyone relate to me? People expect you to be there for your parents no matter what, but how could you ever explain that you yourself are no longer equipped to do so? I lacked the tools as a child to navigate Claire's depression, and though I fought my best to help, it only left me exhausted and realizing a truth; how could I ever help her, if I couldn't even help myself? I avoided my past, not only for the terrible things that happened, but also, because of the terrible person I felt I was.

"I'll go in by myself." I stated, continuing the habit of keeping others away.

"Are you sure?" He asked.

"Yes." I hesitated.

"I don't have to convince you, I don't even need to pressure you either, you do that enough to yourself. But if you'll let me, I'll go wherever you go."

"You don't want that." I assured. "Trust me."

"It's too late. I've been there Gemma, letting me in doesn't take that away."

"No, but it protects me." I didn't want to cry, not in front of him. This wasn't what I needed, not now.

"It doesn't. It only protects the fear you hate. I can't make this choice for you, but I can make this promise." He added, slowly and deliberately placing his hand over mine, "You'll never be alone, so long as my eyes are on you." His promise was convincing and, if anything, an understatement. His eyes had that effect ever since our first encounter. I felt him before I knew him, like that day at Gerard's boutique, when his eyes seared the back of my neck. He was already watching, protecting, defiant to my hesitant nature. If he studied me now, what would he see? According to him, only the possibility to feel relatable.

I looked up at the fourth floor, observing Erin's

Puerto Rican flag that flew below her steel balcony. I always went to Claire's alone and imagined nothing more than that single possibility for the rest of my life. But now, there was Alejandro, not a stranger, not a friend, someone in between—familiar, frustrating, and somehow comforting. His older and assertive nature felt like shelter in a way, much like his hand over mine. Yes, he made me feel small, but everything was when compared to him. Could he make the fear small too?

"Walk with me?" I asked, "The door only?"

He grinned, squeezing my hand with the certainty I needed. "There and anywhere else you want." He nodded at Charles, who came around to let us out. Sheltered by the shade of an old oak tree, Alejandro and I walked along three crooked steps to the large-gated door of a brown brick building.

Unlike the developments Mama Meg worked on, this apartment complex remained untouched since the late eighties. If this wasn't apparent enough, then the brown honeycomb linoleum that padded our steps was. Here, everything felt stuck in time, exclusive not to the walls and yellow paint, but to me as well. As we reached the green chipped door of Claire's apartment, I felt unsure of my decision. I didn't want to knock; I didn't even want to enter. Down the hall a child cried, and for a moment, I wasn't sure if it was real or just a memory.

"It's ok." Alejandro spoke, his permission more like a lullaby. "The hardest part is here, and I'm here to bare it. *We* are." He assured, giving me a subtle nudge to knock just once. At first, I wasn't sure if I hit hard enough, the noise from my fist dulled to the beat of my pounding heart, but I was certain I heard scurrying on the other side.

The door opened.

"Gemma?" Half of Erin's face appeared in the gap of the chain lock. "Happy to see you, *mija*." She said, quickly shutting the door to unlock the chain. She opened it back up.

"Erin…" I tried to smile, but the stench of pungent cigarettes from inside stopped me. I couldn't help but swallow the excess spit in my mouth, which suddenly felt too full to even speak.

"I told her you were coming, but she said nothing." Erin replied, looking over her shoulder, then back at me, "You can fix this? Right, *mija*?" She asked more in a plea, but depression isn't something you fix, it was something that was survived. I was only an observer, but the fear of becoming Claire, a disposition to the disorder, made me want to run in the opposite direction, as if the proximity was infectious. I couldn't tell her how she was feeling, just like no one could tell me.

"We'll talk." I assured.

Erin reached for my hand, but then noticed Alejandro by my side. Her eyes traveled up from his boots toward his broad shoulders, drinking in an image she probably had only ever seen on T.V. The pause in her reaction signaled a delay, but the sudden realization became almost startling as her brown eyes expanded.

"No puede ser…" She muttered in what felt like a prayer. Alejandro ran his hand along his stubbled cheek, staring down at me, and once again, only me.

"Por hoy no, solamente una sombra." He responded, his

gruff voice somehow deeper in Spanish than English. "For Gemma." He added. Just as before, I wasn't sure what he said, but it seemed to affect me nonetheless. All I needed was the tone, and that was enough to feel what he was saying.

"Will you come in?" Erin asked, making way in the darkened apartment for us to enter. I stared inside, wanting to hold Alejandro's hand to keep myself anchored. I resisted but didn't want to be absorbed, and temporarily felt more scared than ever before. If Parker were here, I'd probably let him in as well, but instead, I had the man who found me in the dark, and what better person to have considering the shadows inside.

"You can come in." I looked back at Alejandro, unsure if it was the right thing to do. But I did it. "If you want." I added quickly.

"Of course. I'll be out of sight, but here if you need me." He followed behind as Erin shut the door. Everything seemed as it was before, though it was difficult to tell given how little light there was. The yellow curtains in the kitchen were shut, though the barely visible sun seemed to cast its tempered hue through the crack of the window. I could make out the brown couch, matched with shag carpet and a wood paneled T.V. Even that was the same; big and clunky, its knob still missing as it was from when I was a child. That was where Dad watched his movies, the action flicks that played a little too loud, but not louder than the arguments he had with Claire.

"She's in the kitchen." Erin advised, leaning into my ear. Contrary to the living room, the kitchen seemed to glow, radiant from the teal cabinets and yellowed counters. Cautious as to not startle Claire, I approached quietly. She sat with her back turned at the table, smoking Marlboros, the cigarettes we somehow afforded while growing up, despite the food we never had. My knuckles cracked, alerting her attention as I wrung my clammy palms together.

"Of course," she announced with a drone, not once turning around, "of all the times to come, you choose now." She took a drag of her cigarette, flicking its ash down onto her powder pink robe.

"I'm here for you," I replied. "I need to make sure you're ok." For whatever reason, she laughed but then got quiet, and without the ticking clock above my head, I'd figured I'd gone deaf.

"Oh, Gemma." She drawled sarcastically, clearing the smoke from her throat, "As if that were any possibility."

"Maybe." I added, "What happened today?"

"Oh just fucking save it." She sniffed, twisting the butt of her cigarette onto the table. "Things are piling again, one on top of another. You don't call, you don't visit, yet here you are. A savior?" She scoffed, still avoiding my eyes. A cabinet door sat wide open, its mouth a trajectory to a bag of sugar that lay on the floor. Her steps had tracked over its powder, trotted like blots of snow, leading to her foldable chair.

"I'm not trying to be a savior," I replied. "I'm just who they call when there's no one left."

"What a short list." She flashed a fake grin.

"Short, but necessary."

"Well, good for me. I know how to get you home now." She said sarcastically, resting her head onto her palm. She fished out another cigarette from the loose carton, sticking it between her cracked lips. I leaned in and noticed what was scattered around her. I stopped in my steps, observant to a collection of photos, all of which were of my father.

"Where did you find these?" I asked.

"Who cares where? They're here, and it's all I have left of him."

"You shouldn't be looking at those, you know what it does to you."

"Yes, but at least it's something, and I can't help but imagine someday I'll do the same for you; the absent daughter who avoids her mother."

"I don't avoid you." I lied, somehow more uncomfortable with the truth. She knew I did, but how could she blame me?

"Erin shouldn't have called you." She snipped.

I sat by her side, but she turned away, "Erin didn't know what to do." I replied calmly, collecting the photos I tried not to stare at. Dad was in them all, tall with sandy brown hair, dark eyes. He appeared to be in his early forties, possibly even Alejandro's age, a photo taken not too long before he left. I was by his side, the top of my head barely reaching his chest. He was so tall, capable of protecting me, yet he did the opposite. He left like a coward, leaving me here with Claire, after what she had done. "Why don't you look at me?" I asked, my brows knitted.

"I don't have the strength." She mumbled.

"Strength or desire?"

"Neither!" She hissed, finally turning to face me, her stare more startling than I remembered. She aged quicker than most with her bad habits, the grey in her hair more pronounced and frizzier, but not as much as the heavy bags under her eyes. When was the last time she slept? Her lips curled from years of disappointment as she reached for her Bic lighter, rolling the flint wheel with her thumb. It snapped with a flame.

"That's it. I'm taking these away." I folded the photos in my hand. Her eyes locked onto my quick movements as I pulled them out of sight.

"You don't see it, but I do. You're just a mirror, baby girl. When I look into those naive eyes, I see myself. A complete fool, forgetting the boy you moved in with is really a man. You're everything I used to be, don't think otherwise." The tip of her cigarette flickered with orange heat.

"Parker is just a friend." I corrected, her feelings about me living with him were completely unfair.

"Doesn't matter. I know how you look at him. I was your age when your father left. You know he had a gambling problem, right? And I tried to stop him from leaving. I tried."

"Those two things aren't related, and you don't need to talk about this." I interrupted, not for her own mental health, instead my own.

"He persisted though," she shook her head ignoring me, "and I had to put my foot down. We both did."

"I didn't do anything." I whispered, "I was just a kid, Claire."

"Yes, you did, we were a team. I thought I could keep him around, but I needed your help, guess we weren't enough, but I tried! You didn't though. You let him walk out that door without a thought. Without a fight." She was speaking too quick to keep up, her eyes no longer avoidant, but angrily fixed onto me. I glanced away, picking at the skin along my thumb.

"What was I supposed to do? You scared me!"

"Convince him! You were supposed to convince him! He's the catalyst to this, don't you see? Don't you realize we were meant to keep him here? That's why I did what I did, but you can't see my efforts." She lowered her voice, "Gemma, you know I was desperate, I didn't mean for things to happen the way they did, but I needed you to prove a point."

"Don't bring him up, not now. Please, can we talk about anything else?" My voice shook as I pleaded.

"I didn't think he'd leave his precious girl behind, but guess what... he did, because somehow we weren't enough. How could we even live with that?"

"Stop! I'm calling your doctor." I rose from my seat.

"You cannot trust a man, Gemma, not with your heart, not with what *we* were willing to sacrifice."

"We?" I asked looking over my shoulder, assuring we were alone. In the dark of the living room, I saw nothing, but I knew Alejandro was there, his eyes present like a spirit in the shadows. He didn't need to hear this, but I didn't want Claire to continue. "There is no 'we', there is you and the thing you did. And I can't go back, and I cannot sit here and relive it with you."

"And I'm to be punished forever?" She scoffed, "I

already apologized for what I did. What more can I do?" She gritted her teeth, the tears in her eyes almost as red as mine.

"You can't apologize! You can't even say out loud what happened! That takes courage."

"And you can?" She accused, "We weren't good enough anyways, he had to know what he was losing."

"A child?" I retorted.

"You were my partner, and I needed you! I still do, but you left like him, and I'm here suffering!"

"No!" I screeched, sitting back down. "I was your child, not your therapist! But that didn't stop you, and even now when I ask you to stop, you don't listen. I can't be blamed for leaving, and you can't say '*we*' weren't good *enough*. Enough? That would have been a mother who had the sense to see she was hurting her own daughter."

"Everything that has happened has made you the person you are today! Is that not enough? I gave you everything I had, and now I need the same back!"

"You don't get to ask that of me!" I shouted. "It's not my job to be your daughter, it's your job to be *my* mother!" The screech of my words failed in comparison to Claire's pounding fist as she slammed her hand onto the table and screamed.

"I was broken!" She shrilled, rocking a ceramic ashtray off the surface and onto the floor. Instantly my shoulders clenched as if guarding my ears from the shatter it made. If I wasn't crying already, I was now, not sobbing but rather, choking on a tear. I gripped my neck, frightened by her voice. Claire opened her mouth to speak but hesitated as a large hand gently wrapped around her wrist.

"Gemma doesn't like loud noises." Alejandro asserted, his voice rolled like a wave, deep and penetrating. He squeezed her softly, letting his presence be known, felt without threat. "We're going to be quiet now, because that's what she needs." He nodded, until Claire did too. He knew what scared me, just like at The Met, when the thunder cracked, and I ran into his arms. For the first time I was thankful for allowing him in, even if it was just a little.

"Gemma?" Claire asked, her mouth parted, confused and in awe. "I know this man." I sat still, my shoulders hunched, rattled by the shattered ceramic. I didn't even reply.

"Can we be gentle?" he asked calmly. "I can't leave this room and have your voice be raised again. I won't allow it." He stared as I finally looked up, his eyes locked onto mine. He said it all, not with words, but with the provoked gravitas of his stare; *I take care of you now*.

"You're Alex Rivers." The once solemn look in her eyes melted. Her voice purred as she patted the knots in her hair. "Gemma should have said something," she scolded, but somehow seemed delighted. "I'm Claire."

"So I've heard." He replied, his friendliness enough to ease her back into a calmer state. She covered her mouth as her mood spun quickly like a manic leap. This was a trait of her disorder, the hot and cold mood swings. Some lasted weeks, others only moments. I dropped my shoulders as Alejandro looked away, observing the high pile of ash and cigarettes lying on the table. He studied them, making mental note, indexing their meaning and their assignment to me. He was so intuitive; he could sense my distaste.

"Gemma?" Erin called my name near the hall as Alejandro took a seat, distracting Claire as I walked away. He kept his eyes on me, but Claire never noticed. She stared at him with all the conviction and yearning she had for my father. Was this a sign? Her fear of what men could do was never displaced by how poor her judgment was. She gravitated towards troubled men, just as she possibly did now.

"Sorry about that." I apologized, approaching Erin as quickly as possible.

"No, hunny, no need to apologize. I think your mother's behind on a refill…" She stated, being sensitive with her words as she handed me an empty orange bottle. I stared down, looking at the date and label, wondering how long it had been since Claire took her last pill. I looked up at Alejandro, while Claire still laughed in a euphoric cloud.

She told me she was taking these; she gave me her word. Was this a new problem? On top of everything else, did I need to fear this too? I had the choice to scold her, to remind her that never once was she a mother, but instead it was me who carried those responsibilities. But what good would that be, other than to reinforce the guilt she produced? I was expected to be here, I was born for her, not for me.

"I'll call now." I assured, taking the bottle from her hands, leaving down the hall. It was dark given there were no windows, but the length seemed shorter than what I remembered as a child. I didn't realize how small the place was, forgetting already from the time I visited while working with Gerard. I suppose I just tried to block it out, each moment here was an unpleasant surprise.

I approached my room, hesitant to enter, but doing so regardless for privacy. I tried not to dottle, dialing the pharmacy to place the order. As the call rang, I caught myself in a large mirror by the corner; the one whose frame was outlined with photos, most of which were Parker and me.

It was like a piece of us, held in the past, preserved in faded old snapshots. I moved closer, smiling at one in particular, an image of a determined Parker winning Andy, a stuffed giraffe from the county fair. He saved every ticket he had that summer, ensuring I got the one toy I truly wanted. He never gave up on me, but I couldn't help but feel like a part of me gave up on him. Was it wrong to shut him out on this part of my life, after all he'd done, didn't he just want to be as close as he could? We were friends, truly, and maybe that's all it would ever be.

"Shit." I muttered to myself as the phone rang to voicemail. I shut it off.

"Nice room." Alejandro's compliment took me by surprise, along with his sudden appearance. How long had he been there?

"Hardly, but thanks. We should probably just go." I stated, stepping forward as he blocked the door.

"How are you?" He asked, not once moving. I wasn't willing to squeeze by, so instead I focused on the floor.

"Ok, I think," I admitted. "How's Claire?"

"Better, I think. But right now, all I care about is you."

"It's nothing new," I promised. "She just... has her moments."

"I'm familiar." He walked past me to enter my room. He looked around, studying the mirror and walls as he made his way to my bed, taking a seat at its edge. The springs creaked, as the weight of his body creased my purple comforter with stars.

Unlike my room at Parker's, my walls were mostly colorless, absent of any St. La Vie magazine clippings. A few things were still on display though, such as the *Twilight* poster I got at the theatre on my thirteenth birthday. This was subjected to Alejandro's eyes, along with the cup of milky gel pens that had surely lost their ink. He didn't linger long on these things, or the Hamptons postcards that sat thumbtacked by his side. "Sit with me." He requested, nodding to the space beside his lap. I curled the bottle in my hand, tucking it away from his eyes, following as he ordered.

"I'm not sure what you heard," I started. "I don't think it was very professional of me to bring you here." I wiped my eyes, feeling bad about what I'd done. This was my job, and maybe Claire was right, I should have been here to prevent this whole mess. I wasn't enough, I'd failed in so many things, and Claire was quick to point out the worst of my flaws, not being a good daughter one of them.

"I'm not interested in professionalism," Alejandro cooed, "you're more than capable of that, and not just that alone." He reassured, guarding me already from the doubt I had. I stared across from the bed at the sliding closet door, whose railing was falling off the track. It was where I hid alone when I was scared, plotted with worn teddy bears and childhood clothes that could no longer fit. I made out a familiar yellow shirt, one with a large smiling daisy on its front. It was an ironic and cruel contrast to the little girl that once wore it.

What if I had an Alejandro back then, when I was just a child? Would he have held me, or would he have pulled me out from there and carried me away? It was likely the latter, considering how persistent he was, or who knows, maybe he would've been there by my side, just like he did for his brother in the dark. I touched my neck from the memories, the night it happened, when my dad left, and I hid.

"Why do you do that?" he asked. "Touch your neck?" It was a simple question but lacked a simple answer. Maybe this was his chance to save me, but I couldn't risk it, not now. No matter what he'd seen or what he saw in me, time felt like the only remedy I could consider before talking about that day, so instead, I revealed only what I could in this moment.

"Cigarettes." I answered, "Just like how cherries remind you of your mom, cigarette smoke reminds me of mine… but in a bad way."

"And when you touch your neck around me?" He asked.

"Just a nervous habit I suppose." That was true, I had done it so long it expanded beyond where it came from. "But not just from you… sometimes I get scared."

"Like loud noises?"

"Mhmm… or…" I opened my fist to the empty orange bottle, showing what I held, "Are you ever afraid of becoming something you can't control? A victim of something bigger? Something… inherited?" My words popped out like a quiet blast. Everything was silent around us, except for the rise of his chest, which slowly collapsed as he watched over me.

"Like a disease?" He asked, almost in his own world, but I didn't answer right away. How could I explain what I hated to hear out loud?

"Well," I mumbled, "a disorder, technically." He looked down at my hand, observing the empty bottle.

"If you're asking if I've ever been afraid of such a thing, then the answer is yes." He stated, reaching his hand for my palm, closing it shut. He held it tightly.

"So, you do get scared?" I asked, relieved by his candor.

"Absolutely. I hope to never be the things I saw while growing up, nor the people who caused it." His eyes no longer fixed on mine, but rather our hands. There was so much more to him than he shared, but he was here for me. Could I ever be there for him? That night at The Met, the photo of the man he slashed, it was a frightening and raw glimpse of how he felt. Alejandro wanted to grow, that was clear, but how could I ever be more than what I was, a failure with my dreams, a failure with love? Claire thought I wasn't enough, so would it be the same for him too?

My phone buzzed by my side with Parker's name flashing across the screen. Was this some cosmic interjection, a sign to run away? He was in the room, but even now I couldn't speak, I couldn't answer his questions. I pressed the button, silencing his call, feeling guilty again for shutting out the man I loved so dearly. I couldn't be who I was, which was less than what I felt I should be.

"I'm not enough." I admitted out loud, reaffirming what Claire led me to believe.

"*Enough?*" Alejandro questioned, the intensity in his voice unchanging. "That's a definition only I can speak on, and what I know is best. Tell me again you're not enough, and I'll fix it."

"It's not that simple." I replied.

"Correct, when alone nothing is, but here I am, so I dare you to think otherwise. You don't need to feel guilty for surviving." He caressed me with his words alone, "When I call you a good girl, Gemma, I fucking mean it." His hand lifted to my chin, directing my gaze towards his.

A *good girl?* He saw me as such, and maybe more than one to be broken, a manifestation of his urges, but also, the infatuation of his heart.

"I don't even know where to start." I said hopelessly, genuinely lost in his eyes.

"*We* can start today. I might not be able to take the memories away, but I can replace them with new ones. Together, that is, something new for each other." He pulled the bottle out from my hands, tucking it into his pocket, "I'll get this arranged for Claire. *I* take care of you now."

I swallowed easier now, my neck relieved at his

words. His protection was foreign and more astute with age, complimented with an affirmation I never knew. It was less work hiding these things, accepting already that he shared this life. Maybe there *was* something he saw, and now I could see it too, through small steps and patience, there could be a way out. But was it through him, or was this another let down in the making?

"I won't let you be defined by anyone's eyes other than mine," he announced, his thumb tracing my jaw. "Not your friend, not your mother, not anyone. And know this when I say it, Gemma, that when I look at you, it's because I can't look away."

Chapter 20

The walk down Parker's hall was the first quiet moment I had all day. I was exhausted, but now, finally off the elevator and at his door, I found peace. I slid the key into the lock, giving it a twist, possessed by a sudden thought before walking in.

Alejandro, in the most punctual and commanding ways, did something I never knew was possible. He made me feel relatable, and on top of that, he extended some sense of normalcy to my life. Maybe I wasn't alone in my experiences. I wasn't sure if he would be able to live up to his expectations, the idea he proposed of replacing my memories. It sounded sweet, but I knew too little about his capabilities thus far, excluding the ones he controlled over my body. What would the memories he promised look like? I wasn't sure yet, or willing to admit, which I desired more. Was it the prospect of freedom from my past that excited me, or was it the fact that it came from the dark brooding man himself, Alejandro? Both felt nice, yet different.

I walked in, surprised anyone was even home, signaled by the dim lights and music. I put my coat on the hanger, and Parker turned around from the kitchen corner.

"Gem…" He pulled me in, wrapping his large arms around me. His greeting felt both excited yet relieved. I didn't question it. I was consumed in the subtle spice of masculine cologne, much like fresh leather, but sweet like the gardenias on the dress I'd worn for him weeks ago at the play. It was as if he knew my day was long, making his embrace more secure.

"Rattlesnake!" I pressed myself against his firm chest. "What's going on?" I asked, curious as he lowered me down gently.

"I just couldn't stop thinking about you today."

"Me?" I asked.

"Only you. I was useless at work, completely unsure what was going on." I was unsure why he was like this, or what I did different. The excitement in his emerald eyes were soon replaced with concern.

"What do you mean?"

"I called you. I heard where you were at, who you were with." His hands fell to my waist as his grip secured my body. I looked away, worried he knew, that he'd be upset. It was no secret how much he loathed Alejandro, and the suspicion he had of him. "With Alejandro?" I asked shyly, unsure of his reaction.

"Yes, but more so with Claire." He discerned. He stared into my eyes, noticing the red puffy bags lying beneath. I'd been crying, and I was sure I looked look like a disaster. He licked his lips, as if to taste the tear that his large thumb brushed away from my cheek.

"How did you..." I started to ask, but Parker stopped me.

"Alejandro was supposed to show up for another meeting but didn't. He advised his lawyers where he was, and it wasn't difficult to figure it out. Out in

Bushwick with an auburn-haired beauty." He confirmed so confidently with their sweet description.

"Beauty?" I laughed, but Parker tightened his grip.

"As if there was any confusion." He shook his head, probably noticing the wide expression in my eyes. "I called, but you must have been busy." He noted, admitting he also knew I ignored his call.

"I was…" I replied, glancing down at my hands, unsure of what to say.

"I could have been there, you know? I could've helped. I know you know this, but I guess it doesn't change things. I understand it's a sensitive subject and it's your choice who you bring or don't bring. It's just… if there's anything I can do to help, tell me." Parker was always protective, but respected my boundaries, such as when I kicked him out of Claire's house when we were kids. Now was no different, but I could tell it hurt him, nonetheless.

"So you don't care that Alejandro took me?" I asked, still shy at his reaction. The thumb that just wiped my cheek now caressed along my jaw.

"Butterfly," he lulled out, "don't ever confuse my dislike for him as disappointment in you. Right now, I care only about how you are, and little on what he is. Tell me, are you ok?"

Outside of Claire, I wanted to tell him the truth. I was confused, conflicted even. I wasn't sure if I could control the physical attraction I had for Alejandro, and though I was resistant, I wasn't sure how long I could fight it. In that same thought, how could I ever truly divulge, if I loved Parker so much? Love for me was not a choice, but a curse that brought me to the most caring man I couldn't have: Parker.

"I'm ok, now." I confessed, "But it has been a long and draining day."

"I understand. And Claire?" He asked, motioning to the stool by the kitchen as he walked to the fridge.

"She's better now. It was one of her... cloudy days." I muttered. Parker handed me a soda, popping its tab with a quick fizzy snap. He opened one for himself, taking a long sip.

"Do you know what happened?" He asked quietly, fully aware of Claire's patterns, "A trigger?" He leaned closer, resting his body against the counter, the vein of his bicep appeared lost in the sleeve of an old, faded Columbia shirt.

I took another sip. The burn of carbonation was a unique sensation that challenged the exhaustion I felt. "It was simple, she stopped taking her pills." I sarcastically rolled my eyes, as if the whole thing was a minor mistake, though it was a huge ordeal. "Charles was kind enough to pick up the refill, amongst other errands." I blurted out, not even realizing what I admitted.

"Charles?" Parker asked, his eyebrow arched at the name. I toyed with the open tab of my drink, flicking it with my finger.

"Alejandro's driver."

"He helped too then?" Parker asked, his emotions stilled.

"Feels weird admitting, but yes." I said.

"It shouldn't," he stretched his thick neck, his

Adam's apple bobbed with the swallow of soda. He almost sighed, "I know what it's like to hide a truth, so I can relate. I respect you enough to control the things I struggle with, such as not knowing more about your past. I ask questions because I'm desperate to know, but I'd never push you to answer, or at least, I hope I never do."

"You don't." I comforted.

"Good, because believe me, Gemma, honesty is not only welcomed, it's admired. I know what it's like, even if you don't think I do." I felt unsure of what he truly meant, if he was alluding to the details of a lawsuit he couldn't talk about, or something different, something from the boy turned man that held my heart. This was his effect but maybe Alejandro's was different, a way to encourage a future where I'd no longer need to hide. Maybe I could speak some truth, be the good girl Alejandro wanted me to be.

"Alejandro was actually why things got better today. He caught Claire off guard, made her manic again, which was better than the reverse…" Parker took a sip, unable to respond as the last words fell out of my mouth. The slightest wince subtly appeared, concealed in a pain he hid in his eyes. He wanted to do that for me, but I somehow denied that from him.

He cleared his throat.

"And does that make you happy?" He asked, genuinely curious. I suppose it did. I thought of what made me calm, what put me at ease, and whether it was a lie or not. I knew the moments we shared—the fantasy of Parker and me as a couple—was what made me happy; it was the fantasy I protected, as much as he protected me.

"You make me happy." I replied, watching as he stopped chewing the inside of his cheek, and grinned.

"You make me happy too, and I'm happiest when you're safe. I'll see to it that this doesn't happen again. You won't need to go back to that house, not for an emergency, not for anything." He sipped his soda, his words confidently sure that he could make it happen.

"Don't be silly, Parker." I laughed, not at him, but at the relief such an idea already brought.

"You doubt me, Butterfly?" His throaty voice challenged me. "I never break a promise, especially with your safety. I made it before, and I intend to keep it, no matter what, even from…" He stopped, lost in his own words, sucking in his lip. He squeezed the can in his hand, playing with anything that could fill the void of silence.

"Parker?" I asked, "From what?" I searched his eyes, hoping to find the answer he wished to say.

"Just…" he smirked as if realizing some mistake. I opened my mouth to ask again but stopped as his phone buzzed loudly against the counter. It sat there, illuminated like a slim brick with Camilla's name displayed on its front. She was calling, and we both just watched as it vibrated with a ring. Parker finally reached out, silencing the call.

"Aren't you going to answer that?" I scrunched my face, speaking quietly as if she could hear me.

He shook his head. "No, not tonight. I took off work to be here with you. Let's just hang out like old times.

Maybe movie and a pizza?" He shrugged, "We can do anything you want." I nodded, concealing my unabashed smile.

"Pizza from Joe's?"

"Extra large," he confirmed, two words that reminded me of him and that night I took a bath. The muscles in my stomach tensed at the memory, as he dialed to place our order.

"I'll get changed!" I exclaimed, eager to get comfortable. I made my way back down the hall and into my room, shutting the door. It was easy to be excited, finally having a moment to be alone with Parker, though I found it odd how he promised to keep me safe, especially with his unfinished thought. Was this another trait of his, a big brother looking out for his little sister? Our history said yes, but his conviction was confusing. To ignore a call from Camilla without thought, just to spend a night with me. What did that mean, and what did that look like to anyone on the outside? I slipped off my shirt, tossing it across the room as I went into the closet.

Quickly, I pulled over a loose crop top, pinning my hair into a small bun. I was wise enough not to get too excited, because I always had a habit of getting carried away. My imagination had always been colorful, leading me into expectations of how a night could go. An ignored call, a lingering stare, and a breathtaking hug. How could I not get excited? At minimum, my sad fantasy was still being fulfilled, and wasn't that what I wanted? I was unsure of what to wear, pulling out two silky shorts from my drawer: pink or red. I bit my lip, slipping down my pants, kicking them off my feet. I hitched up my panties, asking out loud to myself, "Which one should I wear?"

"I prefer black." A deep, haunting voice whispered from behind, startling me.

"Parker?" I gasped, spinning around, my lips rushed with the pressure of a strong hand. I attempted to scream, but instead was lost in the glare of a godly ghost.

Alejandro.

Chapter 21

His stern eyes seared into mine as a single finger raised to his lips. "Ssssshhhhh," he hushed, slowly releasing my mouth, "be my good girl, now."

"Alejandro! What the fuck!" I choked at the sight of him, his knuckles tightened from his grip on the door frame. He smirked, as if he were the devil sent to tempt me.

"I've come to take you." He declared, the black ink on his hand was as dark as his eyes. "Tonight, we start."

"Start what?" I asked. He scanned my body, stopping along my exposed hips and legs. I squeezed them together, as if to make myself smaller, but that only intoxicated his grin.

"The replacement of bad, and the start of good." He bit his lip, his stare fixed right on my panties. The infectious promise of his eyes never failed. He stared as if he wanted to nip them off, his teeth clenched so deep into his lip, that I feared he would draw blood. "Perhaps we can start here." He warned.

"You sure you aren't the bad, replacing the good?" I concealed my screech, floored by the fact he snuck into my room.

"Both are a fine fucking line. You'll take each and learn soon enough, that my bad is just as good."

"You're crazy!" I panicked, "My friend is outside, he's waiting for me."

"The best friend? Then let him wait," he stepped closer, his head peered down towards mine. He licked the corner of his lip, the fang of his tooth presented in a snarl. "Or better yet, let him hear." He reached out, one hand placed under my chin, the other sliding along my bare waist, caressing a set of nerves that placed me into a trance. It wasn't enough to touch my waist, but he had to be closer. His thumb slipped along the band of my panties, desperate for the skin that blocked his path. He brushed it with a small stroke, enough to make my head fall back. "Tell me you feel that?" He asked, his thumb snapped the silk elastic around my hip before grabbing it again.

"No…" I moaned, echoing the warning he gave me in the trailer, that he would stop me with his lips if I said it one more time.

"No? You're my mouthy girl, aren't you? What'd I tell you before about saying no?"

"That you'd correct me?"

He pulled harder, causing my panties to ride up my ass, to be pressed tightly against the lips of my pussy. A weakened moan escaped me, threatened by the small silky liner that he twisted into a string. Had he pulled any tighter, it'd slip right between me and onto my clit. He was punishing me, and if he wanted to, he could rip them off with his strength alone. I could practically hear the tear of fabric in my mind.

"That's right. Run your mouth off again and see what happens. Tell me no, once more."

The allure of his voice aroused every sense of my body, chilling me into the most sensual fever that made me sick. Saying no to him meant I'd descend into his burning world. Saying no meant taking a risk on my heart and ignoring all my responsibility.

"And if I say no…" I dared to find out, the prize or punishment to come.

"You say no this time, and I'll wedge my fat cock between those pretty lips of yours. You'll forget about your little friend once your crop top is covered in sloppy wet drool." He grinned so viciously as if the fantasy had tortured him for centuries.

"Alejandro, I'd choke…" I whimpered at his description, hoping for mercy or possibly not.

"That's right. Because when I go in, Gemma, I go in fucking deep. Now do as you were told, and describe it." He commanded, "Tell me what you feel." He grazed his knuckles on the bare skin of my stomach, causing me to react with an uncontrolled shiver. I wanted to faint, from fear and the thrill of uncertain danger. The hush from my mouth already felt too loud, what noise would I make if he touched me more. Maybe it'd be like Camilla and Parker, except this time it would be Parker who'd hear the *thuds*, not from my bed, but rather, my back shoved deep into the closet. I'd scream, I just know it.

"Feel what?" I cried, my eyes fluttered shut. My shirt lifted, expanded by my ribs that sucked in the air of his scent.

"The collapse of everything you thought you knew about the truth," he whispered, "but soon, you'll find out." He leaned in, his stubbled cheek grazed mine with a poke.

"The truth?" I asked, a provoking word that revolved around everything we were, which still I knew little of.

"Yes, of what pleasure really is," he recited as his words slipped into my ear, slick like the bath water where he made me come.

I tried not to moan, deprived for a release I needed as I squeezed his wrists, "I can't," I stuttered, pressing my tongue against the roof of my mouth, resisting the temptation to stick it out, to have it sucked.

"But you want to. I can smell it. I can feel it," I allowed his mouth to graze my ear, subtly nipping my lobe with his supple lips. If I let him, he'd suck me up like a loose noodle, bending me into the position that would fill his need. If he were to break me, I knew it would hurt, but I wanted that. The soft smack of his lips popped like the slap of patent leather, reflective and wet. "I can fucking taste it." He leaned me back into the closet, pushing the weight of his large body as clothing surrounded us, concealing our dirty secret.

"I need more time…" I hesitated, growing increasingly weak at his stare. "He's expecting me, just wait." Alejandro pressed himself tightly against me, as if refusing to let me go. He had me right where he wanted, and I'd be lying if I said I didn't want him too.

"That boy can wait," he snipped. "What does he know about a good night? He doesn't even see what I see." His teeth gritted together, drunk with the lure of my body, my flesh on display for his eyes, "A woman to worship." The sincerity in his words evoked a new sheen of sweat to form on my palm. I wasn't warm, I was on fire as he squeezed my upper thigh, barely grazing his thumb over my covered mound.

I stared at the door, hoping this was real and not my imagination. How long did I have before Parker came knocking? I looked back at Alejandro, anxiously unsure of what to do. Stuffed in the small confines of my closet, I knew my moans would be muted, still, the nervousness ached in my groin, overcome with the impulse to reach for Alejandro's hand, to guide him between my legs to test my wetness. One finger was all I needed, already vulnerable with my skin exposed.

"I'll be back, I promise!" Quickly, I pressed my palms against his chest, creating the awful distance I wished to close. "I can't leave him waiting. I just need a few minutes."

"Only a few. Otherwise, I'll come out and take you myself."

"You wouldn't…" I hissed.

"I fucking would, and I would delight in it too." He gripped the strap of my panties, twisting it along his finger like a strand of hair. "No silk shorts." He demanded, "Not for that boy. I've claimed these legs, they're mine to praise."

"They belong to no one." I asserted.

"If I can't have them, then I'll take his eyes." He grinned, "He'll never see what he's missed out on… that is, now that a man is here." I concealed my excitement, but his was unguarded, his hard erection constricted in denim, stiff against my navel. "I insist." He continued, reaching for a folded pair of black sweats. "Lift your legs for me."

"I can do it myself." I whined, feeling more anxious.

"And deny me the pleasure? You're the crazy one now. Now lift." He commanded, kneeling towards the floor, dragging the sweats up slowly from my ankles. He moved with both delicate and purposeful speed, his eyes fixed on each inch of my legs, as if to memorize them for later. I was unsure where I started and where he began, whether it was my skin that was cold, or his that was burning hot. The combination of flesh was a compliment, a key to the goosebumps that rose in place with each demanding touch.

As he stood, his fingers pulled at the waist of my sweats, assuring the accessibility of his reach. He slipped his hand down the back, the entirety of his palm gripped my bare ass, squeezing it into an almost painful pinch. I moaned, as my belly tightened with the soft touch of his large pinky. He pulled my cheeks apart, daring to inch his fingers closer, as if to stick them in my ass.

"When I say I want to break my good girl, I fucking mean it. That includes every inch of your body, every tight hole that could mold to my size. These sweats are temporary, and remember one thing before you leave…" He made me feel fucking dirty, like he wanted to measure the tightness of an opening I myself never even played with. "What goes on, must come off. Keep me waiting, and I'll rip these off your body." He slowly pulled his hand away, leaving me numb and uncontrollably buzzing.

"Not another word." I insisted, my thighs already ached from his touch, "And don't move!" I worried at what he would do, and his promise to take me felt more like a reality. I knew this was no bluff, he'd kick down the door and steal me away if I took too long. I walked quickly past him, eyeing the open window and fire escape where he climbed in from. Of all the possible ways to find me, he had to choose this. I knew Parker would kill him if he ever found out, which was why I needed to make sure he remained on his best behavior. I looked back as I reached my door, cringing at the springy squeak of my loud bed. Alejandro was lying down at its edge, flashing a final warning of a tense stare. My clock was officially starting now, as Alejandro quietly began to count me down.

Yes, I was in trouble, and maybe in the best way possible. Had Parker come in, what would he say. I wasn't allowed to wait any longer as I heard a shout from down the hall.

It was Parker...

Calling for his Butterfly to come.

Chapter 22

"In forty minutes, Gem!" Parker shouted from the living room. "Pizza is on its way!"

"Coming!" I replied, opening the door slowly, squeezing through the crack to hide what was inside. I scurried down the hall, appearing as Parker turned the TV on. He scratched his chest, his taut abs ripped on display, much like the arm that dug under his shirt. I gawked for a moment, admiring the distinct cut of his pelvis whose trunk dipped into a pair of loose grey sweats.

"There you are?" He laughed, "I thought you needed some help." His glasses were on now, a studious look to his otherwise rugged jaw.

"No help needed in there." I nervously giggled, shaking my head. Why did I always crumble with pressure? He arched his brow at me, slipping his hand out of his shirt.

"Monster marathon?" He asked, clicking the first movie of a collection of black and white classics. "Since I missed *Phantom of the Opera*, we could at least watch the thing we were expecting as kids." I nodded too hard. There was no way I could make it through this, not with Alejandro in the room. Still, I agreed.

"Sounds great!" I squeaked, pulling a blanket off the

chair. I looked up at the clock, checking the time, mentally preparing for my departure.

"Let me get in on that." Parker signaled for the blanket as I made my way over, opening it just for him. He leaned on his side, pulling the massive blanket over his body. The room grew dark as he clicked a remote, queuing the opening credits of a three-hour marathon. I couldn't even concentrate, staring up at the clock, down to the hall, then back down towards Parker. I repeated this cycle, determining the amount of time that felt least suspicious before Alejandro would storm his way out.

What was he even doing in there? Lying on my bed, stretching along my comforter? There was so much for him to see in my room, and here I was, hopelessly stranded. What if he peeked around, what if he found my vibrator in the nightstand? First Parker, now him? He'd know that his good girl masturbated, possibly making him even more impatient than he already was. Would my vibrator qualify me as the bad girl now? I wasn't sure. Knowing Alejandro, his correction would be more of a foreplay than an actual discipline. He'd probably make me use it in front of him, whispering his praise, showing me the best way to come. He was assertive and hungry, I doubt he'd stop at that, surely insisting that he'd be the one to fuck me with my own toy.

"I got the peach rings." Parker announced, scooting closer. He reached over with the bag, resting his arm near mine. "I'd slip it on your finger, but then I'd have to bite it off." He grinned, a playful but almost alluring tone. His forearm brushed along my leg as his weight creased the already small space of cushion between us. I sat straight up, which gave me the advantage of seeing his large traps peek from his collar.

"Just like old times." I mumbled, accepting the idea.

"The best of times." He slipped the candy right over my ring finger, "Sweet, isn't it?" He asked, not taking a bite this time, instead placing my finger inside his mouth. I watched him slowly suck the candy off. I blinked quickly, his lips pressed against my skin, teased by the heat of his fruity tongue. The electric pulse radiated from my finger and steeped into my legs, the ones Alejandro commanded me to conceal. If Parker knew that these pants were worn only because of Alejandro's command, what would he say? I feared to think what would happen if Alejandro came out. His perception of Parker being just a boy was a serious misconception, and a dangerous one at that. Parker was big, comparable even to Alejandro; the two being mirrored clones of size and strength. And although Parker was vocal in his assertion, there was no mistaking that my Rattlesnake was more like a bear. If Alejandro came out, there would be chaos, and I wasn't sure who would actually survive.

"Hmmmm," Parker hummed, "you smell different."

"Different?" I asked, my voice croaking. "How?"

"Sweet, but not like normal." He pondered, his senses more in tune than a wolf with its prey, "Cherries," he stated confidently. I forgot how to blink, feeling already caught with Alejandro's cherry scent stuck on my skin.

"New perfume." I laughed, grabbing a peach ring

from the bag. "Trying something new." He was close enough to smell me, but I had to throw him off, grabbing another gummy, slipping it into his mouth as he took a bite.

I wondered why Parker felt so close as his hard body and tussled hair leaned in. His expression was sharp, despite the round rim of his thin glasses, causing me to tighten every muscle in my core while watching him closely. He made me nervous, almost as if he could sense what was happening between my legs.

Fuck.

I could feel it, sitting here in the dark, a silky wet drop leaking from my lips and onto my panties. I shut my eyes, thinking of the closet, of what Alejandro said and its clear effect. He wanted me in my black panties alone, and he would see to it that they came off. As delicate as his touch was, I knew it was a facade. He was restraining himself, and if I gave permission, he would break me like he'd promised. No one had ever dressed me before, and though I protested at first, there was care in his touch which made me weak. Was he a protector or a provider? I crossed my legs, squeezing them shut. Parker adjusted himself, even closer than before. He was next to my dripping wet slit and didn't even know it, which turned me on. I was ready for a man, either man, both if possible. The more I thought of it, the worse it got.

Parker rung his hands together, twisting the blanket into a sturdy and threatening rope. He seemed tense, ready to bind either himself or possibly even my wrists, or so I fantasized. My heart pumped between my legs, making me swell with each passing beat. I squeezed my legs tighter, feeling the leaky wet drip pinch out from my lips.

"Are you getting horny?" Parker looked up at me, saying the four words that made my nipples perk.

"What?" I choked. I was ready to spread myself, to be taken and claimed by the men in this house, but his question drew me back.

"I asked, are you getting hungry?" He grinned.

I laughed, my nervousness an appalling giggle. "Very!" I answered, mortified by my feelings.

I looked back up the clock, the time passing quickly, keeping me in an eternity of worry. I couldn't help it, there was something about the nervousness that twisted inside, causing me to squirm with anxious lust. I stared at the screen, unblinking and consumed. Two men, one giant problem.

If only it were so simple, if only I knew why there was such a tear between my heart and my head. Outside of being caught, I couldn't focus on what was best, or the signals being fed to me.

Alejandro was clear and precise. I loved this, I needed this. But Parker... I thought he was clear on what we were, but I always felt like something was there. Why did he hug me the way he did, keeping me tightly wrapped around his arms? Even now, he placed his lips around my finger and sucked the candy off for a bite. I wasn't crazy or a fool. He always made me feel like he was on the cusp of a confession. Parker inched even closer, and now his gentle touch and tender words felt so different. Was there more to Parker than he'd ever admit?

I had to ask. I had to have the clarity as my mind spun with uncertainty. What was it about me that made him see me only as a sister?

"Parker?" I asked.

Just then, a loud rolling thud echoed from the hall.

Alejandro!

Parker shot up, peering into the dark hall, "What the hell was that?" He exclaimed, gripping the couch. Even in the loose-fitting Columbia shirt, did he fill out its size with tense muscle. "It came from your room."

"I…" I stammered, caught off guard, looking at the clock and then back down at the hall, "I… balanced a box of shoes on the top shelf, when I changed into pjs!" I thought I was going to puke, "I think they fell!"

"Jesus!" He groaned with a laugh, "I thought someone was in the house." He leaned back into the couch as I shook my head.

"Nope, just us!" I replied as I sat back into the cushion, my ears on full alert. Clearly this was a warning from Alejandro, a promise he'd steal me away at any given moment. *I can't wait*, I thought, *he will come out at any…*

The front door pounded with three quick knocks. I screamed, startled once more by the noise. Parker looked confused, pausing the movie.

"Pizza?" he questioned. "There's no way." He got up from the couch, slipping the dimmers back on for warm light. I turned around, squinting over the cushion as he answered the door.

I wanted to run back to the room, to check on Alejandro. I was worried he'd sweep me away with his hungry hands, enraging a primal Parker. There was no time, I only sat and listened intently.

Parker blocked the doorway, murmuring, keeping it mostly shut as his head peeked through the crack. His voice was soft, almost concerning, his calm demeanor sorting out what I thought was a mistaken resident. A woman responded with sultry intrigue. I bent forward, feeling nosey, stealing a glance.

Camilla?

She stood at the door, shielded by Parker's broad shoulders. I bit the corner of my thumb, staring at the clock, feeling an impulsive urge to shout.

"Camilla?" I rang out, my voice sounded surprised. "Is that you?" I tilted forward on the couch, "Come on in!"

Parker turned back, opening the door wider to a confused Camilla. She stood in a slim black dress, her makeup sleek with cat eyes, dark red lips, and glam.

"I was just telling Mila about our plans," Parker replied, massaging the back of his neck. "She's actually about to leave." Camilla shot daggers at him, but Parker paid no attention.

"Don't be silly," I waved her in, concealing my bare torso with the grey blanket.

"Well, this looks cozy." She studied the blanket that covered my crop top, not realizing how dark it was just moments ago. I imagined it wasn't a good look but assured myself that my fantasies were just that. I knew the truth already; I had only always been Parker's sister.

"If Parker had just answered his phone," Camilla announced, narrowing her eyes at Parker, "I would have known not to surprise him." She scanned the room suspiciously, discerning if there was any hint of romance. Did she sense something too, or was this all in my head?

"It's totally fine," I stood up from the couch. "Honestly, Park, I'm so exhausted from the day. I think I'm gonna just go to bed."

"But, Gem?" He paused, as if he wanted to say more but was incapable because of Camilla. His green eyes appeared lost, a look that made me question everything. What was behind the wall of Parker Jones, and what was the promise he made to keep me safe?

I grew quiet, staring at him and Camilla, and honestly, they looked great together. If Parker was happy, then I could be happy for him, or at least, I'd try.

"It's ok, Park." My words slipped out, telling him goodnight in the best way I could, "You better shake, Rattlesnake." I stepped back, still watching him before turning around.

"Bye, bye, Butterfly." He mouthed back, as I made my way down the dark hall.

I opened my door, quickly stepping inside, locking it shut. Alejandro sat at my desk, looking through sketches I drew for his suit. All he cared about was my work, even though my room was covered in the renderings from my idol, St. La Vie.

"I like what I see." His eyes peeked toward a covered mannequin, which held his almost completed suit. He shot a curious glance at me. There were a few surprises attached to it that I didn't want him to see.

"That's not ready for you yet." I kept my voice low as I dropped the blanket by my side, exposing the toned curves of my tight tummy. His knuckles tightened from his grip on the armrest, absorbing me in.

"What about you?" He asked, giving me a long once over from my stomach to my chest. "Are you ready?"

I hesitated, but only for a second, making what felt like a permanent decision. Could I end the fantasy I had with Parker and start a reality with Alejandro? Possibly, but not without its bumps, that I was sure of. Either way, I was willing to try.

"I'm ready." My finger poked his chest. "Though you're not the one taking us out tonight," I glanced up, giving a final grin, "I am."

Chapter 23

Alejandro kicked a small latch beside the descending fire escape. The additional steps hidden below slid down with a loud clank. "Nice and slow," his eyes peeked through the drops of mist in his hair. He was quick to move, almost swinging down, popping his hoodie over his head as he landed on the wet pavement. A small light buzzed in the rather dark alley, catching subtle rain that fell more like a haze.

I wore my leather skirt just for him, knowing he'd have a peek of my bare ass and panties as I descended down. His strong arms reached for my waist, his touch appearing almost like a sting. First, he grazed my leg, then squeezed around my thigh. I wanted the attention, not of a movie star, but of the older man who wasn't shy about his intentions. For the first time, I felt seen.

I let go, closing the distance, allowing him to swing me down in his arms.

"And what's your grand plan?" He asked. Even with my heeled boots, he was massively tall, my head still needed to peer up to his height.

"A secret." I hummed, still unsure where to go, but leading Alejandro felt like a test of his patience. I liked it.

"A tease?" he asked, disappointed we weren't staying in the dark alley. "You better take me then, good girl, before I take you myself." How could I resist any further, as if he hadn't weakened me enough? His words and his eyes were like a wrecking ball to my nerves. I pressed my back against the wall, tugging at my skirt.

"And if I protest?" I asked, assuming the answer.

"I'll correct you." He lured, his finger trailed along my thighs, raising my skirt with a flick of his wrist. The cool air pressed against my body, my panties slicked with the wetness he caused from earlier tonight.

"And if I scream?" I reminded, recalling him to repeat the warning he gave that night at The Met, when I promised to leave. Only now, I asked it with a naughty grin, still nervous with how forward he was, something I'd never experienced from a man before.

"If you scream, it'll only be to beg for more." His return was a seething confidence, as if he knew my resistance was on the brink of total collapse. He knew I picked this skirt for him, but what he didn't know—and nor did I—was the uncertainty of what I'd allow. If I had a choice, I'd keep my legs held together, but maybe he had other plans. "Just a taste," his fingertip slowly traced the line outside of my panties. He was so close, the tip of his curled pinky was right at the cusp of my wetness. He would know then, what a good girl I was, eager to please the assuring god that praised my hard work. I bit my lip, almost leaning in as bright lights blinded along the alley. It was a car, making its way towards us.

"Not yet." I gripped his hand, laughing nervously. I wondered what the driver saw as I pulled Alejandro out of the alley and into the busy sidewalk. He ran his thumb along the back of my hand, his daring smirk unbothered whether we'd been caught or not.

"Just in time," he warned, "god knows the sweet mess we would have made."

I pulled myself close to his body, not realizing that I looped my arm around his, as if it were natural. Suddenly, I felt subconscious of it, like I should pull away, but before I could, Alejandro squeezed the security of my placement. I couldn't leave now, and I didn't think he wanted me to either. He felt safe, unlike the things I'd read about him, and considering what just happened in the alley, this seemed tame, almost romantic.

We blended amongst the crowded street, walking along the unknowing residents and bright bodegas. "Are you used to this?" I asked. "Just walking around in the open?"

"Not without these," he pulled out a pair of thick black sunglasses. He covered his beautiful brown eyes, keeping his head slightly lowered amongst the misty air. "Can't cause a scene, now can we?"

"Is it really that bad?" I asked, familiar enough, but ignorant on the scope. It seemed almost miserable.

"Like every moment is a risk, an opportunity for things to get crazy." He stared ahead, "Watch." He lowered his eyes as a group of laughing women approached. They peeked up, hitching their mini dresses, clicking their heels along the pavement. Alejandro clutched his hand over mine, leaning lower to whisper. "This, Gemma, isn't a group of people. This is a wave, and you either sink or float."

Sink or float? A foreign idea to me, but an articulated one I understood instantly. That night after the play, just escaping the crowds to get to our car was chaotic, a distance no further than a hundred feet. We were swallowed alive, and without the aid of security, I wasn't sure if we would've made it at all. I looked towards the group, studying what Alejandro couldn't even look at.

One girl stared for a while, wrapped up in Alejandro, whose hood fell loosely around his face. Her expression held curious wonder, almost as if asking, could that be Alex Rivers? Alejandro tightened his hand around mine, using me as an anchor not to run. The girl never said anything, and as soon as the moment came, it left. "Today we float." He declared, his hand loosening its grip.

"I can't believe it." I shivered.

"Believe what?"

"My heart! It's racing!" I really felt it, the tipping point of chaos. Each move he made, each stare he shot, was like snipping a wire to a bomb. It was so simple, the act of being out, using our feet to get around. I did this every day, I even dreaded it at times, yet there was an inherent privilege to it. He couldn't enjoy that, his experiences were usually limited through the window of a car, or possibly a high rise.

We crossed a large street with long white lines, making our way amongst the unassuming tourists and gift shops. Did he ever have the urge to go into a place like that, to get something simple such as a snow globe or a magnet? He was visiting after all.

"Do you miss it?" I asked, staring through the large window of a glowing convenience store. "Life before Alex Rivers?" Alejandro was quiet, soaking in the question as we made our way across a lighted path of flowers and canopies.

"I miss the mundane," he grinned, "to grab a drink, to be where I want to be, to see and eat like you and others do," he looked over, his lips almost twisted, "to do that, all without a photo, all without strangers wanting my name scribbled on a poster."

Amongst all the benefits he had, the power and wealth, was there room to feel sorry for such a thing? I thought so. What is the cost of wealth, if it couldn't be spent in peace? We turned a corner of the quiet street, pausing for a moment to stare down its path. From afar, the large glowing beacon of Times Square felt distant, like an island of light and noise, too crowded for the likes of Alejandro.

"It's not that great, any self-respecting New Yorker actually hates it." I comforted, leaning my head against his arm. He allowed it, maybe even encouraged it. His hand raised to brush my hair. "The crowds are too big; the stores are kitschy." I assured.

"Still, it's a piece of normal I could never have again… unless," he paused.

"Unless what?"

"Unless I had to for you, like that night for the *Phantom*. Like I said, a small price to pay to get what I want."

"More time with me?" I asked, remembering the words he said, how at that time his persistence frustrated me. Alone on a quiet street, I suddenly felt bad for him, along with the unpleasantries of the world's attention. I had the sense that neither of us wanted that, but instead, something ordinary. "A piece of normal." I repeated his words, my attention on something even the biggest celebrity could still enjoy. I let go of him and ran closer to the corner of the street. He followed.

"Gemma?" He called out, staying close as I opened my mouth.

"Two hotdogs, please." I approached a small glowing cart, sheltered by a yellow umbrella and photos of food. I turned to Alejandro, "This here, this is normal, a dirty water dog with ketchup and mustard." I stared up, making my eyes big for his view.

"A dirty water dog?" He laughed.

"A staple." I nodded, approving the order to be continued. The man behind the cart lifted the lid of a silver tray, allowing a cloud of steam to plume into the air. You could smell it, its salty promise wafted along the display of assorted sodas. "It's almost as New York as pizza. Tell me you're not tempted?" I asked, slipping the man a five, taking the foiled dogs from his hand.

"Oh, I am." He replied, fixing a strand of my hair, staring at me rather than the food.

"Well, I hope you're hungry then!" I looked back, linking my arm into his.

"Starved."

We made our way towards a brick wall. Alejandro unwrapped his dog, taking a big bite as he leaned against a decorated pillar.

"I mean, come on." I laughed, my mouth filled with a bite.

"You can't beat it," he confessed, actually reaching up to remove his glasses. I could see his eyes, those perfect dark bowls, more illuminated by the glow of window light. He winked, taking another bite, staring at my own enjoyment of something so simple. "If you like this, then you'll love Pink's." He covered his mouth.

"Pink's?"

"You've never heard of Pink's? Not too far from Santa Monica Boulevard. Los Angeles, that is," he distinguished.

"Oh, I've never been," I admitted. "Actually, I've never really been anywhere too far from New York, to be honest."

"I'll take you." He motioned, wiping mustard from my lip and licking it off his thumb. "After production, that is. I'll show you lots of things out in California." His plans were matched with a stare, one that lingered from my lips and up to my eyes. For a moment, it took me out, forgetting almost that he wasn't from New York. He would have to go back to Los Angles eventually, how did I feel about that?

"I'd like that," I replied, "someday, maybe." Not disillusioned by another fantasy of being whisked away. Not that I needed it or sought it, but his command did have a charm to it that I would possibly miss. It was nice to be around a person who knew what they wanted, who had both a direction and a plan.

"Someday." He added, his tone as coy as it felt. He presented himself as though his mind were made up, a decision I wasn't yet privy to. The night was so different than what I expected, assuming it would have ended with Parker, curled on the couch. As much as I loved that idea, I recognized this was nice too, possibly even better. It was new, and new was refreshing. Old meant repeating a cycle that'd probably hurt me as much as it helped. For a moment, I felt foolish again, remembering I almost asked Parker why he saw me as a sister. Would his answer have changed anything, or would it have been just another confirmation?

If confirmation is what I needed, then why did I need to look further? Alejandro was here, and though I tried to fight it, I was willing to accept what my body felt. Was there more than just the urge to be touched, to please the older man with compelling dark eyes? He wanted me, I knew it, and his plans seemed greater than what his production time allowed. We chewed silently, my gaze averted by the loud blare of a determined fire truck. It passed quickly, its siren screeching along the quiet brick walls behind our backs.

"There goes trouble." I mumbled, taking another bite.

"Hmm," Alejandro hummed, "perhaps trouble is already here." His eyes peeked down towards my feet, the heel of my boot stuck on the sticky cover of a *New York Prestige* magazine. On the front was Alejandro's smoldering face, posing with a finger over his lips, showing the black rose on his hand. Big bold letters read across the headline, warning like a wanted poster.

I lifted the magazine with my heel, peeling it off. *Thirty Million Dollars Sought from Bad Boy Alex Rivers-*

Redacted Police Filings Bring New Questions About What Really Happened At The Pierre Hotel: (Pleads innocent amongst long history of destructive behavior).

How could this be true, what does this even look like? I winced up into his eyes, seeing the brooding expression focused on the magazine. What happened at The Pierre Hotel, and why was Parker so disturbed by the events of a party gone wrong? Was Alejandro truly dangerous, or was he just reckless? Maybe the truth was somewhere in between, and if he saw a future for us, what would that look like? A yes to being by his side meant accepting the good and the bad. Yes, to his charm, yes to the paparazzi, yes to the lawsuits and leather.

"Do you do these things often?" I asked, almost concerned, inquiring about the magazine in the most conservative way possible. "Lose control?" I thought of The Met, that night he lashed out, smashing the photo.

"There are always two truths," he answered, "one for Alex Rivers and one for me."

"And which one should I be afraid of?" I asked.

"For you? Neither. No one alters what I give you, which is the truth to the best of my ability. But sometimes those truths cross paths, and things get messy."

"Messy?" I asked. "Like The Met?"

"Yes, just like then."

"And who was that? Alex or Alejandro."

"The latter, as it will always be," he said, almost swearing it with his tone, "just for you, that is."

I combed a piece of my hair, staring down at my hot

dog. It seemed easier to ask, looking away from the eyes that sucked me in. "The man in the photo that night, he meant something to you. Like a feeling?"

"Yes, he did." He replied quickly.

"And that feeling is the truth, and when you see me, you see the things I try to hide, just like you?"

"Yes."

"Just like when I asked about the tattoo on your chest, or why you slashed the photo, the reason is always hidden. If you're like me, then I know the answer. Something or someone hurt you but admitting that takes time."

"Time and trust." He added, "Both of which we can have."

"And you want that?" I asked.

"More than that," he growled, "I need it." The struggle in his voice gave me pause. Maybe he was reckless, maybe he lacked the tools to say what he wanted. I expressed myself through the fashion I loved, but I'd always been more shy, more reserved. Alejandro, on the other hand, was clearly assertive in his aggression. When he expressed himself, it was the eruption of everything he bottled up inside, but the absence of what he needed: the courage to speak.

"Your family?" I asked, "What do they think of this? The tabloids and news, all the bad things that others say?"

"Nothing."

"That seems odd." I questioned, his walls possibly thicker than mine. "Tell me about your brother." I decided to start somewhere small.

He thumbed a piece of bun off his hot dog, sticking it in his mouth. "What would you like to know?"

"Anything about him. What's he like?" I asked, inching closer to his body. My proximity garnered a smile from his face, but he twisted it with a sigh.

"My brother…" he hesitated, "he's a great man, unlike anyone I know."

"Are you two still close?"

"I'd say so," he mumbled, "we're practically the same person."

"So he's cocky?" I played, rewarded with a small laugh from Alejandro.

"He's hard-working," he corrected. "Lives in Mexico now and has helped me more than I could ever repay."

"Helped you?"

"Mhmmm…" he looked away. "He runs the tequila business from Jalisco, a harvester like me. But much better."

"Must be pretty good then."

"He is."

"You told me before he's your little brother. How old is he?" I asked.

"He's probably closer to your age."

"What do you know about my age?"

"That you're clearly much younger than I am." Alejandro was a clever man for not outright asking. It wasn't like he could Google me and have all my stats right there, like I could for him. Although, I never much bothered to really see all of that. I enjoyed the air of mystery between us.

"Tell me his age, and I'll tell you if you're close."

He smirked, looking upwards, "He's thirty-two."

"You're not wrong, he's much closer to me in age than you," I let out a laugh. "I'm twenty-six for another few months… but ask then, and I'll say twenty-one."

"Either way you're young… and that makes me want to show you all the things I've learned with time and age."

"I'm sure it's a lot." I teased.

"It's experience…"

He was luring me in a new direction, a technique I've used myself. It was tempting to continue, but I quickly changed the topic. "What about your parents? Are they with him in Mexico?"

"No…" He said, losing the air of playfulness.

"So, they live in California still?" I asked, unsure of his distance and this new reaction. He scratched above his brow, rolling the foil from his hot dog into a ball.

"Not necessarily." He swallowed, clearing his throat. I watched as he sawed at his lip, digging with the pressure of his striking white teeth. Nervously I pressed, his eyes no longer on me as mine were on him.

"Where then?"

"Nowhere, Gemma…" He hissed. "They aren't anywhere because they aren't anything anymore. They're fucking dead." His eyes shot back to me, daring and dark. He spoke with a strong pause, his final words defiant, punched like a stamp. I wanted to ask, I wanted to know more, but couldn't, as my eyes turned around towards the shilling scream of his name.

Chapter 24

"**A**lex Rivers!" A girl with thick glasses dropped a small bag of macaroons, covering her mouth as she screamed. One of the desserts rolled to our feet, alerting the presence of every fan along the block. She was their siren. A man started running across the street, pulling out his phone, struggling to swipe it open. This was the wave, the feeling Alejandro warned of.

"We'll float." I announced, gripping onto his hand, yanking him urgently around the corner. His pace quickly mirrored mine as I guided him, but soon found myself being pulled by his hand rather than my own.

"I got you!" He huffed, his arms pumping with each passing sprint. I made the mistake of looking back, realizing that the sudden horde of onlookers began to pursue us, passing the seated guests of an outdoor restaurant. Their cameras flashed with a series of photos, causing our shadows to grow like giants amongst the wall. I tried to signal the passing cabs, but none were wise enough to interpret my running waves for help.

"I know a way!" I commanded, motioning near an alley a street ahead. Our sight was blocked, disrupted suddenly by a pair of gold swinging doors that opened wide. It was a theater, it's showing completed, as guests poured out like eager cattle. Alejandro slipped his shades back on, and our running halted as we pushed our way against their direction. We broke through, collecting angry stares of the people we shoved. This was it, this was our only chance to escape.

"Don't let go!" He warned, breaching the other end, yanking me along.

The screaming fans became tangled, lost in the mess of theatre junkies who shoved back. We crossed the street, enduring the blaring horn of a passing car who skidded past our path.

"In here," I exclaimed, pulling Alejandro under the yellow caution tape that blocked an alley.

"Gemma?" He questioned, "Where the hell are we?" We zig-zagged through the dispersed construction equipment, passed the cones and machinery that stood like dark shadows.

"Here." I instructed, leading him behind the large tire of a crane. We kneeled, watching from the cracks as straggling fans passed the entrance, sprinting towards nothing.

"If they find us, I want you to run," He demanded. "Nothing is worth the attention."

"Somethings are. Besides, that's for me to decide." I snipped, pulling a page from Alejandro's book. I shushed him, allowing the silence to pass as he for once complied, watching me more than the entrance of the alley.

"If you say so." He said impressed, "It appears you're right. Today we stay afloat."

"As if there was any doubt."

"Another lesson learned," he eyed me with interest.

"Are you sure you're not a celebrity? You hide like one." He stood up to turn away, linking his arm in mine. "Maybe my good girl is finally breaking." His sentiment was both a compliment and an observation. Perhaps he liked both of my sides, the confident girl and the shy one as well. Maybe it was my outfit, an homage to him—dark leather boots, a skirt for easy access—all of which made me feel extra naughty, broken as he said. Maybe a part of me enjoyed this perception, a devious but playful light Alejandro conjured. It was both the potential he saw in me, and the one I saw in myself, which I found exciting. I wanted it to continue, the chasing, the screaming, the breaking of Alejandro's good girl.

"Wait." I stopped briefly, pulling his arm. "We're here for another reason." I looked passed my shoulder at the dark entrance into the renovation. "It's my turn to sneak you into a place."

"Ms. Harrison," he groaned, "you're a rebel." He pinched his thumb along the lobe of my ear, caressing it.

"Maybe you're just a bad influence."

"The worst." His hands found their way around my waist as we stepped inside. Our boots clanked loudly in the gutted warehouse, decorated in graffitied logos of slithering snakes. I ran my hand along the wall, pressing against coarse chips of peeling paint that flaked and fell apart. It was dark, just as we liked, an atmosphere familiar to The Met. There wasn't much to see, but I was fond of this place, remembering what it once was—a vibrant auditorium, a sanctuary of dreams.

"They used to have fashion shows here," my eyes stared at a massive, windowed ceiling. The city sky sat above, seeping through the room. "We would come here, back when I attended F.I.T. It's where I spent most of my internship," I murmured.

"Internship?" He questioned. "Did you design?"

"No… I watched others though, some of the greats even. Have you ever heard of St. La Vie?" The question provoked a gentle laugh.

"I'm familiar. If I wasn't already, then I would be now, considering he was all over your walls." He motioned, signaling how expansive my magazine clippings truly were.

"I'm a fan. I mean I didn't get to meet him, but he had one of his shows here. I was fortunate enough to attend." I said shyly.

"A fan? It should be the other way around," he corrected. "Soon you'll be much more famous than me."

I laughed really hard, the idea almost impossible. "I don't think that's true."

"Why not?" He asked, "What makes St. La Vie so special?" The question was valid, leaving me unsure of where to begin. He was a brilliant designer, yes, but he was also one of the first ones I truly knew. Mama Meg used to wear one of his dresses all the time, an orange tulle piece with a navy ombré fade. It reminded me of vacation—not the beginning—but rather the end of our stay at the Hamptons. She'd always wear the dress on the car ride home, and I knew instantly how she felt. It was both happy and sad, the colors reminiscent of a sunset fading into the ocean. To me, it embodied a memory. That dress was a postcard, taking the sunset she loved from the Hamptons back home to the city. I loved that dress and, therefore, fell in love with St. La Vie.

"It's my truest form of cherry cigarettes." I replied, comparing the feeling Alejandro had while smoking, and how the flavor reminded him of his mother. It was all a soothing thought, a memory like the dress.

"What a feeling that must be. A better one than most." He seemed happy, possibly from a memory himself, or maybe more sweetly, because I had been here by his side. One wouldn't have assumed just moments ago he snipped at the revelation of his parents passing. Was this what pained him all along? Perhaps, but the way he smoothed over it, as if nothing happened, made me hesitant to ask. Maybe he was just as guilty as me, living in a fantasy, but if we were to grow, wouldn't we have to face the things we feared?

"It's not the only feeling." I cooed, "This place gets better. I'll show you." I reached for his hand, initiating a need to be touched. He reached back, allowing me to lead, taking the first step on an old steel staircase. Alejandro climbed by my side as we made it towards the ceiling, pressing against the flat bar of a metal door. It propped open, screeching loudly as the cool air pushed itself inside.

"It's not much, but you see a lot," I quickly prefaced, "It's one of the darkest parts of the city I've ever been." Hinting at our shelter, the shadows where we'd learned to talk. "It always feels like I'm watching from a different world, floating in space, staring back at the city." We moved along the graveled top, getting closer to the edge.

"Floating in space," he repeated my words. "A place to hide." He almost questioned it as if finding some meaning. Floating into nothing was a familiar sensation, such as the moments when I'd cower inside my sliding closet. Now was kind of like that, but not out of fear, but rather, the exploration of us. The wind brushed through his wavy hair as he stared out into the glimmering city. Bringing him here was an extension of trust, sharing a space where he, too, might feel free.

"Thank you." He announced, "Sometimes, it feels better to be so far away. If you can't be with them, then it's best to be away from them. There is no in between." Alejandro stared at the cascading towers in the distance; each box of light was a window, a story of a life concealed.

"No in between." I repeated. Maybe what he said was true, especially with Parker. Could I imagine a life without him, a moment we could ever be apart? It'd be difficult, but would it be impossible?

Currently the fantasy of him and I was just that, a true 'in-between'. If I couldn't be with him, would it be best if I stayed away, for good? To do so would take courage, maybe something I didn't have, but possibly could learn. Or perhaps, what we could learn, Alejandro and I. Would he be open with me, and could he show me the way to be honest? I wasn't entirely sure. His eyes expressed a look only in the shadows, that he'd rather die than say the truth.

"Alejandro, what happened earlier? When I asked about your family, I was afraid I'd upset you." I carefully questioned. I didn't want to pry or be so abrupt, I only wanted what he wanted, a chance to be inside, to see him for who he was. His gaze became more distant, cooled by the chilled wind that picked up around our bodies.

"It's messy." He sighed, "Just like my life, there's a lot of versions of what people think happened.

"Maybe all I care about is your version." I said softly, sensing his urge to hide.

"My version comes with more questions than I can answer, so instead I'll ask you, and maybe you can see… Gemma, what will you do when you become famous?" His head craned towards mine.

"What does that have to with your truth?"

"More than you think, a price always has to be paid."

"I won't be famous." I murmured, unsure of his question. I struggled to find the connection, how it related to me, an idea I could never grasp.

"You will be, because you're with me, and what will you do when it begins to take things away? Your choices, your freedom, your loved ones. It steals it all. It takes and takes until nothing is left. Until they've hollowed you out, spitting out a corpse of who you once were, leaving you to rot." Alejandro looked back at the city, lifting his foot, placing it on the edge of the building. "Like I said, a price to be paid. What does it cost to chase a dream?"

"Alejandro?" I asked, swallowing the spit in my mouth. My feet stung like hot needles, burning from the sight of his on the edge.

"And what will you do when you realize that it's all

gone, maybe not so sudden, but slow like a disease, much like the ones we fear from our past? How will you cope?" He lifted his other foot, placing it at the edge, the wind blew along his leather jacket and hair.

"Alejandro!" I shouted, this time more assertive. His feet balanced on the rim of wobbly bricks. He stared back at me, his eyes completely fearless.

"It costs a life and not just your own sometimes." He mused, his existence almost slipping with the dangle of his foot. "You want to know what it feels like, what it's like to be me? Well, let me show you." He reached out his hand, his eyes dared me to take hold.

"Goddamn it!" I screamed. "Alejandro, please! Just come back down!" I begged. My heart felt wild in my chest, aching even the muscles along my neck.

"Take my hand, or you'll never know." He commanded with all the authority of a deity, and the confidence of one as well. This was him. This was his expression. Just as I'd thought, this was the explosion, the lack of words he couldn't speak, manifested in a single way to show me who he was. This wasn't me, but who I was lacked the courage to move froward—not only in business, not only with Claire, but with Parker. I was stuck, hopelessly dependent with no way out. What if the only way to be free was to take a chance, to see things from a new perspective, even if it was from the top of a building. My eyes stung as I reached out with a shaky hand. He held it, squeezing it tight as I placed one foot on the edge.

"I don't think I…" I whimpered, the blood rushed

out of my head and through my legs. They felt heavy, like bags of sand.

"You can. I will never let anything happen to you. As long as I'm around, you and me together, we'll keep each other afloat in this crazy world." The impulse to pull twitched in his impatient hand, showing the strength he had to protect. "Trust me." My foot left the floor, lifted from his strength as I stepped up, dangerously close to the edge. Alejandro held me so tight against him, stilling my position with the strength that wrapped around my waist. I screamed as the wind whirled around my hair, burning my eyes with tears that seeped from the corners. He said he'd never let anything happen to me, and I believed every word of it. Call it callous or reckless but trusting him felt natural.

"Open your eyes." His words got lost in the buzz of my head, swirling in the cerebral cocktail of adrenaline and fear, but I did as I was told. My palms clammed up and my knees ached, seeing the possibility of how life could change in an instant. Honestly, the city felt miles away, complete with tiny pools of lights and ants, commuting like little dots. Alejandro tilted my chin up, holding my eyes as firmly as he did my body. I shook once more, as a piece of gravel slipped from the heel of my boots.

"Do you feel that?" He asked, his voice low and booming. My toes tingled, mirroring the dull ache of my clenched jaw. His hand reached up, his palm placed firmly on my chest as I stared into his eyes.

"Yes!" I shouted, trembling with the strangest thrill. I wanted to laugh, I wanted to cry. My heart hammered, stronger and stronger, intoxicating me with a dizzy feeling. I was in a dream.

"This is me." He swore, his voice louder than ever, "This is fame. It's heaven and hell. It's fear and panic! Every moment more impossible to tell, did I choose to jump, or was I pushed all along?" Alejandro leaned in, his eyes and tone far more intimate than anything we shared in the closet, seeking something much deeper than my body alone. "It has given me so much, but it has taken everything as well. Family and all." He caressed my face, holding it softly. "But you, Gemma…" he leaned closer placing his head onto mine, "for the first time in a long time, I don't feel afraid. For the first time, I think there can be something else, there can be change, and maybe it's not fair to put that on you, but fuck if I won't try." He didn't just hug me, he held me as if I were the only thing stopping him from falling, and because of that, I held back just the same. "You, Gemma, you're my only hope, and I will never lose that, I'll never lose you. I need you; I knew it the moment I saw you, that you were my good girl."

"Yes…" I exhaled breathlessly, captivated in the spell of who he was and the vision he saw. A man who knew what he needed, a man who took me in his arms to show me the best way he could.

"Just what I like," he whispered, "and I'll fucking show you that." Alejandro pulled me in, his lips pressed into mine, dissolving my body into a thousand burning suns. The beat of his heart, pulsed from his kiss, his hands securely wrapped around my waist, peeking through my shirt and onto my flesh.

I was everywhere and nowhere at once.

My mind and body were lost in his final words, claimed to be his, destined for his touch and lips. It was like nothing I'd ever imagined, but for once, better than the fantasies I had.

Finally, an expression, one words could never resolve, but sealed with a kiss, a promise, more profound than what I was prepared for. His hands swirled in my hair, tugging a strand as he dug deeper, parting me with his tongue, which slipped inside my mouth. This was what I'd been missing, what I couldn't have with Parker, the kiss on the roof I never had back in college. Alejandro was the true opposition, the one I'd melt for over and over again. I was a fool to deny how I felt, my body clearly craved his touch, every embrace, but stifled by fear.

Slowly, he pulled away, our lips parted with a gentle suck. I stared into him and felt everything I was ever missing. I wanted him, in every sense of the word.

"Alejandro…" A tear rolled down the corner of my eye. "I see it too."

"Say it…" He gently commanded, brushing my cheek with the back of his hand. "Tell me you belong to me."

"You and I, we…" I confessed, ready to admit more, but was startled by the sudden loud clank of the rooftop door.

I turned, completely terrified by the noise and shouts.

"Freeze!" Two bright lights beamed in our face, concealing the shadowed figures that approached, "Put the girl down, asshole!" One of the figures commanded, his voice hoarse from the shout. Alejandro glared, his eyes intrigued by the arguable men.

"Alejandro?" I questioned, his authoritative figure calmer than the screaming men.

"There's nothing to worry about. They're more scared of us, than we are of them, or at least they will be." He spoke as if they were frightened animals, unsure of their inevitable fall. I took a step down, raising my hands in the air to the approaching figures. It was the cops, armored with heavy vests, but even heavier guns.

"It was my fault!" I admitted quickly, absolving Alejandro of guilt. "I broke us in."

"Don't listen to her," Alejandro stepped forward. "I took her myself, I showed her the thrill."

"Shut the fuck up." A cop commanded, yanking Alejandro's arms behind his back, cuffing his wrists.

"Hey!" I shouted, shocked as the cop gripped his neck, slamming him against the wall. "What the hell are you doing?" Another cop hovered his hand by my chest, pushing me back.

"Ma'am, I'm going to need to see some ID!" He warned with a dominant voice, scaring me more than the edge I just stood on. Alejandro appeared delighted, his face pinned against the wall. He gritted his teeth, amused like a captured devil, dark and alluring.

"They don't realize the hell they just caused themselves," He looked up at the cop delivering a promise that made his eyes grow, "I'll take everything from them." It was apparent the cop finally realized who he cuffed but gloated when he found something of interest while patting Alejandro down.

"He's got a knife." He barked, pulling out the blade Alejandro used from the night at The Met. I stared, unsure if that was bad, my hands trembled as I reached for my ID. I handed it to the cop that flashed his light in my eyes, teasing my name.

"Gemma Rose Harrison?" He mused, reaching up to his walkie-talkie. He clicked a button, sounding a loud beep, "I have a match on a ten-fifty-seven, missing persons."

"Missing persons?" I exclaimed. "I'm not missing, I'm here, what are you talking about?" The other officer pulled Alejandro away, back into the building.

"We're taking him to the station for processing, until all this gets cleared up." He reached for my arm assisting me towards the door. I shook my head, demanding answers.

"Who the hell would report me missing? This doesn't make sense." I asserted there was a mistake. I was the concern of no one; the shy girl, the sister, and now, possibly the interest of a Hollywood star. But despite that, I was me, I was free to do what I wanted when I wanted. My legs locked at the realization as the cop looked up, assuring the answer right on his lips.

"We got a call from a higher up," he said smugly. "This was filed from a Mr. Parker Ellis Jones."

Epilogue
PARKER

As Gemma walked down the hall with the blanket wrapped around her shoulders, it took everything in my power not to call her back. I wanted to follow her, to pull her into the living room, or possibly worse, her bedroom where I'd lock the door behind us. It was a wicked thought, especially with Mila by my side.

"We ordered pizza." I stated, correcting the disappointment in my voice. "Are you hungry?"

"No appetite," Mila replied. "I had about five nigiris at Kosaka's."

"Sushi?"

"Of course!"

"And is five a lot?" I asked, unfamiliar with what a nigiri was, but figured its taste to be something fishy or sour.

"For me it is." She blinked, her dark eyes even larger in the darkened apartment. "I'll take you sometime, it's very romantic."

"Is it?"

"I think so," she affirmed but took her time to look around the room. "Though, maybe not as romantic as how you have it here now." She raised an eyebrow.

"Stop." I sighed but couldn't blame her for noticing. What the hell was I even doing? I knew better than to do what I did, but I couldn't resist. Gemma came out in that loose crop top, its bottom bellowed above her navel. Fuck if I didn't want to get close, to brush my arm against her, to lean in as we watched the movie. Did she know how that affected me, seeing even the slightest bit of her skin?

I stared down the dark hall, remembering her by my side. She seemed preoccupied, even breathing heavier than normal. I noticed and not just because it made her crop top rise higher than what I was prepared for. It was her lips, how they sucked in the air, full and ready for mine. What I wouldn't give to press against them, to feel the pressure of a kiss so hard that bordered painful. Had Mila not knocked on my door, what would have happened? I shook my head. "Come sit with me. We were watching a horror movie."

"Monsters?" Mila asked.

"*Dracula*. We like the classics," I shrugged.

"You and Gemma?"

"Yes, us."

"You two are so weird." Mila scoffed, pulling her hand in mine as we walked to the couch. "But I like that, you're a little nerdy. And thank god you're hot." She added, resting her head that barely reached my bicep. She made me laugh, mostly with how silly her comment sounded. She justified my interests by qualifying my looks, convincing herself that I made up for it. It was cute how she said it, and her teasing was mostly harmless, though I wasn't sure if she really cared for the things I liked.

"Well, I'm glad you like me."

"Sometimes…" she bantered, sitting where Gemma sat just moments ago. That was her seat, and part of me wanted to move Mila to a different spot. That wouldn't be fair though, in fact it'd be rude, if not completely noticeable.

"I like me sometimes too, but not always." I joked back, but maybe it was truer than even she anticipated. I felt guilty being with Mila, almost desperate to find a connection. I was willing to try anything to see the good in someone else, to form a bond that I felt was only possible with Gemma. Was that wrong, seeking a chance with another person, despite how I felt? Maybe, but I had to try, in order to keep the promise I made Claire long ago. And when I make a promise, I never break it. "Have you ever had one of these?" I nodded, pointing to the bag of peach rings.

"No, but I'm more of a chocolate girl." She admitted.

"Try one." I persuaded.

"I'm watching my weight."

"That's a silly thing to say. Maybe you're just as weird as me."

"That's not weird!"

"Yes, it is." I laughed, "I want to share something with you, and you're worried about your weight."

"It is New York, everyone always is." She affirmed.

"Maybe." I added, "I won't discredit how you feel, but you're missing out on a candy. What if it changed your life?"

"A candy could never do that."

"I think so," I replied softly, almost offended. "What

if it was so good that it changed how you felt about everything you ever knew? What if the flavor alone reminded you of someone, or maybe a memory? Wouldn't that be enough to take a chance and eat a single candy?"

"Easy, Mr. Wonka." She laughed, but my assertion was anything but teasing.

"I never take it easy." I fished out a gummy ring from the bag. I couldn't remember how many times I'd slipped one of these on Gemma's finger, only to bite it off. I felt guilty, having her by my side tonight, knowing goddamn well what I was doing. Her finger was so small and delicate, the candy itself consumed its size. I often thought of that finger of hers, how skilled it was while sketching designs and the limitless potential I knew she had. Even that small piece of her was deserving of praise, something I obsessed over.

Yes, that finger was made for more than just talent alone. I could never admit my guilty confession, how I'd fantasized about her and how that finger had probably been inside her silky wet slit. If she touched herself, then I wanted to taste it, but much more, I wanted to be the reason for it.

If only I could keep her stuck between my lips, her soft white skin sweeter than any candy itself. It was all an excuse to get close, small doses that were required to keep my urges at bay. I was hopelessly desperate for her, and for that reason, I fucking hated myself. I passed the gummy to Mila who hesitantly chewed it in her mouth.

In the brief moments before she swallowed, Mila appeared to be assessing her feelings on what the candy meant to her. Her otherwise expressive dark eyes rolled to the ceiling, as if digging deep for a response she couldn't find. "Nothing," she shook her head, "just a candy."

"Nothing." I mused, repeating her own words to myself. I wish it was nothing, but to me it was everything. Having Gemma live with me was supposed to be easy, but now it was more difficult than ever. I wanted to keep her safe, but to do that involved ignoring my own feelings, which lately have been almost impossible. I hadn't realized how vulnerable I'd be, sharing this space with her. Now I got to see her walk around in her robe, her face perfectly washed without makeup, revealing a more tired expression I had never seen before. I loved it though, such as the small creases near her eyes or the tangled bun of hair she'd get from a good night's rest. These were a few things I'd seen, the mannerisms I'd hope to capture quietly. I observed more of her, which was something I always wanted but prevented myself from in the past. I'd already fallen so deep, I didn't think I could possibly get deeper.

"What do you think of when you eat them?" Mila asked. I hesitated, thinking of all the ways they reminded me of Gemma and, without saying that, tried to describe it the best way I could.

"Comforted," I started. "Like how the sun feels when you leave the water of a cool pool."

"That's unique."

"Yes, laying out to be absorbed, allowing it to dry me off. It brings me back to life, plugging me in, charging me up. In those moments, I could fall asleep. I could stay there forever and die happy."

"You'd burn, Parker." Mila ignored my sentiment, eating another peach ring without thought.

"I know I'd burn, but it's tempting, isn't it?" I asked, more for myself.

"You should have picked up your phone," she scolded as if it were a second thought. "When I called, you sent me to voicemail."

"Tonight was important, I wanted to be here for Gemma. I told you what happened."

"That she had a bad day?"

"Yes, but no. You make it sound so simple, and it's not." Mila wasn't privy to Gemma's life, nor was I for that matter. But I knew enough, and I had seen more than maybe Gemma even realized. Her life at home had never been great, and as a child, there wasn't much I could do, but I'm not that anymore. Maybe the thought was naive, but I felt like I could protect Gemma from it all, even from Claire, who was responsible for the promise I made as a child. Could I ever tell Gemma about that day, and would she ever understand?

I'll never forget her face the morning after her father left. There was a difference in her eyes, more swollen from tears than I had ever seen before. That wasn't Gemma, that was remnants of her, pieces left behind from whatever happened that night before. I fucking hated it and what that expression did to me, having stayed burned in my mind even to this day. What I wouldn't give to go back, to wipe her red eyes, my little Butterfly.

If only I could keep her in my hands, to protect that beaming smile of hers, the one that hung in the frames of my home; *our* home, or so I wished. I'd do anything for that smile, including getting rid of Claire. I'd see to it that she'd never be a problem again, just as I promised Gemma.

"Sounds like your day was worse than hers." Mila continued as she laid back, resting her feet across my lap. "I heard about your meeting with Alex's lawyers."

"How much did you hear?"

"That the family of the girl they found at Alex's hotel is not wanting to settle."

Fuck. There was more to Alex's case than the public even knew, and a lot was kept private, despite the interest of reporters like Mila.

"How did you hear about that?" I sighed.

"Tommy." She laughed, "It only took a few bats of my eyes, and he spilled the beans."

I shook my head, annoyed that Tommy—my own fraternity brother—would so easily divulge in private information. It was a bad look for the firm, one that could ruin our case if it ever leaked out. "I don't have to tell you this, but you know not to say anything." I warned, squeezing her foot in a massage. She purred sweetly but gave a mischievous grin.

"Is it true then. They found the girl in his bed?"

"I'm not telling you anything."

"You should…" she toyed. "If not me then at least tell your precious Gemma. I'm sure she would want to know what happened with her boy-toy at The Pierre Hotel."

"Gemma is smarter than that." I spat, unaware of how harsh my tone was. Mila pouted, and that expression made me feel remorseful, almost like Gemma's. I continued to massage her foot, growing more upset. I wasn't annoyed with Mila but more so myself. The way she labeled Gemma as 'my precious' made me feel both transparent and foolish. Outside of that, the indication that Alex Rivers was somehow her boy-toy made me sick. I couldn't tell Gemma a lot of things, exclusive not only to Claire, but also to Alex. I knew she could take care of herself, but that didn't make me feel better. Maybe I needed control, maybe I was just incapable of caring any less than what my entire heart felt.

"You're the one that said he was dangerous." Mila reminded me.

"Yes, I know." I reflected, trying to ignore the fact that Gemma brought Alex to Claire's house today. Why him? I had always been there for her, yet he was invited to a place she never let me see. I was jealous to say the least, and a part of me was hurt. I suppose it was selfish, expecting the complete truth from her while keeping secrets myself. Still, I watched from afar, anticipating Alex's moves before he could take them. I wouldn't let him hurt her, or anyone for that matter. I never wanted to see that sad little face again, the one that made me want to find Gemma, to hold her and tell her everything I ever wanted.

"Well, if you're making her feel better, who's making you feel better?" Mila asked.

"Myself." I answered quickly, "That's no one's job but my own.

"Wrong." Mila corrected, "It's my job now, and I would do it happily." She pulled her legs back, sitting up on her knees along the couch. Her tight black dress creased along her hips, hugging every line of her gorgeous body. "How can I make you feel better?" She asked, her soft fingers traced my chin. The natural rasp of her voice was tempting. It was something that momentarily distracted me from the things I felt but, of course, came with its own unique sense of remorse.

"Gemma's in the next room." I whispered, telling Mila but reminding myself.

"I can be quiet, not like last time." She reached down, her small hand wrapped along my thigh. "A part of that was your fault though." She narrowed her eyes, "You fucked me too good."

Maybe that was true, and maybe I fucked her good because of the angst Gemma gave. Only with Gemma in mind could my cock curve with such an erection, almost painful without her imagined touch. Mila didn't make it easy to say no, her own breasts pressed together, aching to be sucked. I chewed my lip, discontented with my urge to be a decent person, but to relieve the stress I felt with not having the woman I truly wanted.

"Only cause I fucked you hard." I admitted, remembering how frustrated I was that night. Mila was sexy, even I could admit that, but I couldn't help but feel that our relationship was more about convenience than passion. Gemma needed to see me live a normal life, and Mila needed insight into Alex's case. We seemed to help each other out; me with the legal information, and her with the appearance that I was a taken man. I didn't feel good about doing it, but maybe I cared more about Gemma feeling assured, than my own sickening guilt.

"We need to take things slow." I added, knowing that last time we slept together was a mistake. I was already frustrated as it was, not having Gemma how I truly wanted. It was as if I couldn't get her out of my head, especially the visual of her changing in the closet. I watched her that night, invited into her room, lying on her bed as she dropped her robe. My cock grew stiff at that thought, the visual of her round ass that tempted to be touched. What I wouldn't have given to reach out, to have yanked her close by the straps of her panties alone. Zipping up her dress, god that visual, it was an insight into the future I'd wanted for so long. Could she tell I was on edge, that seeing her bare shoulders being covered up drove me mad?

Even tonight with her outfit, I wanted so badly to pull her hips down into the couch, to lay her on her back. I'd slip those pajama bottoms off her legs, if not rip them off with the strength of my hand. I begged to feel the warmth between her legs, to lick her like a dog. Fuck if I didn't feel like a piece of shit, and how my erection twitched at the fantasy.

"What if I suck you off?" Mila asked. "I'll let you come in my mouth." She stuck her tongue out, as if to show me the perfect place to come. It made me grow harder, the unique cocktail of shame and arousal. I wanted to bend her over, to plow myself into that little pink pussy of hers and have her scream my name.

Maybe then I could lose myself, if not just for a moment. My sweats were no longer loose but tightened by my sudden growth.

Without thought, she pulled my pants down my hips, springing my cock loose. She squeezed my shaft, constricting the steady flow of blood that pumped harder against her grip. Resisting sex was damn near impossible, and though I said our relationship was convenient, it didn't mean I hadn't hoped for something more. This idea of a normal life was not only for Gemma, but for myself.

"I want to be kind." I assured, a vague request to let me off easy, her temptation left me both guilty and undeniably hungry.

"What if I want to be fucked?" She asked, "Will you make me feel better?" My answer to that would be yes. I wanted to be sweet to Mila, I wanted to care for her just like she deserved, but I knew I needed time. Would there ever be enough? Yes, I could fuck her, I could make her come like I did that night. But I'll never forget walking in on Gemma, her body wet with bubbles in the tub. I wouldn't admit it, but I saw her perfect little tits, peaking from the water. If I could've, I would have pulled her out of the bath and slipped her right over me. I'd suck those perfect nipples, making those little nubs red with the nip of my teeth.

It was bad enough that I already came to the memory of her, beating myself off into a sputtering mess while in the shower that very next morning. If only she'd been in there with me, I'd shoot myself all over her stomach. I'd watch as my filth dripped down to her beautiful cunt and into the drain. I wanted that now, maybe alone in the bathroom.

Mila straddled my lap, placing her hands around my cheeks. She leaned in for a kiss, her dress pulled passed her panties, whose chic black lace pinched between her lips. She was warm, or at least her pussy was as it pressed against my cock.

"Do you care for me?" I asked. I wanted her to say no, and maybe that would make me feel like I had more time to develop feelings.

"I think that's apparent." She shrugged, "I'm having fun, aren't you?"

"Yes." A half-truth, focused on the promise of sex rather than the pain in my heart.

"Then let's enjoy that. Just like you told me about your candy, I'm trying to show you something." Her sultry whisper was sweeter now, more caring, "What if it changes your life?"

"Then it would be worth it." I aspired, coaxed by the slide of her hips. She rubbed herself against me, pressing into a dry hump against my cock. There could be something here, and maybe I would just have to work for it. Maybe it was just physical, and perhaps it could bloom into something more. I wanted to fuck Mila, but not like how I would Gemma, not yet. With Mila, I used a condom, I was more careful about the consequences of our actions. With Gemma though, I don't think I could. I'd only fantasied about being in her raw, not wanting to be deprived of even the slightest of wetness against my skin.

To admit in my head was easy, in fact it echoed over

and over again. If I were inside Gemma, I'd leave every drop of my cum, deep between her legs. I'd fuck her till she was hungry or thirsty, stopping only to feed her, to massage her aching muscles, so that I may fuck her again.

Yes, I would be reckless, considering any consequences of our actions would only make me happy. She could be the mother to our children, and I would remind them every day how lucky they were to call her Mom. I had always felt this way about her, but it was becoming uncontrollable now, her scent like fresh linen, marked on the cushion by my side. I smelt it, shutting my eyes, still thinking of her as Mila kissed my lips.

If there was a hell, I was going there, and I knew I deserved it.

I kissed Mila, still thinking of Gemma, the peach flavor on her lips a reminder of what I wished was true. She was asleep, and it wasn't sex I truly wanted right now, admitting that I'd much rather just lay by her side and hold her while she dreamed. What a thought, what a fucking tragedy.

Not a second after this fantasy did I jump. I thought it was a scream, something far more terrifying than any horror movie Gemma and I ever watched. It was the blare of a screeching alarm, ringing through the room, almost honking.

"Fuck!" I shouted, rising from my seat, holding Mila in my arms. She screamed as I placed her down softly, her hands reached for her ears.

"Parker, what is that?" The alarm continued to ring, emitting a bright flashing light that popped in a pulse.

"Fire alarm," I replied quickly pulling up my sweats. "Something's wrong." I heard the slamming of doors outside, the neighbors already leaving their apartments.

"Seriously, a fire?" Mila whined.

"I don't know." I sighed, "Yes, I'm guessing so." I was already making my way down the hall; I couldn't leave just yet.

"Where are you going?"

"I'm getting Gemma." I affirmed, already calling for her attention. "Gemma!" I shouted, banging on her door. I pounded with three sharp knocks, surprised she hadn't come out already.

"She can take care of herself." Mila ran to my side tugging on my arm. She was panicked, but I wasn't there yet. I flashed her a strange look. Maybe I was the crazy one, not wanting to leave right away, but I could care less about how I looked.

"What's wrong with you?" I asked. "We're not just going to leave." I banged on her door, more confused why Gemma wasn't responding.

"It's probably not even a real fire. It's just loud." Her determination to pull me away irked me, but I ignored it, twisting the handle to Gemma's door. It was locked. I banged again, calling for her name, but she didn't answer.

"Your phone!" I commanded, pulling it out of Mila's hand. I swiped it open, as she covered her ears once more.

"What are you doing?" She asked, but I ignored her

as I dialed Gemma's number, the only number I knew by heart. I didn't know why I thought she would pick up, and actually I wasn't sure what to think. The siren roared in my ear, warning me to leave. I'd never listen.

"Gemma, wake up!" I slammed my fist against the door, so hard that Mila jumped. The call went to voicemail, her sweet message chirping with an apology.

"You've reached Gemma! Sorry I missed your call, but I'd be happy to return it as soon as I can!"

Fuck. My stomach burned with a knot, a dread like I had already lost her. It was a strange thought to appear, as if it were more permanent than I realized. She wasn't answering, and what if something did happen to her? How would I cope?

"Let's go!" Mila shouted, but I hissed quickly.

"Goddamn it! Don't ask me to again because I won't!" I couldn't help but shout, clearly losing the cool composure I had just moments ago. Gemma was on the other side, and she needed me, or more so, maybe I needed her. Was this secret I kept worth it? It didn't feel good keeping it inside, and if something ever did happen to Gemma, then it would remain in me forever, rotting like once ripened fruit. Who would want me then, and what good would I be?

I couldn't live with that.

It was a premonition of my future, flashing within the milliseconds between my pounding fists. Would there ever be a time where I wasn't just locked out of her room, but ultimately her life? I pounded my fist harder, not just once or twice, but repetitively. I would stay here till my knuckles bled, until the place burned down if I needed.

I didn't want to be closed off, I didn't want to just be her friend, but how could I explain the reason behind it all? That night I cleaned her up in college, when she confessed her love to me, I was tempted to kiss her, to tell her the same, over and over again. I always thought I was protecting her, but maybe I was protecting myself too. If we remained friends, nothing could ever ruin that, but if we were a couple, everything could go wrong. What if her feelings eventually changed? How would I deal with that then, having tasted her, knowing I could never have her again?

I'd rather not know at all, I'd rather not risk the possibility of her ever getting hurt, even from me. But this felt wrong, and maybe it was my panic, maybe it was everything coming together like a swarm of angry crows. Mila, Alex, Gemma's mother. The promise Claire made me keep no longer felt worth it, but I had to hold on, I had to keep her safe.

"I'm leaving!" Mila screamed.

"Then leave!" I shouted, louder than the alarm, turning to face the door. I leaned back, my thick muscles tensed with rage, kicking the door harder than I kicked anything ever before. It exploded, shattered into fragments of wood that collapsed along the dark floor. Mila screamed again, but I gripped the door frame, peering inside like a mad man. "Gemma!" I shouted, running my eyes across the room, immediately focusing on her open window.

"Parker, she's gone, we need to leave!" Mila tugged

on my arm as I stared at it, the curtain blowing from the fire escape. She was gone, and I wasn't sure why. Did she leave, was she taken, and how did that make me feel? I wasn't just scared, I was tortured.

"Gemma?" I asked myself, my voice quivering from my chest. I was lost, but fuck if I hadn't felt this way forever. I always worried about losing her, feeling that I could keep her close, keep her hidden from my world as much as she hid me from hers. It wasn't fair what Claire asked me to be, not the future boyfriend for Gemma, but the supporter of something more important. Could I be just that alone? I wasn't sure anymore.

I wanted more, but what I wanted above all else was to keep her happy. Maybe it was selfish of me to think it could be so simple, that I could deprive myself any longer while she lived her life. She was gone, but I was here, watching as her curtain whipped in a cold wind.

If everything was already falling apart, couldn't I fall apart as well? Maybe I could lose myself, take the chance I always wanted, despite Claire's wishes. Fuck if I couldn't control myself any longer, physically sick at the idea that she was out there, away from me, away from the words I wished I could say. I would tell her how I felt, only as a last resort, and maybe it would cost me everything. But I didn't care anymore.

I love her.

I always have.

I always will.

Lawsuit and Leather,
Mine to Keep Series
Book 2 is coming…

Until then, be a good girl.

Alejandro

* * *

Did you enjoy Lawsuit and Leather? Did you know reviews/ratings help indie authors be noticed by more readers?

If you enjoyed this book, please spread the love on your favorite platform with a review! It can be short and sweet, or anything you wish. Thank you for reading.

* * *

Subscribe to my newsletter for exclusive updates, new releases, reveals, and more: https://www.vivianmae.com/newsletter

Bonus Content

Want bonus content from Lawsuit and Leather? New York Prestige was kind enough to provide us with Alejandro's scandalous news articles.

Please be aware, if you have not read Lawsuit and Leather *(if you made it here, I'll assume you did)* please know this is your spoiler warning!

Visit the page below for some extra goodies!
https://www.vivianmae.com/ll-bonus

Acknowledgements

Wow, oh wow! This has been a wild ride and I want to thank the following people:

I want to thank my street team for being such a rock that I could lean on, especially when I needed guidance. You were always there for me when it counted the most and I absolutely adore our little community! Thank you for always taking the time to promote my book with equal parts love and generosity. THANK YOU!

I want to thank my beta readers, without you, I wouldn't have known where my weaknesses or strengths lied within this story. You were my light though it all. Thank you SO much!

Thank you to my social media community, including Instagram, TikTok, Pinterest. I see everything that you do, and I love you for it. You take the time to engage, like, comment, share my posts, and I couldn't be more thankful for having such a strong community backing me up and making me feel valued when I doubted myself the most. Thank you!

To my dearest husband, who has truly taken my breath away and who has supported me above anyone else in helping make this dream come true. Having you by my side—not only as my partner in crime in marriage, but as my editor—has been such a joy in my heart. *I love you truly, and just as Parker said, *"always have, always will."*

Also by
VIVIAN MAE

Burning Little Secrets

A secret romance filled with devious secrets, angsty lure and breath hitching steam. Burning Little Secrets divulges the forbidden journey of an engaged woman's encounter with a sexy small town hero.

Turn the page for a peek into chapter one of Burning Little Secrets...

Burning Little Secrets
CHAPTER 1

There was always a damn issue with Robbie. He had a way of spinning my mistakes into psychological code, as if forgetting to water the plants was actually a red flag, signaling a lack of relational attention. It was so exhausting; so crazy.

As a journalist living in New York City, my work demanded late hours, working the occasional all-nighter for a nail-biting deadline. There was a promotion available, and I had been busting my ass off to earn this. The type of promotion I dreamed of, to be taken as a serious writer. I'd already come so far, living with Robbie and his skyline view, versus my old apartment, which faced the neighbors who fucked at their window. I'm sure they enjoyed the audience, me watching, crunching on a bag of Lays. How fitting.

When I moved to the city for school, I'd always dreamt of independently paving my way to success. Never had I thought I'd earn a shortcut to life when I met Robbie. His wealthy parents paid for his schooling, and he lived in a beautiful penthouse, gifted to him after his graduation of course. *I know, right?* My dad got me a stuffed graduation bear, which I now squeezed to death during stressful days at the office.

When Robbie romantically swept me off my feet and invited me to live with him after grad school, you could imagine my feeling, realizing my shortcut to success stemmed from the man of my dreams and all his familial connections; or, so I thought.

Now? I had found myself overly dedicated to my job. Oftentimes, I forced my body to survive off hot coffee, cold bagels, and noodle cups—which may or may not have peas in them; at least that's what I told myself whenever I encountered the squishy green balls.

I loved work more than anything, and being in the city was alone what allowed me to thrive. The hustle and bustle lifestyle, the one where you secretly grew ten new gray hairs overnight, only to paint them in before work the next morning — that was part of the exhilarating charm of it all. Overworked, stressed, yet successful.

The agency I worked for was small, maybe even microscopic. We were always in search of the next big story, the scandal that would tip us over the edge, or so my boss, Mitchell, always said.

"It only takes one story, Julia. Then we'll be the next media sensation for the news. Twitter-famous kids will retweet our every dramatic article into stardom." His eyes gleamed with proverbial dollar signs. He would write a segment about his mother's sex life if he knew it would help the company. I get it. We all have dreams, but those were always his sharp reminders at every morning huddle. The script had been practically engraved in our minds.

But my soon to be husband — Robbie? He didn't

understand my job, the insanity of it all, and he faulted me. You'd think as a stockbroker he'd be the first to understand. But lately, his once accepting approval of my work seemed displaced. He used to be so kind, patient, and supportive. Now that man was replaced by a looming psycho. He was a complete stranger, always on edge.

I didn't know what happened between his proposal last year to being a week away from walking down the aisle. It was as if he regretted asking me, or as if he wasn't ready for the commitment — you know, for better or worse. I would even imagine us in our old age, sitting in the countryside, retired, complete with rocking chairs and a large porch. Now? I don't even think we can make it through dinner.

Cold feet?

Maybe? Maybe not?

"Where you going?" Robbie barked at me when I placed my hand on the door looking for a quick escape. The annoyance in his eyes was evident. They narrowed, like a suspicious metronome, ticking back and forth between me and the door.

"I'm going downstairs to grab a coffee." I half-smiled and nodded politely; my eyebrows cowered a bit, and I quickly glanced down to avoid his stare. "Need anything from there?" I asked innocently, shifting my feet in place, attempting to hide the real truth for my trip away from him.

"It's late, don't you think?" He snipped at me, shaking his head.

"Not really, I mean... it's barely past seven." I

opened the door to leave, but Robbie slammed his body against it. "Robbie," I closed my eyes and inhaled my frustration. "I mean it, I'm going downstairs." My voice quivered, which only made him louder in response.

"No, you're not. I know what you're doing behind my back, you whore." His face leaned so close to mine. He spoke in a breathy whisper, and it felt hot against my face.

Knitting both my brows, I straightened myself up and gave him a hard stare — one long enough to make him back off. My daring eyes spoke what my lips could not. I would stare all night if I had to, just determined to see his next move, to call his bluff. He slowly eased off the door, and I stepped right out, flipping my hair over my shoulders. *Gotcha.*

The soft breeze of passing people sat in contrast to the stuffy room I emerged from. I needed this time, this moment away, savoring each step as I made my way to the coffee shop below Robbie's home.

At this rate I needed at least three shots of espresso after being inside that tension-filled house. The one I felt too uncomfortable to call home.

Only Robbie could drain my energy every damn moment. I wished it was different, like how it was before when we first met and fell in love. Maybe fireworks hadn't exploded behind us as we shared our first kiss, but his sweet and secure nature for our future hooked me.

For now, I had to get away from the madness for a minute — just one.

The aroma of strong espresso beans and the season's

latest pumpkin spice filled the welcoming shop. I didn't order right away, I spent time observing the dimly lit loyalty mugs on display. The same soft music seemed to play every time I entered. I loved how their obscure jazz laid hushed against the muted traffic outside. It felt like a fuzzy dream. Regardless, the patrons were a bit pretentious, but I couldn't resist their banana nut muffins. So worth the unprovoked scowls.

"Large pumpkin spice with three espresso shots." I paused as the barista took my order. "Shit," I shook my head, "make it four shots instead." I rummaged through my large laptop bag. The handsome young barista blew through his messy golden hair which covered his eyes. He arched an eyebrow and looked at me as if I grew an extra head.

"Wanna make it five?" His flirty grin was a warm surprise that I needed. I smiled and shook my head, then placed a couple bucks in the tip jar. "Thanks," he nodded excitedly as if he was rocking out to the elevator music playing, "I'll throw an extra shot in there for you. Looks like you could use it."

Fuck, did my forehead display the entire list of my problems? Maybe it was the dark circles under my eyes. Maybe he's psychic. Oh god. In my frantic state of transparency, my thoughts turned into a puddled mess. I glanced at his big, dark brown eyes as he pulled his hair back into a bun. He was way too cool for me. I'd be a neurotic mess around him.

"Yeah… thanks, I guess."

His pale face turned the reddest shade I'd ever witnessed, and I tightened my lips to keep my giggle inside. "Ah, sorry, not like that. I'm an asshole. Uh coffee's on me tonight." He reassured me, and he spoke rapidly with his hands. His chestnut eyes widened, seemingly embarrassed. My heart warmed as it skipped a few beats faster than normal. Is this what flirting was like? It had been a while. I twirled a ring of hair around my finger.

"Thanks," I said. I waved and smiled like a damn idiot and moved myself to the other side of the counter where drinks were being slid to their owners.

Shortly after I placed my order, my cell rang, blaring Christina Aguilera's "Come on Over Baby." My cheeks warmed up instantly as she belted that tune inside the painfully quiet corner where I stood. It was enough to make me move elsewhere from embarrassment.

"Sorry," I mouthed to those nearby, attempting to avoid the evil eyes dotting at me from all sections of the shop.

"Julia!" My best friend, Eve, shouted through my phone. Almost as loud as Ms. Aguilera herself.

Damn it.

Luckily, my order was immediately placed onto the counter, almost as if the cute barista was shoving me out the door, but politely. Embarrassed, I swiftly waved my hand as I yanked my coffee and muffin off the counter, while clutching my singing phone against my chest.

Temporarily muting Eve, I turned the volume from a ten down to a one but could still hear her yelling at me for placing her on mute. She knew me too well.

"Julia, I'm not kidding. Unmute me!" She cried out.

I pushed past the wooden door, bringing my phone

up to my mouth, "Ok, ok, I'm here Eve!" I exhaled out loud hoping to find peace on this journey. "What's going on? Aren't you supposed to be at work right now?" I found a nearby bench and sat down to enjoy my coffee and warm muffin. It was complete bliss.

"You're never going to believe this, but… I bought you a ticket to come see me! Well, me and your dad. You leave tomorrow morning." She chirped excitedly in a proud tone.

"Eve! What? I thought nurses didn't take time off work? Or is this one of those trips where you'll be working the whole time and I'm just alone with my laptop?" Actually, that didn't sound like a bad option.

"Well, this bitch has saved enough lives this year to earn herself a couple weeks off. Besides, I desperately need my best friend; it's been too long. Please." I could feel her puppy dog eyes on the other side of the phone. Funny, how you can know someone for so long, that you can feel their expressions radiate without seeing them.

I sighed because Robbie would frown upon it. Especially it being last minute. He was a complete control freak, and I dreaded imagining what our conversation would entail.

Besides if he didn't trust me enough to go get coffee, why would he agree to this? I must have been silent for too long, or Eve could read my mind; one of the two.

"Anyway, I know what you're thinking, and it's non-refundable, tell Robbie. Besides. I need to see you before you decide to walk down the aisle. Fuck him." I bit the inside of my cheek in thought.

Decide. Interesting word choice. However, with how I'd

been feeling lately—like a trapped prisoner inside this relationship—I deserved to go home and visit. Alone.

"Fuck him! You're right. I need to see everyone." Being in the city had been a nice change, but I hadn't felt so far away from home until these last few months.

My little family of two, I missed them more than I could stand, and I needed my dad's famous bear hugs right about now.

"Pack up and come back to sweet home North Carolina!" Eve shrieked and clicked off. She loved being dramatic.

North Carolina.

It felt like a universe that was far away. I left North Carolina because I was never fond of small-town living. Part of me didn't want to go back to see the sad life I once fled. Even my accent flew out the moment I began my life as a city girl. Not sure I wanted my southern twang to come back with vengeance. I did love Dad and Eve, but their love wasn't enough to keep me trapped there. New York on the other hand — I'll do anything to keep my life in one piece, even if it may be complicated. Complicated was normal, right? It seemed that way in the city at least; chaos was its middle name after all.

Suddenly, my heart sank into my stomach knowing that the conversation I would have with Robbie wouldn't be great. I chugged my drink back, threw my trash away, and headed back upstairs.

One of the great things about New York was how you could step out and you were seconds away from a cup of coffee, cream cheese filled bagels, or cheap slices of Joe's pizza. The phrase 'the city that never sleeps'

360 | LAWSUIT AND LEATHER

couldn't be any truer. People drank until four in the morning, or until they passed out before closing time.

I turned the corner of my apartment hallway, and Robbie was waiting at our doorway like a scolding father. His brow furrowed as he watched each step I took, judging me up and down, until I passed him.

"Hey… Robbie." I softened my voice a bit. I lunged at him, attacking him with a big hug. "Guess what! I'm going back home for a week." I squeaked out, and his eyes narrowed in on mine. "Eve got me a ticket to go see her, and I'll be able to see my family as well right before the wedding. It's been a while, and I need this." I paused. My index finger circled around the exposed part of his chest. I exhaled loudly, almost out of breath at my fast speech. "I leave tomorrow morning."

A few silent moments lingered in the cold air between us. Not knowing which way he would go as his angry furrowed brows relaxed into a sad glance.

"Ok," Robbie softly replied, almost defeated. His eyes sunk low, viewing the floor beneath us. Did he really just agree without a fight? Although we have had more great moments than not, my old Robbie was shining through in his own way again.

"Ok?" My voice pitched at the end of my sentence, in surprise of his response. *What gives? Oh fuck, why did I care? I'm going home.*

* * *

Want to continue reading, Burning Little Secrets? Read Julia and Nathan's secret

romance in this angsty, spicy, quick read, insta love story!

One click, Burning Little Secrets, today. Available to buy now at all major retailers, or visit my website, www.vivianmae.com for more details!

About the Author

Vivian Mae is a Latina indie author, living out of Phoenix, AZ who writes sexy contemporary romance for her naughty readers.

She is married to her best friend, fulfilling her own trope of best friends to lovers.

When she isn't writing, you can find her laughing alongside her husband, binging trashy TV, sneaking chocolates, reading her favorite naughty novels, and dreaming about pizza and wine.

Subscribe to my newsletter for exclusive updates, new releases, reveals, and more:
https://www.vivianmae.com/newsletter

Follow me on Facebook, Instagram, Pinterest. Better yet, tag along on my daily Instagram Stories for a peek into my daily shenanigans.

Made in the USA
Coppell, TX
18 July 2022